WASHINGTON WEIRDOS

A Claire Gulliver Mystery

Also by Gayle Wigglesworth

GAYLE'S LEGACY,
RECIPES, HINTS AND STORIES CULLED FROM A LIFELONG RELATIONSHIP WITH FOOD

TEA IS FOR TERROR

WASHINGTON WEIRDOS

A Claire Gulliver Mystery

by
GAYLE WIGGLESWORTH

Copyright © 2005 by Gayle Wigglesworth

All rights reserved. No part of this book may be reproduced or transmitted in any form or by any means, electronic or mechanical, including photocopying, recording, or by any information storage or retrieval system, without prior written permission from Koenisha Publications, except for the inclusion of quotations in a review.

This book is a work of fiction. Names, characters, places, and incidents are the product of the author's imagination or are used fictitiously. Any resemblance to actual events, locales, or persons, living or dead, is coincidental.

Library of Congress Control Number: 2005906448

ISBN-13: 978-0-9759621-4-5

ISBN-10: 0-9759621-4-0

Koenisha Publications, 3196 – 53rd Street, Hamilton, MI 49419
Telephone or Fax: 269-751-4100
Email: koenisha@macatawa.org
Web site: www.koenisha.com

Once again my thanks to my best friend and husband, David, who not only helped me research locations and settings for this book but ruthlessly edited it. And to my daughters, Janet and Danielle, who again proofed it, and my son-in-law Dave, who volunteered to read it without having read the first book so that I could be sure this book could stand on its own.

But I'd like to dedicate this book to my sister-in-law, Linda Coates, who is more than a relative and more than a friend, she is both. Linda loves a mystery, perhaps even more than I do, and she loves Washington, D.C. So Linda this book is dedicated to you. Thank you for your encouragement and support over the past four plus decades.

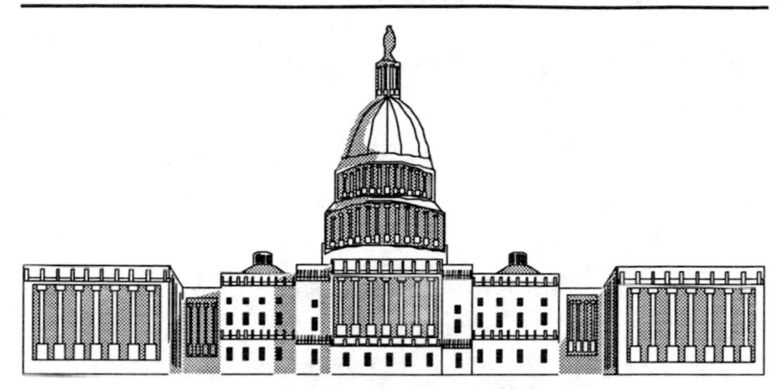

PROLOGUE

Going through the mail was never Claire's favorite task, so the plate of ginger snaps and the mug of tea were meant as a bribe. She dutifully sorted the accumulation in the basket until she reached the embossed envelope from Vantage Airlines. She felt a clutch of fear grip her stomach as she turned it over, examining it carefully.

It was strange how quickly things had returned to normal after she came back from London. The story for the other tour members, her mother and friends was readily accepted. And why not? No one would have guessed what really happened.

Of course, Lucy, Mrs. B and Claire all knew the truth and were haunted by what had *almost* happened. But then as the weeks passed, and they became involved once more in the details of everyday life those fears gradually receded.

Claire studied the creamy stationery. This was no normal promotional offer she could tell. She used her letter opener to cut through the top and unfolded the letter to scan the contents. She read it a second time more carefully.

The CEO and President, David Burlington Lickman was inviting her to be Vantage's guest in Washington, D.C. They wanted her to attend a special meeting of the Board so they could show their appreciation for her efforts on behalf of their corporation. Additionally, the Lickmans would like her to be their guest for the long Labor Day weekend in their home in Maryland, where they were hosting a Gala to celebrate the end of the summer.

She was stunned. Who would expect a major corporation such as Vantage Airlines to issue such a personal invitation? It was a really caring thing to do. It made her feel like they really did appreciate what she had done. She decided right then that the Lickmans must be very nice people. But she still felt a little guilty about Vantage's appreciation. Truthfully, she hadn't given a thought to saving the airline. She had been totally concerned with her own safety and that of the others on the plane. The results, of course, benefited them all. Doug Levine, who had been the State Department's representative assigned to protect her interests through all the interrogation and investigations by the British, kept telling her how grateful the airline was for her action. That had planted an expectation in her head that she could receive some formal thank you and perhaps even a gesture of appreciation, like some free bonus miles or a complimentary ticket to somewhere. But then as the weeks passed without hearing from Vantage she had dismissed the idea. But never had she expected a personal invitation such as this.

Yes, she admitted, she had always wanted to see Washington, D.C. She had vowed someday she would go to the Vietnam Memorial because she identified so much with that era while she was growing up in San Francisco. And she had heard so much about the Smithsonian. It would probably take a week to even make a dent in the museums. And, of course, what librarian (albeit ex-librarian) could resist an opportunity to visit the Library of Congress?

She toyed with the idea of getting on a plane again. It was so soon. She kind of rolled it around a bit in her mind, but strangely the thought didn't seem to alarm her. What did concern her was her business. She had a bookstore to run and it needed her. She couldn't just be running off on trips every few months.

A Gala, she thought. What was that precisely? It sounded rather posh. She decided to ask Lucy about it. Lucy, her travel book author friend, was the one who knew just what Claire should wear when she had been invited to an afternoon society wedding several months back. Surely she would know what a Gala required and maybe she had even heard of the Lickmans. Or, Claire thought, she could check the Web. David Lickman, as the head of a major corporation, could surely be found on Google.

The invitation was tempting. Maybe she'd discuss the trip with Mrs. B, her assistant manager, when she came in this afternoon. Maybe there was a way. Maybe it was possible. It seemed that this was a unique opportunity, something not to be missed.

And Labor Day was only a month away.

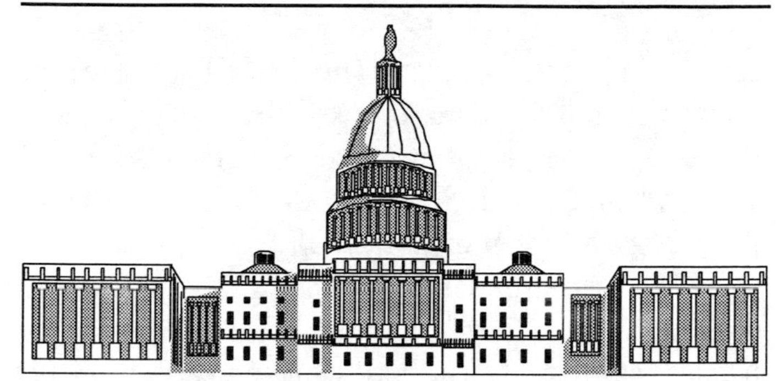

CHAPTER ONE

The evening was balmy, not hot and humid as Claire had been led to expect. She took a deep breath, looking around. It wasn't yet dark, but very shadowy between the bright bluish white glows emitted from each light stanchion lining the paths which ran along each side of the long park the locals call the Mall.

She was glad she had come out. She had spent too many hours cooped up in a plane. And while it was dusk here in Washington D.C., her body was still on West Coast time.

And she wasn't the only one who didn't want to be indoors with this great city to explore, Claire thought with satisfaction, noting the joggers, cyclists and other tourists taking advantage of the beautiful evening. However, she did notice the numbers were dwindling as the evening wore on. Then she noticed, for some reason, there were fewer people on the path she was on. Perhaps the other path was more popular because it was closer to the busy street it paralleled. And noticing how deserted her side of the park had become stirred a feeling of unease so she walked faster, suddenly anxious. She glanced over at the other path, considering cutting across. At the same time she scolded herself for being spooked. But when hairs at the base of her skull prickled, she paid attention. That's when she noticed the sound of someone coming up behind her rather quickly.

She stopped under one of the lights and whipped around to face the person approaching. The man paused, startled, then a hard smile spread across his face and the blade on the knife he held clicked into place.

Sharply she sucked in her breath. Her heart thundered with fear.

His grin widened at her gasp. He was enjoying this.

She hadn't brought her purse; but desperate for something to offer him she thrust her hand in the pocket of her windbreaker, reaching for the few bills she had grabbed in case she wanted to take a cab back. Her fingers closed over a chunky object and dimly she registered it was her screech alarm.

His eyes never left hers as he began advancing. He appeared to be savoring his control over the situation. She was so frightened she couldn't breathe. Her fingers clumsily twisted around the little alarm in her pocket until the trigger came free and the sudden deafening screech shattered the evening.

He jumped back. His eyes darted around nervously. Then recovering, he moved forward again. His knife was ready.

The body came out of nowhere, slamming into him sideways with a force which sent them both to the ground. The knife flew through the air; the streetlight gleaming off the blade traced its trajectory. She wanted to run, to scream, to cry for help but she stood mutely rooted. Her eyes were riveted on the men on the ground in front of her. Her would-be attacker rolled free and came up on all fours. He was poised, looking at the knife, which lay temptingly only a few feet away. But her rescuer's hand protectively hovered over it, his gaze fastened on the attacker's eyes. The evil grin had been knocked off his face and he sidled off a few feet before he made up his mind. Quickly he gained his feet and ran for the other side of the Mall leaving his knife and his intended victim behind.

Claire's knees buckled suddenly and she sat on the path with a force that knocked her breath out with a whoosh. Stunned, gasping for air, she tried to make sense of what had happened.

Her rescuer climbed to his feet, shouting over the ear damaging screech, but she couldn't make out his words. However, when he cupped his hand to his ear she understood, groped around in her pocket, found the alarm and the dangling pin and after a few futile attempts she managed to insert the pin and silence it.

They stared at each other, ears still ringing in the stillness. Then, he leaned toward her. "Why are you down there? Are you hurt?"

She shook her head, dazed, sure she was dreaming.

No chance of that, she told herself, the stones on the path biting cruelly into her butt were too real for this to be a dream.

"Jack? Jack, is it really you?"

Then gathering strength, she demanded, "Jack, what are you doing here?" She had thought when she bid him farewell in London several months ago that they would never meet again. Yet, unbelievably, here he was.

"Here, in the park, or here in Washington?" He was being facetious, an annoying habit of his.

She tried to keep impatience out of her voice. "Either, both! What are you doing here?"

"Well, I knew you were coming in today, so I stopped by at your hotel but just missed you. The concierge said he showed you on the map how to get to the Vietnam Memorial, so I headed this way to see if I could catch up. Luckily! I was across the park," he gestured in the direction of the path on the other side, "when I saw you. Then I saw him skulking after you. It looked rather sinister so I headed this way as fast as I could."

He looked at her sternly. "How many times have I warned you not to walk alone on dark deserted streets?" He shook his head in disgust.

Somehow his scolding made her feel defensive. "I had my screech alarm." It sounded rather feeble even to her.

"So that's what it was. Well, it was a big help." He waved at the empty space around them. He was right, no one had responded to the alarm.

Her face paled. "He was planning to use that knife. I could see it in his eyes." She shuddered and pulled the lightweight windbreaker close around her. She felt chilled. "He was going to kill me."

Jack reached for Claire's hand to help her to her feet and guided her toward the bench at the side of the path. He sat next to her still holding her hand tightly in his, stilling her trembling somewhat as they both contemplated her brush with violence.

"You don't think it had anything to do with Guiness, do you?" she whispered horror apparent in her shaking voice.

"God, I hope not!" He paused, then continued, "I wouldn't think so. What would be the point?" Then he went on. "This looked like a rather nasty, but normal, mugging to me. Unless, of course," he said with concern, "you've had any other strange incidents happen to you recently?"

She shook her head, "No, no problems; no scares. I lead a rather staid life."

"I've noticed," he teased, then shaking his head in frustration, "I'll get some of the guys to run that knife and see what we can get." He turned toward her. "You don't have a hanky or a Kleenex, do you?"

She felt in her pockets and dug underneath the screech alarm to come up with two wads of tissue and offered them to Jack.

He hesitated looking at them suspiciously.

"They're clean," she assured him.

He took them and straightened them out, then went over to where the knife still lay on the ground. He used one of the tissues to pick it up by the blade and managed to close it, wrapping it carefully in the other tissue to preserve any prints before slipping it into his pocket.

"I really need a plastic bag but this is better than nothing." He returned to the bench looking at her earnestly, "I don't think there's any point in contacting the local police now, do you?"

She agreed. Her attacker was long gone.

He sat down again picking at some of the debris that had been caught in his shirt while he was on the ground. He looked about the same. Maybe his sandy hair was a little grayer, but maybe it was only the light. She had forgotten that he was attractive. He was only medium height, really about the same as her five foot, nine inches. She remembered crashing into him, nose to nose, when they first met and it hurt. She hadn't liked him then. But somehow during the two weeks they had traveled together they came to respect each other and, eventually, they came to like each other. In fact, she remembered, they had progressed to a mild interest in flirtation before she left.

"What are you doing here?" She looked at him thoughtfully, realizing she had been caught up in violence once again, and Jack was on the scene. Was it only a coincidence?

"I was rotated back last month for some specialized training and, since I was here, I was invited to represent our group at the meeting you're attending tomorrow. Supposedly I'm to be there in case there are any questions that need answering, but I suspect it's meant as a bit of reward for my work with you." He grinned. "That's how I knew you were coming."

That's when she noticed he no longer spoke with a British accent. "And are you still Jack Hanford? You don't sound the same."

He shook his head, slightly embarrassed. "That was an alias. Actually, my name is Jack. Well, John. Really I'm John Rallins. But you can call me Jack, most people do."

She stared at him. "You probably change your name for every assignment. It reminds me of a movie with Audrey Hepburn and Cary Grant. He kept using different names."

He laughed. "I know. *Charade.* Great movie! And she kept asking him if there was a Mrs. Whatever. So, just for your information, no matter what name, I have still been divorced for many years. I still have a grown daughter I try to stay in touch with. And I do have an interest in British history, although I confess I was never a teacher." He looked at her closely. "Okay?"

It was completely dark now and she felt much calmer. Jack apparently thought it was time to leave. "How about taking a rain check on the Vietnam Memorial? I'll buy you a bite to eat and you can catch me up on what's going on in your life. Sound good?" He got to his feet, reaching a hand out to her.

She stood for a moment testing her knees to make sure they would hold this time, and then let Jack lead her across the Mall and out to a street where he flagged down a cab.

They arrived at Georgia Brown's after the dinner rush was over, so they were seated right away. Claire sat down at their table looking around the vibrant crowded room with curiosity. It was attractively decorated; the ceiling was covered with what looked like copper strands of seaweed floating horizontally through the space. Most of the tables were filled with smart and important looking people, but no one she recognized.

Her mind was too frazzled; she couldn't even make sense of the menu. She threw herself on the mercy of the waiter. "I'm not very hungry, what do you recommend?"

"She-crab soup. It's our specialty. That and some of our cornbread make a great meal."

She agreed. "Sounds great but I need a glass of wine." She thought a minute, shaking her head, unable to make a decision asked, "What do you recommend?"

He suggested a Kendall-Jackson Chardonnay they were offering by the glass and on her agreement turned to Jack. He ordered Scotch on the rocks, and then hesitating, he added the peach cobbler. Sheepishly he reminded her he was on local time and had already had dinner.

The waiter came back with their drinks and after a healthy swallow, Jack sat back and looked at Claire carefully.

"Are you okay? That was pretty scary. I wouldn't blame you for having hysterics or something." Then he smiled. "But knowing you as I do, I'd be surprised. You're pretty cool in an emergency, aren't you?"

"I don't think cool describes my reaction, frozen is more like it. Of course there are those times I just pass out cold or my legs give out." She smiled ruefully, remembering prior occasions. "I think I'm okay but I won't guarantee how long it will last."

She drew in her breath with a ragged shudder. "I just can't believe that on my first night in town I was mugged. But then, I don't suppose it mattered to him that I had just arrived."

Jack shook his head. "Don't suppose," he agreed. "Well, how is everyone? Have you been in contact with the rest of the tour group? Is Lucy's leg better? Have you heard from Betty? And how's my friend Joe?"

She laughed at his eagerness to know what was going on, only too glad to fill him in on the lives and happenings of the other members of their tour rather than continue to dwell on the encounter on the Mall.

Earlier in the year, Lucy Springer, her travel book author friend, had organized a tour for novice travelers to follow the route through England and Wales she described in her newest book, *An Armchair Traveler's Adventure.* Claire who had never traveled outside the States offered her bookstore, Gulliver's Travels, as a co-sponsor for the tour. She, of course, would also go along. It was a great publicity gimmick for both Lucy's book and Gulliver's Travels. It was unfortunate that Lucy broke her leg rather severely just before they left and couldn't go. So Claire ended up in charge. It was the trip from hell. Fortunately, Claire, novice that she was, didn't know until the end what danger they had been in. She thought the many problems they had were normal.

Jack was the tour director assigned them by Kingdom Coach Tours. But of course, as it turned out he had a bigger role than just tour director. Claire didn't know who he really worked for but assumed it was the C.I.A. Somehow it hadn't seemed appropriate then to ask him a lot of questions, and he wasn't given to volunteering much.

"Vern and Mike are scheduled to go to Paris for Christmas. They said they didn't know why they hadn't done more traveling over the years and felt they had to make up for lost time." She continued, trying to remember if she covered everyone.

"And, Lucy? How is she doing? I still want to meet that lady some day," Jack inquired as he dipped into the steaming cobbler with a large scoop of ice cream melting on top.

"She's really remarkable. You know Rosa didn't verify any of the data in the book which was, of course, the initial purpose for the trip. Lucy about had heart failure when she found out. But desperation drove her to be creative and she contacted Kingdom Coach Tours and hired them to verify the data. She was determined to meet her deadline. She's a professional. I really admire that in her."

Jack's eyes had darkened at the mention of Rosa, and Claire asked him for an update. He shook his head, an expression of disgust on his face.

"Still no clues. It's like she walked off the edge of the earth. But don't worry, we're looking for her. She almost got away with her little plan. But thanks to you, she'll think twice about trying anything as bold as that again.

"And we had her, that's what's so frustrating. We had her and she still got away!"

Claire paused between spoonfuls of the delicious soup. "But surely, you can't believe you're at fault for that. They stopped at nothing." She paled, remembering the horror she felt when she heard about the ambush in Miami, which facilitated Rosa's escape. "They killed all those people just to rescue her."

Then, she made a determined effort to think of more pleasant things. "Look, let's not talk about it. Tell me more about your daughter. Where does she live? What does she do? How often do you see her?"

So they finished their meal talking of personal things and gradually Claire relaxed again.

Finally Claire remembered her ten o'clock appointment in the morning would seem like seven to her because of the time difference. She pulled her windbreaker off the back of the chair. "I need to get back, Jack. Tomorrow is the meeting at Vantage Airlines and I need to be bright-eyed and bushy-tailed.

"It was so nice of the Lickmans to invite me. I just can't believe a Fortune 500 corporation would do something like this. It's so thoughtful. I wasn't interested in traveling again so soon, but I just couldn't turn them down."

When they were in the cab she continued as if there had been no interruption. "I've never been to a Board Meeting before. I don't even know the protocol. Do you?"

"Not really, but by this time tomorrow we will. Doug will be there. You remember him, don't you?"

"Doug Levine? Of course, but I thought he lived in London."

"Oh, he does from time to time, but he spends a lot of time here and he's been acting as the liaison with Vantage for the State Department. So of course he was included."

"Now I'm getting a little nervous, it sounds like this is a big deal."

"Are you kidding? Of course it's a big deal! If it hadn't been for you, Vantage would be in dire straits right now, say nothing of the 335 people who were on that plane. The Board of a big corporation usually meets only certain times of the year and apparently they intend to show their gratitude to you, albeit, quietly. And as well they should."

They finished the ride in silence; each thinking back to that time in London when Claire, convinced that Rosa had planted a bomb on their plane, insisted the flight, already on the runway in line for takeoff, be aborted.

She had been horrified at the seriousness of what she had done and was terrified she had acted foolishly, afraid it was all her imagination. When she was informed the bomb had indeed been found she didn't know whether to be hysterical or relieved. Then there was the danger to herself for being the main witness but she had been assured, when her deposition was captured on video, it would no longer be of benefit for anyone to eliminate her to prevent her being a witness.

But, of course, Claire had to assume Rosa and her friends knew of that videotape. Otherwise they might mistakenly rid themselves of her anyway. Hence a strange man with a knife might approach her out in the Mall.

Jack got out of the cab with Claire at the door of the hotel. "Look Claire, get some sleep and don't worry about this incident. I'm sure it was just a coincidence. Washington, D.C. has a very high crime rate, they are in a crisis. And you know I've warned you about walking alone on dark deserted streets."

She nodded. She knew. She knew, but she was probably still going to be worried for this whole trip. She wished she hadn't come. In California she had managed to put the whole London incident behind her. Now it was all back, including the worry about where Rosa was.

"And while you're here, I hope you'll have dinner with me. Remember, we never got the one we planned in York?"

"But you just bought me dinner."

He shook his head, "No, I mean a dinner date. Okay?"

She nodded, smiling, and got into the elevator, more than ready to end this day.

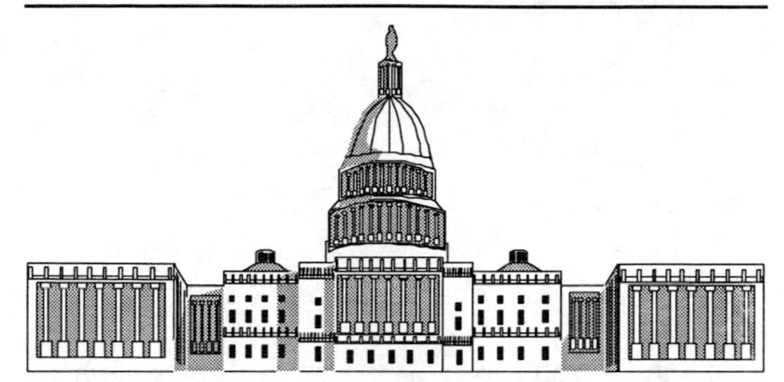

CHAPTER TWO

"Darn!"

She jumped at the shrill ring and dropped the tiny back to her earring. She tried to see where it fell at the same time backing up to reach for the phone on the bedside table.

"Ms. Gulliver, this is Ramon downstairs. Your car is waiting for you," the polite voice announced.

She smiled broadly at the message. She wasn't used to this kind of service, but she was learning to like it. Still she had to find the back of her earring, so she got down on her hands and knees and combed her fingers through the nap of the carpet until she found it. Finally, the earring in place, she took one final survey of herself in the mirror. Her friend Lucy was right again. Her suit was perfect for this meeting. Cut out of navy gabardine with tiny white stripes, the white linen collar and cuffs made it very stylish. She had bought it at Loehmann's discount store more than three years ago and, while she seldom wore business attire, she knew she had to have it. And she told herself then its classic style was not likely to be out of fashion soon. Today she wore it with a simple navy silk blouse, Lucy's borrowed pearls and earrings and a jaunty red silk poppy pinned on her lapel. Her red soft leather pumps and red fabric tote bag kept her from looking too somber.

She smiled at her reflection. Not glamorous, not young, but she thought she looked good. And, she admitted to herself she was a little excited about attending a Vantage Airlines Board Meeting. She felt like one of those people she saw in Fortune Magazine, a mover and a shaker. She tucked the plastic key card in her purse and sailed out the door, ready for anything.

"Good morning, ma'am. I'm Charlie Watts. Mr. and Mrs. Lickman asked me to drive you to the meeting this morning." He smiled, transforming his sober face to friendly. He then inquired with interest, "How are you enjoying your stay?"

"Oh, it's a wonderful city. I just got in last night, so I haven't seen much. But I'm looking forward to it."

Charlie ushered her out the door and into the long, dark blue Lincoln Town Car. When she was settled on the buttery cream-colored leather, the car pulled smoothly out into the traffic. Claire watched enthralled.

This was the political hub of the nation. The streets were crowded with pedestrians, including power brokers in business attire, bicycle messengers in their eclectic garb, tourists in shorts and sandals gaping and pointing, with taxis zipping through the melee and wall-to-wall cars. This city was teeming with life. It had a vitality that seemed present only in the truly great financial centers. It certainly was different than the pokey little street her bookstore sat on in Bayside California.

Charlie pulled to a stop in front of a solid Art Deco building where Vantage Airlines was etched deeply into the granite above the doors. He came around to open her door and help her out. She felt like a gawking tourist herself as she entered the building, trying to take in the details of the ornate lobby all at once. But remembering Charlie's instructions, she approached the young woman at the reception desk and gave her name. She was issued a name badge which she attached to her lapel. Meanwhile a young woman was summoned to whisk her up to the top floor in a private elevator before leading her into a small tastefully furnished conference room where Jack waited with Doug Levine.

"Doug! How nice to see you." Smiling, she grasped his hands warmly. Then, "And, Jack, how are you this morning?"

The men were both dressed in somber suits, but that's where the likeness ended. Jack, shorter, lean, sporting graying blond hair, was attractively tough looking. While Doug, tall, dark hair peppered with distinguished gray, and a dark tan, looked as if he could be an international playboy.

She smiled fondly at these two men who had cosseted her through her ordeal in London during the earlier part of the year. Jack had hovered protectively about making her feel physically safe in spite of the danger which seemed to abound. But then she knew him, having just come off of a two week tour with him acting as the official tour director for Kingdom Coach Tours. Of course, by then she knew he was really an agent along for the ride and to watch everything they did. It hadn't done much good as no one noticed anything amiss on the tour. It wasn't until she was on the return flight, waiting on the runway that it all came together. She had almost blacked out with fright, but somehow she got to the stewardesses in the front of the plane and insisted they abort the flight. That had been scary. And until they determined she was correct and they found the bomb on board, she had visions of spending a long time as a guest of the British prison system.

Doug, on the other hand, had been a complete stranger when he appeared at the request of Vantage Airlines. His role was to make sure she was accorded the proper respect and comfort while working with the British authorities. He was with her whenever the British authorities had talked to her, and during the long hours of videotaping when her testimony was recorded. He said he was there to protect her rights and she felt he was fully capable of doing just that. He was attached to the State Department and he made her feel, and the Brits, too, that he had the authority of the entire United States government standing behind him. She had quickly come to trust him and was very grateful for his support.

She and Doug chatted as one does on seeing someone familiar far from home and then Jack inquired, "How are you this morning, Claire? Did you sleep well?"

She smiled wryly. "I'm fine. But I have to admit I didn't get much sleep. With the excitement of this meeting looming and the letdown from my adrenaline rush I didn't expect much more. To tell you the truth, at about 3:30 this morning I was seriously thinking about forgetting the whole thing and just going home." She looked sheepish. "But I changed my mind. It would have been terribly rude."

Doug looked at them both puzzled. "Adrenaline rush? Did something happen?"

"Claire had an incident on the Mall last night."

"It was scary." Claire closed her eyes a moment then looked at Jack, carefully composing her face.

Jack nodded, agreeing with her, and proceeded to tell Doug about the attempted mugging, only to be interrupted by the door opening.

"Hi, I'm Suzanne Queensley. Claire Gulliver?" She approached Claire with her hand outstretched. "I'm so pleased to meet you."

Claire clasped her hand firmly, surprised to find the strong authoritative voice from her phone conversations belonged to this wispy, dusky, thirtyish woman. Suzanne's physical presence might have been more diminutive than her voice indicated, but her professional manner wasn't a disappointment. She was obviously in control as she turned towards the men.

"Jack and Doug." She read off their name tags as she shook hands with each.

"I'm so sorry you've been kept waiting but we're running a little over. Neil Pinschley, our Chief Financial Officer, is just finishing, and then everyone will break for a few minutes before the meeting resumes. As soon as they break, I'll take you in to introduce you to the Lickmans. They're so excited about meeting you. You are really special to this group of people as I'm sure they'll tell you themselves in a moment."

Then she changed the subject inquiring of Claire, "How was your flight? Are you comfortable at the hotel?"

Claire smiled. "Fine, fine. Everything and everyone was perfect. I'm getting spoiled riding in first class. I don't know if I'll be able to adjust to steerage the next time I take a trip."

"Good. Good." Suzanne laughed then returned to the agenda. "Now, after the break there will be a presentation from Wiley Blackford. He's one of our senior vice presidents and he's the Director of Safety and Security for Vantage. After his presentation he will introduce each of you and then open the discussion to the Board. I'm sure there will be questions. Don't worry; it will be very informal at this point. If someone asks something you can't answer, just refer those questions to Wiley. I suspect they will have lots of questions on this subject. Wiley has a lot to explain."

She looked at each of them and seeing no questions, continued. "After Wiley's presentation we'll all adjourn to the Executive Dining Room for lunch, and after lunch we will continue back in the boardroom with a presentation of the new advertising campaign. I think you may enjoy that. Then it will be over."

Just then the young woman who had ushered Claire upstairs poked her head in the room and nodded at Suzanne.

"Okay, they're on break. Follow me please."

David Lickman was a pleasant looking man with white thinning hair and a tanned face and scalp. He was dressed expensively in a charcoal gray suit, snowy white shirt and attractively patterned red, black and white tie. He looked like an actor who was perfectly cast in the role of a CEO. He was very gracious and greeted them warmly before turning to introduce them to his wife, MiMi.

Claire felt as if she had been enveloped in a warm hug even though Mrs. Lickman had only clasped her hands and smiled at her. She liked Mrs. Lickman immediately. She looked like a very stylish grandmother, slightly round and kind of short. Her hair was short and fluffy; its natural silver didn't look as if it had been introduced to a bottle of hair color. She wore a light mauve suit with burgundy shoes and gold jewelry. And while her manner was warm, her eyes radiated her intelligence. MiMi Lickman had an unusual role in Vantage Airline, as Claire had discovered when she researched the Lickmans. MiMi's father had started the airline and passed the reins to David on retirement. However, he continued to provide guidance to his son-in-law through control of the large block of stock he retained and when he died the stock was left to MiMi so she could have a say in the management of the company. While many women might have abdicated the voting rights to their husband, MiMi had not. She had become involved as her father had wished her to. And apparently her husband appreciated her involvement in the business.

The Lickmans were reported to enjoy a unique relationship of friendship, respect and love. They were reputed to be a happy, devoted couple and their track record in managing the airline included conservative but innovative actions that paid off.

"Neil, let me introduce you to our guest of honor." David Lickman gestured to a younger man as he came into the boardroom. "Claire, this is Neil Pinschley,

Vantage's Vice Chairman and CFO. Neil is my right hand man. I sleep better each night knowing he's here for Vantage." He patted Neil's shoulder fondly.

"Neil, this is Claire Gulliver."

"Claire, I can't tell you how glad I am to meet you. Thank you so much for coming to our meeting. Vantage Airlines owes you a debt it can never repay." He looked earnestly into her eyes; his intensity embarrassed her.

Neil was handsome, self-assured and outgoing and, except for the slight tick she saw controlling his left eyelid, perfect in almost every way.

Claire continued to study him while David introduced Neil to Jack and Doug and then another man joined them. David went through the introductions once again. This time he told them how Wiley Blackford, Senior Vice President and Director of Safety and Security would be explaining to the Board about the incident and describing what steps had been taken to correct the breach of their security.

Wiley said soberly, "And I'll be sweating the questions. They love to make me squirm." He was a big man, probably six foot four inches, and while easily well over two hundred pounds, there didn't appear to be an ounce of fat on him. His military bearing gave his conservative suit the look of a uniform. His large coffee colored hand swallowed Claire's in his grasp. "They're going to be successful today. I squirm every time I think about the *what ifs*. I thank you very much for your brave actions."

Wiley's admiration shone from his eyes.

She demurred, "Remember, I was on that flight. I was trying to save my own skin."

Suddenly the Board members were taking their seats. Wiley seated Claire next to him at the large oval table. The water pitchers, the glasses and the little bowls of mints, sitting at intervals down the middle of the table, were filled and waiting. In front of each person lay a little stack of papers, an agenda, a yellow lined tablet and a couple of sharpened pencils.

The faces turned her way were expectant. Claire felt their curiosity picking over her. She took a sip of water, her mouth suddenly dry with nerves. Neither Jack, nor Doug looked concerned and she envied them their panache.

David Lickman called the meeting to order and for the benefit of the guests introduced each member. Claire tried to concentrate so she could remember who was who, noting each one on the list of attendees provided for her with the agenda. Some registered well, the graceful, fifty-something Asian American woman, Bernice Eng-Smith, who was Vantage's Director of Customer Service and, of course, George Warton the former senator from Maryland. There was a Robert Pollack, who needed no announcement that he was retired military, his whole body screamed it, and a stunning woman who was apparently the head of her own public relations firm. As David Lickman moved around the table Claire gave up keeping the Board members fixed in mind, resorting instead to nodding and smiling while she tried to read the names on the badges pinned to their lapels.

When Wiley began his presentation, Claire was intrigued with the story he told. It wasn't a new story for her. She had been there. But somehow Wiley's factual accounting became a suspenseful drama.

"Excuse me, Wiley."

Claire thought the woman who spoke was the one in the public relations business and found her name, Katherine Gilford-Merrith, on her list.

"I don't understand about this Carol Daley. How did she explain her actions? How could she have so flagrantly ignored our safety rules? Why would she allow that woman to pass through to the boarding area without the proper screening?"

Wiley looked very uncomfortable. "Good question, Katherine. One we asked ourselves. Unfortunately, we will probably never hear the answer. Ms. Daley left early that day, shortly after this group was boarded and the plane had pulled back from the gate. Naturally, as soon as her role in this was revealed we conducted an all out search for some answers from her. But too late!"

He looked around the room, his eyes focusing on Katherine. "That day there was an incident in the Tube Station near her house. You might have heard about it? Two groups of rival football fans had a rather severe ruckus. Three people were killed, one died later in the hospital and about twenty were injured to varying degrees. One of the dead was Carol Daley. She was apparently in the wrong place at the wrong time. She never made it home. And we never got the chance to question her."

Shock appeared on Katherine's face; this whole incident had just become more real for her.

Claire felt a wave of sadness wash over her. Somehow when she agreed to come she hadn't thought about it all being dredged up again.

Carol Daley, the Vantage Customer Service Manager, who met them at Heathrow, had been a godsend for Claire just when Rosa refused to have her computer X-rayed at security for fear it would damage the hard drive. Then to complicate matters, Rosa's battery was dead. Had Claire been a more experienced traveler she would have known Rosa needed to keep her adapter plug with her so she could plug into an electrical outlet to boot up the computer for the security check. But Rosa had packed the adapter, relying on the fickle battery. Claire thought she was going to have to leave Rosa and the computer in London until Carol pulled strings to get them through security.

It was only later she had realized what a disservice that favor had really been.

She remembered how she had become nauseous when she learned what had happened to Carol, but then it was only one of many things which had that effect on her during that time.

Neil Pinschley looked sharply at the attractive Asian cast woman. "Bernice, she was one of your people, wasn't she? What's your explanation of Carol's behavior?"

Bernice Eng-Smith spoke calmly. "Carol Daley was one of our best senior Customer Service Managers. Ordinarily she was used to assist our most important customers. No one knows how she got involved with this Springer tour group. Frequently she would get a request directly from a senior executive without going through the usual channels and when that happened she usually reported those to her supervisor either before or after she took care of the situation."

"Are you suggesting that a senior executive of Vantage Airlines instructed her to break security rules?" Neil was outraged. "Wiley, have you had any indication of this?"

Wiley shook his head as Bernice continued, "No, of course I'm not accusing anyone. I'm just explaining how Carol worked.

"One of the ladies on duty in the Advantage Club that day said Carol did receive a phone call before hurrying out. The timing was such that we assume she went directly out to the check-in counter and connected up with the Springer tour. However, there was no indication as to who the call was from or even if it had anything to do with the tour."

Bernice continued in her calm voice. "As you know, delicate situations develop frequently and this group of employees is prepared to fix whatever is wrong.

"Actually, I remember that one of our people took care of one of your clients for you once, didn't they, Katherine? Some emergency situation you had in New York?" She waited for Katherine's agreement. "That's their job, solving problems. Ensuring the customer is being served appropriately. That's the Vantage way."

She paused, looking around the table, then said firmly, "Carol Daley was one of our best. We can't conceive how this happened. All of her colleagues and the people she worked with over the past years had nothing but respect for her. They are devastated at what happened to her."

The room was silent, absorbing Bernice's information.

"Katherine," Wiley addressed her in a respectful tone, "Do you have any more questions, or shall I continue?"

Katherine gestured turning both hands up. "Please go on."

Wiley continued with his story, pausing now and then to answer another question. But Claire's mind had drifted off. She knew this story and frankly, she didn't really want to hear it again. It haunted her, all the questions, all the *what ifs*. Looking back she wondered why they just didn't go home when things started going wrong on that tour. But then it was so subtle, even though now it looked obvious. It wasn't like all of a sudden she knew they were in danger. She kept thinking she was overreacting. She thought experienced travelers knew how to deal with these types of incidences.

She felt a shiver down her spine. It wasn't like that man in the park last night. That wasn't subtle. That was an out and out attempt on her life.

She felt her resolve stiffen. She wasn't going to be stupid again. She was not staying. She would explain to the Lickmans over lunch. They would understand. The incident last night was a warning. This time she would heed it.

"And, as you all know the fate which befell Pan Am subsequent to the Lockerbie incident, I'm sure you understand our gratitude to Claire Gulliver for piecing this together and refusing to be intimidated. She brought that plane to a halt on the runway and for that Vantage Airlines will be eternally grateful." Wiley stood up clapping, as did the other Board members.

That brought Claire's attention back to the meeting. Her cheeks turned pink as she reluctantly got to her feet. MiMi hurried around the table and gave her a big hug.

David Lickman walked up to her and put his arm around her shoulders and faced the group. "As Chairman and President of Vantage, I would like to echo Wiley's words. And I would like to present Claire a small token of esteem from Vantage." He nodded at his wife, "My dear," as MiMi handed Claire a beautifully wrapped box.

Claire's fingers tripped over the wrapping but finally she got to the velvet box, which she opened to find a beautiful gold and diamond Cartier watch. MiMi reached in and took it out of the box, turning it over so Claire could see it was inscribed, CG, *Vantage Airlines thanks you.*

Claire was speechless. Her fingers trembled on the clasp so much that finally she held out her wrist so MiMi could fasten it for her.

"So, let's move into lunch, shall we? We can continue our discussion there." David cavalierly took MiMi's arm on one side and Claire's on the other and guided them towards the dining room.

"I can't tell you how thrilled I am with the watch. I will cherish it." Then she leaned around David to better see MiMi. "But, MiMi, I'm so sorry to tell you I can't come to your house party this weekend. I'm leaving for the coast as soon as I can get on a plane."

"Oh, dear, have you had an emergency?" Her genuine look of distress was too much for Claire's conscience and her polite little lie withered on her tongue.

"Well, not exactly. No." She paused groping for something to cover her hasty retreat. "Well, I had an incident on the Mall last night, and frankly, listening to Wiley I realized I had had so many opportunities to avoid being involved last spring but I never saw them. And now I'm saying to myself, don't do that again. Just go home."

"Incident? What kind of incident?" David's authoritative voice didn't leave room for waffling.

"I was mugged."

MiMi gasped. "Oh my dear, how awful. Did you lose all your money?"

"Well, it was a little more serious than that. He had a knife. I'm pretty sure he meant to kill me." She couldn't stop the shiver up her spine at the memory of the look in his eyes.

"But obviously he didn't. Why?" David demanded the details.

"Well, actually, Jack came to my rescue. He had come by the hotel and when he learned I was heading down the Mall, he followed and caught up with me just about the time the mugger attacked." She tried to maintain her calm demeanor as she could see how upsetting this news was to MiMi. "Anyway, he saved me but the mugger got away. So I think it would be wise for me just to play it safe and go home."

David nodded gravely as he indicated the place at the table for Claire, on his right side. She felt relieved at having told them, knowing that after lunch she could be on her way home.

Claire laid the crisp white napkin on her lap and turned to answer a question put by a pleasant man on her right. He was one of the Directors whose name badge she couldn't see without twisting obviously in front of him.

The dining room was rich with dark wood, light walls and attractive artwork. The staff served unobtrusively. First came a bowl of luscious pumpkin bisque, followed by a Greek Salad accompanied by flaky hot rolls. The conversation flowed around the table, multiple conversations cohering into a single topic; then fragmenting again. She was pleasantly surprised when a beautiful Dover Sole was laid in front of her. She found it tasted even better than it looked, and she did a fair job of demolishing it between conversations.

One of the gentlemen, Cliff Denning, across the table had spent a great deal of time in San Francisco and was enjoying telling her about some of the finer restaurants he had visited there.

"Have you ever been to Bill's? It's a little hamburger joint out on Clement. Probably the best burgers I've ever had," clearly boasting of his knowledge of the hideaway.

She smiled. "And his garden? Have you been there in the spring when he has the garden filled with orchids? I grew up not far from there. Even now my mother and I have to go for an occasional burger fix."

He was so pleased; it was as if he found she was related to him. He wanted to tell everyone. But no one else had heard of Bill's and apparently didn't even think they were missing anything.

Claire knew the meal was almost over when the little dish of ripe berries arrived in front of her with a dollop of heavy cream. She didn't even think of demurring, as she thought they were the perfect ending to a wonderful meal.

Just before they left the dining room David leaned over and whispered, "Claire, I'd like you to stay a few minutes after the meeting is over, if you would?"

She nodded, wondering what he wanted. “Of course.”

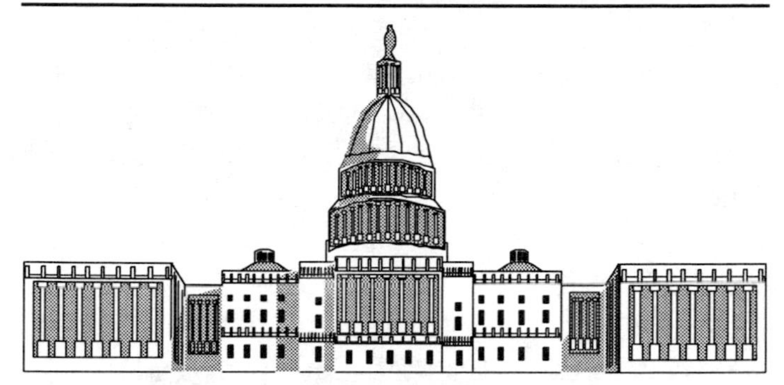

CHAPTER THREE

Claire applied a fresh coat of lipstick, then couldn't help twisting her wrist to better admire the beautiful watch she saw reflected in the mirror. She was thrilled. She had never owned anything so extravagant. And yet, despite the lavish praise heaped on her, she really didn't think she was deserving of it. She had really only done what anyone would have done in the same situation.

She gave one last tweak to a lock of hair which wanted to go its own way and then left the ladies room. She promised to meet with Mr. Lickman and as soon as she was finished with him she was going to find Suzanne and have her get her on the next flight home. And it certainly didn't have to be a seat in first class, she resolved; she was more than accustomed to sitting in coach. She admitted to being a little disappointed about missing the Vietnam Memorial, but she would come back another time. Right now she was more interested in getting home safely.

"Oh, there you are, Claire. I thought I had lost you. They're waiting for you in Mr. Lickman's office. This way." Suzanne moved rapidly.

Claire hurried behind her. As soon as she entered David Lickman's posh office and saw the people, who were apparently waiting for her, she flushed with embarrassment.

"I'm so sorry. I didn't know it was a meeting. I should have hurried." She took an empty chair and looked around the office, recognizing several of the people, including Wiley, MiMi, Doug and Jack.

"Claire, MiMi and I were both very concerned about your sudden decision to return to California."

He waved away her surprised look. "No. No, it's not because you're not coming to the house although, frankly, we were both looking forward to getting to know you better. No, we're just concerned that if what happened to you last night was anything but a random act of violence, going home might actually put you in harm's way, instead of removing you."

The logic of his words hit her and she suddenly found it difficult to breathe.

David continued, softly, "We couldn't bear to have something happen to you after all you did for us. We feel we have to make sure of your safety."

Wiley, on David's nod, began, "Jack gave us a brief rundown of the incident on the Mall. He says after leaving you last night he delivered the knife to his people for a lab check. As of a few minutes ago they haven't turned up anything, although they were able to confirm that they did find several partials and one full print on the weapon."

"When do they think they'll finish running the prints against the database?" Doug asked, concern clear in his eyes.

"And will they check with the locals as well as the FBI and Interpol?" one of the people Claire didn't recognize asked.

The door opened and Neil came into the room and took the last empty chair. He looked around expectantly. "Sorry I'm late. What's up?"

"Neil, glad you made it. I was hoping Suzanne's message would catch up with you." David was relieved Neil made it to the meeting.

Neil listened to Wiley briefly recap what had already transpired.

"Come on, Wiley. This is D.C. How many people get mugged here everyday? And probably most of them are tourists." He shook his head, disbelief showing clearly on his face. "I mean, do you seriously think this incident is part of a conspiracy?"

Neil's scorn actually made Claire feel better. He was right. It was only a chance mugging. They were all over-reacting.

"Neil, if there is any chance of it being something more we have to take the proper precautions." MiMi's voice was soft but firm.

"Yes, MiMi's right, we can't take any chances. Claire is here on our invitation. She has already been exposed to far too much danger on our behalf. We need to be absolutely sure she is safe before we send her home," David chided Neil.

"Of course, you're right, MiMi...David. We wouldn't want to take any chances which could result in harm to Ms. Gulliver." Neil turned to Claire, smiling. "So what is your plan for protecting her until we can determine whether the attack was random or specific?" He eyed Wiley, and then his look swept on to Jack.

"You're with the Company, if I remember correctly. Will your people take on this responsibility?"

Jack looked uncomfortable but shook his head no. "I don't think we can do anything here on U.S. soil. That task would more likely fall to the FBI, or even the local police. Or perhaps private security would be a better option until we are able to identify this guy and determine if he has any affiliations with the group in London."

"But didn't your group take responsibility for Claire's safety in London? All of a sudden it's not your problem?" Neil sounded annoyed; it was obvious he thought Claire's safety was Jack's responsibility.

Jack didn't rise to the bait. "It's not that it's not our problem, it's more that we don't have jurisdiction. Naturally we want to keep her safe. And if the attack has anything to do with the Guiness business, it's ours, even if we have to work through our local colleagues. Doug and I will meet with both agencies when we leave here and see if we can get it sorted out. Meanwhile, I'm afraid Vantage will have to be responsible for your guest."

"This is ridiculous! Claire must be protected. Wiley, what do you suggest?" MiMi was indignant.

Claire sat there, the conversation flowing around her, wondering how she had even thought that going home was going to make her safe. All those years ago when she had been a mystery novel fan she had frequently been irritated when the innocent heroine had unwittingly put herself in harm's way when it was so apparent to the reader that applying a little common sense would have kept her out of danger. And yet, here she was trying to do something stupid.

"Claire," MiMi was leaning toward her, "Claire, why don't you just come home with us. You'd be safe there, and you could come into the city for sightseeing with Charlie. He'd watch out for you. He is really more of a bodyguard than a chauffeur. Isn't that right, David?"

"Of course, why didn't I think of it? It's perfect, Claire. You were going to come out to the house for the weekend anyway. Just come home with us today. I'm sure we can jockey Charlie's schedule around to accommodate you. And perhaps your friends here," he gestured toward Jack and Doug, "can volunteer to take you to some of the attractions you're interested in visiting."

Claire was horrified. "Oh, no. I couldn't. It would be such an imposition. And Jack and Doug have other responsibilities. And, I'm sure Charlie has a fulltime job already without me added to his tasks." Then she turned to MiMi. "And you have to get ready for your Gala. Please, I agree I should stay until we determine where this attack came from, but I'll just stay at the hotel. The people there will watch out for me and I'll be careful."

The chorus of disagreement was emphatic. Claire sat back stunned. On one hand, she was appreciative of the universal concern. On the other, she was appalled that she wasn't going to be able to prevail.

"Nonsense, you won't be any trouble for me! First of all, I already have my two granddaughters visiting while their parents are out of town. If I can cope with them, I won't even notice you. And the house practically runs itself. I have to do very little to prepare for the party. The staff does most of it." A smile spread across her face, as she encouraged Claire. "I think it would be fun. Perhaps not what you expected from a tour of Washington, but we have tennis, a pool and, of course, sailing if you like that.

"Please say yes. I know I'll feel much better about your safety if I have you right where I can keep my eye on you."

Claire had misgivings. She was sure she would be a bother, but she couldn't find a graceful way to escape. And the Lickmans were sure her assailant would be identified within forty-eight hours and then, hopefully, he would be picked up and they would have their answer.

The meeting disbanded shortly after, and everyone left with certain tasks to accomplish. Claire's was to go back to her hotel and pack. Charlie would then bring her back with him to pick up the Lickmans for the drive home.

Later, when the limousine turned onto a private road, MiMi reached across the space between the facing seats and patted her knee. "Well dear, here we are."

David put away the papers he was reading. "Smooth ride, Charlie. Traffic was good for a change."

"Yes, sir. I'm sure glad for Ms. Gulliver's benefit. This way she didn't have to be subjected to that colorful language you use to describe the other drivers' skills."

David chuckled. "Me? Come on, Charlie, you know how good-natured I am."

"For sure Charlie knows, dear. And you may get away with fooling Claire for a few more hours, but I doubt you can hide your true nature much longer."

"Claire," he protested in an injured tone, "I'm being maligned. I'm a very gentle soul and, after I've changed my clothes and had a cocktail, I expect to be even mellower."

They had no more than gotten out of the car when the door on the wide portico burst open and a whirlwind shouting, "Gramimi, Grandpap," launched herself toward MiMi. On seeing Claire, the little girl suddenly shy, stopped, causing the larger girl behind her to crash into her.

MiMi reached out quickly, saving them both from a fall, and laughed. "Careful, careful." Then leaning down she swept them both in a hug. "I missed the two of you too."

Following closely was an older, gray haired woman, scolding the barking, jumping white terrier, who didn't pay the least bit of attention to her commands.

"Tuffy, quiet!" David said sternly. Then after giving each of the girls a hug and a kiss on the cheek, he bent over to fondle the terrier's ears. "Well, Claire, welcome to our quiet home. You know, the one you were afraid to be a bother in."

Claire had to laugh, immediately feeling as if she belonged.

"Oh, Claire, where are my manners? This is Amy and JoJo, our precious granddaughters." She put her arms around the two girls. "And this is Mrs. Kramer, the only sane person in the whole household."

Mrs. Kramer, a twinkle in her eye, nodded her head. "A few more days alone with this group and that won't be true any longer."

The dog barked for attention, dancing in circles around his mistress. MiMi bent over and patted him fondly. "And this is my baby, Laird Tuffus McGee. Tuffy for short."

"He looks just like the white dog in the Black and White Scotch ads," Claire couldn't help exclaiming.

MiMi nodded. "He's a West Highland Terrier. The black is a Scottie."

"He's my baby, aren't you, Tuffy?" The smallest girl knelt down wrapping her arms around the wiggling dog, rubbing her face in his neck while the dog twisted and turned trying to lick her.

"Amy, you know he isn't," her sister scolded.

"He is too. Gramimi said that while I was here he could be my baby, didn't you, Gramimi?"

"Of course, while you're here everything in the whole house is yours, and JoJo's. Right, Grandpap?"

"Right! Now let's go in the house and pretend like we're civilized."

"Mrs. Kramer, which room did you prepare for Claire?"

"The Rose Room. I thought she would enjoy it," Mrs. Kramer told MiMi, at the same time indicating with her head that Charlie should deliver the bags upstairs.

"Yes, that's good. Claire, may I suggest you go up and change into something more comfortable, as I plan to do. We're having a casual dinner tonight with the girls. So when you're ready, come down and join us for a drink in the parlor." She motioned to a door off the large entry hall they were standing in. "And then we'll give you a tour so you can find your way around."

"That would be great. I've been wearing these heels far too long." Claire grimaced, wishing her pinched toes had reached the numb stage.

"If you'd like to follow me, I'll show you your room," Mrs. Kramer said.

"Gramimi, can I show her up?" JoJo offered shyly.

"Would you, JoJo? I'm sure Mrs. Kramer has other things to do, and I know Claire would appreciate it." She smiled fondly at the girl, and then suggested to Amy, "Why don't you take Tuffy down to the solarium and play ball with him?"

"You're so lucky to have the Rose Room," JoJo said over her shoulder as she led the way up the generous curved staircase located at the back of the entry hall. "It's my favorite room."

"It is? Then why aren't you staying in the Rose room?" Claire inquired.

"Oh, no! We couldn't." She was shocked at the suggestion. "We're in the nursery. That's where we always stay. It's where Gramimi stayed when she was a little girl, and my mother did too, when she was little. But the Rose Room is different. You'll see. It's so romantic." The girl sighed. "When I'm grown up and bring my husband to visit, Gramimi promised we could stay in the Rose Room."

Then JoJo opened the double doors so Claire could see. It was beautiful. Soft rose colored silk covered the walls. French windows draped with gauzy white and outlined with a fabric full of large roses made up the far wall and looked over an immense body of water. The bed, tucked into an alcove was covered with the same material as the drapes. The white gauzy fabric floated down from the canopy. Two chairs flanking a small table in front of the fireplace were covered with more roses, not quite so big and against a soft green background. The tables and bureaus were a combination of woods but all blended together as if picked precisely to compliment each other. The deep pile rug was more flowers, roses of course, and instead of overwhelming the room it seemed to pull it all together. This room was as airy and beautiful as a spring day. Claire felt herself relax, sensing she would sleep well in this delightful room.

"JoJo, you're right. It is beautiful."

"And romantic, don't you think?"

Claire looked around her thoughtfully and then smiled. "Yes, I do. It's very romantic. It was very nice of Mrs. Kramer to put me in this room."

A discreet knock on the open door interrupted them.

"Can I just put these down for you, Ms. Gulliver?" Charlie had Claire's bags. He went into the attached room which opened into a luxurious bath and opened the closet, pulling out a luggage rack on which to place her large wheelie bag. "If you'd like some help unpacking, just hit star-seven on the phone and Mrs. Kramer will arrange it. She will also take care of any laundry or ironing you need done." He smiled and winked at JoJo as he hurried out.

Claire looked at the bag and sighed. She would have to unpack. Maybe her clothes hadn't had time to wrinkle again as she had only packed them a short while ago. And she needed to find her other shoes.

"JoJo, Gramimi said for you to go get changed for dinner." Amy popped her head in the open doorway.

Claire wondered if the little girl ever slowed down; she was like a whirling dervish with her eyes sparkling, her toes dancing, every bit of her was in constant motion.

"I thought we weren't dressing." JoJo was clearly reluctant to move, hovering expectantly over Claire's suitcase and waiting to see what treasures would come forth.

"Not *dressed,* but Gramimi said no shorts. We can pick. Come on, I'll race you to the nursery."

With that she was off and JoJo, refusing to be beaten, was on her heels. Claire was left in peace to look more closely at the room; to peek out the windows at the sloping lawn ending at a dock stretching into the bay, or inlet, or whatever it was; to change into a casual dress, a soft print with a longish skirt and matching soft blouse; and finally, to plop in the comfortable chair and rest a moment.

Maybe she dozed, but suddenly she was conscious that time had been moving along and she wondered if she was late. She punched in the number star-seven on the phone and, sure enough, Mrs. Kramer answered.

"I'm sorry to bother you, Mrs. Kramer, but I wondered what time dinner was being served."

"No bother, none. And a good thing you called or you might have missed cocktails. Dinner is at seven tonight. You know, because of the girls' schedule. Cocktails are being served now in the parlor, so any time you're ready will be fine."

It didn't take long, because suddenly Claire felt the need for a cocktail.

"Hello, dear. Are you settling in?" MiMi turned to her husband. "Get Claire a drink, love. She looks as if she could use one."

David was sitting in a comfortable looking chair with a glass of amber liquid in his hand. He good-naturedly got to his feet. "What can I get you?"

"White wine would be great, thanks." Claire looked around the room with appreciation. "What a wonderful house you have MiMi. It's like some of the great manor houses I saw in Britain but more comfortable, like it's really lived in."

"That's very sweet. We do live in it and we've tried to keep it updated so it's comfortable as well. It's so sad when one of these lovely houses becomes so outdated it is a chore to live in it. Suddenly it's so costly to update that the owners would rather sell it or tear it down. That's what happened to this old neighborhood. When my mother lived here there were more than two-dozen of these great houses. Now we're the only one left." She sighed and smiled. "But we love this place, don't we, dear?"

"We do. But we could have had a couple of new homes for the cost of upkeep on this one," her husband grumbled, then admitted, "but MiMi's right. We all love it, and someday the granddaughters will be living here."

As if on cue, there were footsteps in the hall and Amy arrived in her customary burst of energy. "Did we miss cocktails? Did we? JoJo took so long to decide what to wear, I didn't think she'd ever be ready."

"Shush, Amy. I did not." JoJo arrived more sedately as befitted her ten-year-old maturity.

"You both look very nice, girls. And you have plenty of time for a drink. Grandpap, the girls need a cocktail."

David got to his feet once more, winking at the girls as he mixed elaborate drinks of fruit juice and seltzer. He placed them on a small tray and served them with a flourish they clearly enjoyed.

Dinner was served in a small intimate dining room, separated from the large formal room by slider doors. When they had large parties, MiMi explained, they could extend the size of the larger room by opening the sliders. And breakfast and lunch were usually served in the solarium. She gestured to the room so Claire would be able to find it in the morning.

"In the morning there is coffee, juice and fruit set out there from six o'clock until about ten, and you just ring the buzzer near the serving table when you're ready for your breakfast. That way everyone can keep to his or her own schedule. We find it very efficient.

"Of course, the morning after the Gala the house will be full of people, so we'll have someone manning the breakfast room the whole morning."

"Oh, will there be a lot of people staying here then?"

"I think about twenty. It's easier to have them stay over a few days than worry about getting some of them home safely."

"What MiMi means, Claire, is some of them like to party till dawn, so we may as well give them a bedroom, as they'll be here anyway."

MiMi laughed. "Well, actually some of our friends..."

"And relatives," David added.

"Yes. Some of them don't know when to stop. But it's only one weekend. And since it's the end of the summer, everyone tries to make it last forever."

"Ugh! Gramimi, do I have to?" The disgusted look on Amy's face was comical as she eyed the dish she was being offered.

MiMi took pity and shook her head. "No, dear. Just eat the other things. The spinach soufflé is a special treat for your Grandpap."

"David loves spinach soufflé so this is a sample of what will be on the buffet table on Saturday. I can't say I'm overly fond of it either, but some people will enjoy it."

David helped himself to a liberal amount and Claire was happy to join him, being fond of the dish herself. She was surprised to find herself scarfing down the spinach along with baby lamb chops, tiny roasted potatoes, vegetables and mint sauce. She thought at lunch today she'd never have to eat again and here she was eating as if she was starved. It was a wonderful meal and she told MiMi so.

MiMi smiled at her praise. "Marilou, our cook, did this. She is a wonder in the kitchen."

"You should have been here last night. Cook was off, so MiMi and the girls did dinner. Didn't you, girls?" David's face was serious but his eyes gave away his suppressed laughter.

"It was so good. Gramimi is a great cook, aren't you, Gramimi?" Amy was serious and JoJo nodded her agreement.

"Well, I used to think I was."

Amy shook her head. "She is!" Amy was emphatic. "You are. We made fish sticks."

"And macaroni and cheese," JoJo added. "It was our best meal yet."

The grownups looked at each other and then had to laugh.

"Gourmet cooking is just in how you look at it," MiMi explained. "Actually, the fish sticks weren't bad.

Either they've improved them or I've forgotten how they tasted when I served them to their mother." She watched Amy struggling with her knife and fork and offered, "Here, dear, let me help you cut that up or you'll never be able to finish your meal. Cook made your favorite desert."

At the end of their meal, the young lady who had been serving them brought in a message for Claire from Jack.

"I need to call him. And I need to call home and let them know where I am." She suddenly felt guilty. She hadn't thought about the store all day.

"We'll have our coffee in the solarium because the girls and I are going to play a hot game of Yahtzee. David will be in the library. David, do you want coffee?" At his headshake she went on. "Claire, why don't you use the phone in that little room off the library and when you're done you can join us in the solarium. Then we can discuss what you want to do with your day tomorrow? And we may let you play a game of Yahtzee with us."

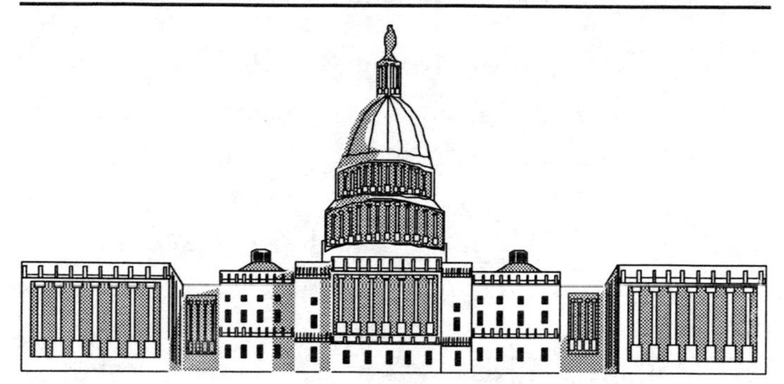

CHAPTER FOUR

He parked his Nova under a streetlight. Even though it was a '77 and the exterior was appropriately dilapidated for a car that age, the souped up car could outrun most other cars on the road. It was valuable to him. When anyone questioned why he kept it parked in his pricey garage he just said he kept it to remind him of his roots but the truth was he kept it for times like this when his hot Porsche would attract undue attention.

This was a skuzzy neighborhood, not one he would ordinarily frequent but the bar down the block was perfect for his meeting. He dressed to match the car with old sneakers, worn jeans, a dark tee shirt and a nondescript nylon Windbreaker. He was invisible on these streets but he still kept his eyes open for unpleasant surprises as he quickly moved down the sidewalk. He was street smart even after all these years and he knew enough to stay alert instead of relying too heavily on the protection of the small caliber pistol tucked in his jacket's pocket.

Most of the neon sign was burned out, announcing only r's Bar. The doorway was littered with trash and smelled as if it had been used as a urinal. When he pushed the door open, the dim interior wasn't any more inviting than the exterior. His eyes roamed the room and saw Tony sitting at a table on the far side, furthest from the bar and the pool table. He indicated to the bartender as he passed he wanted two more, the same as the empty beer bottle sitting in front of Tony, figuring it was the safest drink in this kind of establishment.

He hadn't even sat down before Tony started explaining, "I tried to call you last night. Where were you?"

"Yeah? Well, you didn't try hard enough. It would have been good to have a heads up. When she showed up at the meeting I wasn't surprised, assuming you hadn't had a chance to get to her; but when I found out you tried...and failed, I was speechless. How the hell does Tony the Pickman fail to take out a mark—a little old librarian at that?" He shook his head, his eyes boring into Tony's. "Christ, I thought you were a pro."

"Hey, this wasn't my fault. No, no. It was totally weird. The guy just flew out of the night and bowled me over. Even that wouldn't have stopped me if the damned knife hadn't landed right under his hand. And you should have seen him. He was ready; I could see it in his eyes. So I just got out of there. And I left my favorite knife. Shit, it was bad luck." Tony's eyes sought his face trying to read his reaction. "I didn't really expect to be able to do it the first night she arrived. It was just a fluke. I saw her coming out of the hotel alone so I thought I'd go for it.

"But don't worry. I'll do her. It'll be easy."

"No!" The word shot out of his mouth louder than

he intended. Looking around he lowered his voice. "No, you can't do her now. You should have heard them. They have all these theories. They have her tucked away for safekeeping. They're looking for you. If you had done what you promised, it would be all over with no problem. But now they're all suspicious and any further attempt would be too obvious. No, I can't risk jeopardizing the plan now." He sat back in his chair while the bartender delivered the two bottles and scooped up Tony's empty.

"You were lucky. That guy, the one who tackled you?..."

Tony nodded.

"...he belongs to the Company. He's a friend of hers and was trying to catch up with her. He would have chewed you up and spit you out. Those guys look harmless and act deadly." He nodded, thinking about it. "Yep, it was good you ran. If he caught you Saturday couldn't happen.

"Now they have her with them in the big house. They're waiting to see if any threat develops. No, I think we'll just leave her there. She'll give them all something to focus on, another distraction while we move forward with our plans.

"And who knows, maybe she likes spinach. She'd just be another victim. And, if not, she'll never know how lucky she was." His smile was cruel. Claire had caused him so much trouble with her meddling earlier in the year he couldn't resist the temptation to pay her back for her trouble. "Fair is fair," he decided. It was his own reward system. But it seemed she lived a charmed life, so for now she was safe.

"But what about my money?" Tony whined, not knowing enough to leave it alone.

"You ass," he hissed. "You blew it. Get it? You don't get paid for screw ups."

Abruptly he changed subjects. "Okay, let's go over the plans for Saturday one more time."

"I got the stuff. Doc Yeoman delivered it yesterday along with detailed instructions. I know how to keep it alive and how to insert it in the food. Don't worry; this will be a piece of cake." He chuckled. "I have to hand it to you. What a great idea. No one will ever know it wasn't accidental. The catering company gets the heat and the target will either be dead or as good as..."

"What could go wrong?" He interrupted, tired of Tony's talk, wanting to make sure every detail had been covered. After the aborted incident last spring he didn't want to take any chance this plan could be botched.

"Well, if someone reheated the dish after I added the spores they might die, but that's hardly likely as the heat would overcook the soufflé and ruin it. The real risk is if he doesn't eat it for some reason."

"He'll eat it. He loves it. That's why his wife serves it at their parties, just for him. And since it's not wildly popular we won't have people dying all over the place. But everyone who eats some will get sick. Some will get deathly sick." He chuckled. "Well, life's a bitch!"

Once more he was grilling Tony. "Okay, what about your gig with the catering company? Is that all set?"

"Yeah, no problem. My cousin talked to his friend and I'm in."

"Well, we do have a problem, thanks to your botched attack on Ms. Gulliver. She's going to be there, and her friend, so don't let them see you."

"Don't worry I'm strictly kitchen help. We come through the back door, work in the kitchen and leave the same way. No way anyone at that party will even know I'm there. We're set."

He nodded his head. "Well," He got to his feet, reaching into his jeans pocket he pulled out a few bills and tossed them on the table, "just make sure nothing goes wrong on Saturday and you'll get your money. All of it! Screw up again and you won't need money. Understand?" And he walked out without looking back.

* * *

David looked up from his reading when MiMi and Claire entered the library. "All quiet in the nursery?"

"Amy was out like a light. That's one good thing about all her energy; it does wear her out."

"Can I get you ladies a nightcap?" David was the consummate host.

"Please," MiMi said gratefully, sitting in a comfortable chair while Tuffy collapsed at her feet, his chin resting on her foot. "A little brandy, I think. What about you, Claire?"

"If you still have some of that white wine I had earlier I wouldn't mind another glass, although frankly I don't think I need anything to help me sleep tonight."

"I talked to Jack after you did, Claire," David told her as he handed her the delicate wine glass.

She nodded. He had told her he would call David.

"They still haven't gotten anything from the prints and, in fact, Jack feels they may not, as the one good print was smudged. So, since they don't really believe in coincidence, they have decided they need to consider this as a threat to you." He looked at her. "Not good news for you, huh?

"Jack will be assigned as advisory and will coordinate the efforts to keep you safe. Jack and Wiley will be out here tomorrow afternoon to meet with Charlie. They want to look around the premises to make sure the house and grounds are secure. And then they will want to meet with us all to make sure we know the plan.

"So I suggested they stay for dinner." He looked at his wife for confirmation.

"Of course. Good idea!" MiMi took the news of guests for dinner calmly.

"And I asked Neil to drive me home so he could be here too. I really feel he needs to be kept in the loop on this one."

MiMi nodded. "I'll have the girls fed early so we can talk freely. I don't want to worry them."

MiMi turned her attention to Claire. "Did you get all your calling done, dear?"

Claire nodded. "Yes, thank you so much. Everything at the store is fine. Thank goodness I have Mrs. B to watch over everything. She never has any problems or, if she does, she just solves them somehow."

"I admire you so much for running your own business. It must take a lot of courage, say nothing about effort, to make a success of a little store. I don't know how you can compete with the Barnes and Nobles or Borders Books." MiMi shook her head. "And nowadays everyone is buying on the web too. It wears me out just thinking about it."

Claire laughed. "Remember, it's just a little store. While there are as many tasks to be done as in a big store, they are all done on a much smaller scale. And of course, that's why I choose to specialize. We only do travel books, so it's easier to compete. The big stores have a few rows of travel books, where I have a whole store of them. And everyone who works for me quickly becomes a travel expert, after being exposed to the lecturers and the customers, who love to talk about their adventures. And customers like to come in and look through the books in our comfortable ell before they select the ones they want. So, you see, we add value to the purchases."

"Well, your Mrs. B sounds wonderful. The key to any business is the staff and obviously you have a good one."

Claire agreed. When she had received the invitation from the Lickmans to come to D.C. her immediate reaction was that she couldn't possibly. She had only just returned from Lucy Springer's Untour, and it seemed impossible to turn around and leave again. However, Mrs. B was adamant Claire should accept the invitation, so much so, that Claire accused her of trying to get her out of her way. But, because she really wanted to go, she had let herself be persuaded. So here she was in D.C. and, after being here only two days, she was the cause of all kinds of trouble for the Lickmans in spite of their assurance that she was not a problem.

"Do you ladies mind if I turn on the news?" David switched on the television just in time to get the weather. "Well, Claire, I guess our usual weather is going to be back tomorrow. You'll get a taste of our famous H's, heat and humidity." He turned his attention to his wife. "What do you have planned?"

"Not much, but the girls and I are taking Claire down to Aldo's on the dock for lunch."

"And JoJo wants to show me her swimming, so we're going in the pool when we get back." Claire contributed, "I thought I might take a walk around in the morning, if that's all right."

"Good idea. Just go out through the solarium and leave the door open. Don't worry if Tuffy insists on joining you. He knows his way around and won't stray."

"Well, I think it's my bedtime. I'd just like to tell you both once again how thrilled I am with my watch." She twisted her arm so the light bounced off it. "And how kind you are to invite me out to your house. I'm really enjoying myself. And the girls are wonderful."

"We're glad to have you. I hope you sleep well. Just make yourself at home."

"Night." David's reply was brief, his attention on CNN.

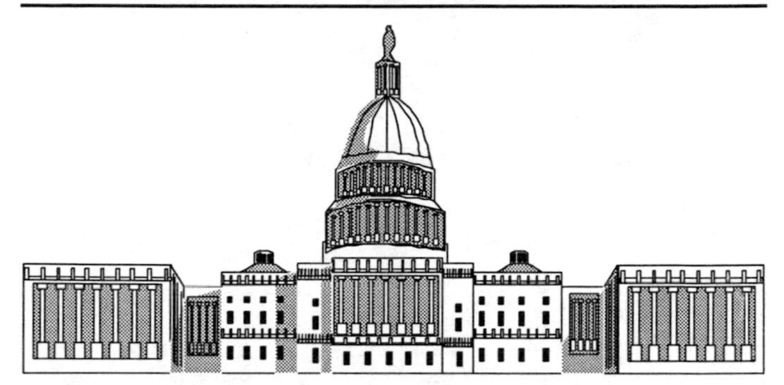

CHAPTER FIVE

The solarium was deserted when Claire helped herself to juice and coffee. But when she headed for the door leading to the flag-stoned terrace, Tuffy miraculously appeared, dancing with enthusiasm at the prospect of going outside.

"You want to go with me?" That was a stupid question, she thought, watching his pointy tail twirl so hard his whole rear end shook.

Claire didn't quite know how to treat a dog, especially this dog, who seemed to be a valued member of the Lickman family. She had never had a dog, or any pet for that matter, only Theroux, the cat, which came to live at the store. Theroux wasn't a pet. She lived there at her choice; she allowed herself to be petted on occasion, but disdained any further attempt at intimacy. And she ruled over the bookstore as a queen did her empire.

"Well, come along," she told him as she headed toward the water and the boat dock she had seen from her bedroom window. He trotted beside her, seemingly as happy as she was to be out on such a nice morning before the promised heat of the day arrived. The dock was sizeable, stretching out into deep water in the little cove. It was much bigger than needed for the three boats tied there invitingly. There was a small rowboat, a snazzy looking ski boat and a small catamaran which seemed to provide a little something for everyone. The cove itself had a sandy beach stretching out from the dock on one side, while the other side was rocky, perfect for searching for sea creatures.

Tuffy tore off barking sharply. Claire jumped, startled, but then had to laugh when she saw he was only guarding his turf from a seagull trying to rest on the dock. She turned and walked along the rocky side of the cove to the formal garden she could see ahead, laid out from the rocks to the house and the trees along the far edge of the property.

Tuffy caught up with her, then scampered ahead to enter a gravel path leading into the gardens, disappearing once more.

The path meandered past a pond, some statues and a nook with a bench inviting her to sit. She didn't succumb to the temptation forging on in her quest to explore but promising she would return later to enjoy that spot. The summer blooms were dying back at the same time fall flowers were starting to bloom. While she was not a gardener she recognized a great deal of planning and work had gone into making this garden so delightful. When she followed the path behind a high hedge she found Tuffy again. The dog was wiggling at the feet of a man stooped over to fondle his ears.

"Good morning," she said taking in the vegetable garden, planted attractively just outside a door leading into the house. She guessed it must lead into the kitchen area.

"Hello." He straightened. "Is Tuffy taking you for a walk?"

She laughed. "How did you know?" She walked forward her hand held out. "I'm Claire Gulliver and I'm staying with the Lickmans for a few days."

He pulled the gardening glove off his hand before grasping hers. "I'm Percy Imamura. I take care of the grounds. We're getting a head start for Saturday. This place takes a lot of work."

"I believe that. But it's beautiful. Do you do all this?"

He was a short, stocky man of Japanese ancestry, not fat, but a sturdy square shape. His face gave no hint of his age but his manners were that of a mature man. "No, I have several sons and nephews who do the work." His eyes twinkled with good humor. "But I usually come to the Lickmans' at least once a week. I like to make sure it remains a showplace." Then he smiled somewhat sheepishly. "And, I admit, I like to get my hands in the dirt a bit."

"I was admiring the flowers as I came through but frankly these vegetables take my breath away."

He was pleased and took a few minutes to show her the herbs as well as to point to the back end of the garden where fruit trees grew. "They use all this for the house. Cook likes her produce fresh. She picks what she wants herself. I've been fortunate enough to taste her work and can attest to the fact she is a master chef."

Claire nodded. "I sampled her work last night." Then she smiled, remembering. "Of course, little Amy says her grandmother is the best cook. Apparently she makes great fish sticks."

Percy's grin matched hers. "That little Amy is something, isn't she? I'm surprised I haven't seen her this morning. She usually likes to work with me while I'm here. She has her own row of carrots over there but she has to keep pulling one up to see if it's grown. I came back and planted some more for her a couple of times while she wasn't looking, but I can't keep ahead of her. She has a few left that may get big enough for her to have at dinner."

They chatted about the gardens for a few more minutes and then Claire was off again. Tuffy led, confidently heading into the thick woods surrounding the estate, anxious to explore the delights waiting in the trees.

The thick woods muted all sounds but the birds and scolding squirrels. It was like another world, yet Claire knew she was only a short distance from the house. She assumed this was originally a bridle trail because Percy had told her the garages had been converted from extensive stables after the Lickmans' daughter had grown. The sunlight forced its way through the thick foliage to pleasantly dapple the path. Tuffy emerged from the brush, panting with enthusiasm, his nose covered with dirt. He had twigs and grass caught in his hair.

"Well, where have you been?" She scolded lightly, "Up to no good I'd bet." He barked and turned around to jauntily lead the way. When the path branched he took the right fork which led them out by the tennis courts.

"Claire, Tuffy! There you are. Gramimi said I could come and see if you wanted to have breakfast with me." Amy was full of bounce even so early in the day.

"What a good idea. Have you been up long?"

"Forever. But JoJo just didn't want to get up, so I finally came down without her." She bent over to hug Tuffy. "How are you this morning, Tuffy? Did you sleep well?" She sounded just like her grandmother.

"Come on and I'll race you to the house," she challenged already running toward the house. The dog quickly took the lead and Claire, with a laugh, followed. She had forgotten the joy of racing all out across the lawn on a beautiful morning.

MiMi laid down the paper when they arrived in the solarium. "Well, you all look as if you had a nice walk."

At first Claire tried to hide her gasps, but finally gave it up; she was much older than Amy, who wasn't even breathing hard. She collapsed in a chair and breathed deeply until she could answer. "It's beautiful out and the garden is wonderful. Are you the gardener?"

MiMi smiled. "It's a joint effort really. David and I both have our favorites. Then cook has her requirements." She laughed. "And, of course, Percy has the final say."

"I met him. He says he's getting a head start on the preparations for Saturday."

MiMi nodded, reaching out to help Amy pour milk into the bowl of oatmeal, which had just been put in front of her.

"Careful, dear, not too full." Disaster averted, she looked back at Claire. "We're so lucky to have him. He doesn't do much gardening anymore. But we were his first clients, so he takes a personal interest in our grounds. All his workers are as committed as he is and they do wonderful work. You'll see his boys Saturday. They will be here to park the cars for all the guests. It was our lucky day when he came to work for us."

Claire's breathing had completely recovered, so she stood and helped herself to some toast and fruit.

"Don't you want something more substantial?" MiMi suggested. "Just push the button for the kitchen."

"No, if we're going to lunch, this will be plenty until then. Thanks anyway." She glanced at her watch. "What time will we be going out?"

JoJo, came into the solarium, still looking bleary-eyed.

"Good morning, pumpkin. Still a little sleepy?" her grandmother inquired.

She nodded, helped herself to a glass of orange juice, pressed the button and asked for oatmeal and then sat down at the table.

"Amy, you made too much noise this morning," she accused in a grouchy tone.

"Did not!"

"Did so! I wanted to sleep longer."

"Girls, girls. Be nice. Claire and I were just talking about going out today. We're going to Annapolis and we'll have lunch there. Do you want to go with us?"

They both nodded enthusiastically.

"Then be ready by eleven, all right? We're having company this evening, so you'll be having dinner upstairs tonight." She smiled at their disappointed faces. "But we'll get a movie for you to watch after you eat. You can pick it while we're in town."

* * *

Claire didn't think she had fallen asleep but when the shadow came between her and the sun, it disturbed her and she was suddenly aware the girls had gone.

"Be careful you don't get too much sun."

She struggled to sit up, certain her mouth had been gaping, wondering with horror if she had been drooling. "Jack. When did you get here?"

"About an hour ago. When I saw you were still out here, I thought I'd better warn you."

She poked her finger on her arm and seeing the white spot it left, she pulled on her shirt. "Thanks, I think I'm almost cooked. I didn't realize how tired I was. Those little girls wore me out today. First Amy had to race me back to breakfast, then they had to look in every store in Annapolis for just the right present for one of their friends, and finally I had to swim laps with them this afternoon."

"I guess you don't know the secret word?" He laughed at her puzzled expression. "You know the word? No!"

She laughed. "Well, why didn't I think of that? At the time it didn't seem to be one of the choices." She started gathering up her belongings. "I'd better go in and get cleaned up."

He walked beside her as she headed for the house. "I thought maybe we could meet tomorrow afternoon and do the Vietnam Memorial, the Korean Memorial and then have dinner. How does that sound?"

"Good. It sounds good." She glanced at him thoughtfully. "You know, I really didn't expect to see you again. I guess I'm still a little surprised."

"What? You didn't get my postcards?"

"Ah. I thought they were from you. But you didn't sign them."

"Well, I'm used to being secretive. I figured you'd know who sent them."

She nodded, "I did."

"Well, I just wanted to keep in touch. I'm not very good at that, but you know it's because of my job... well, it's hard to have a relationship. Anyway, that's why when I found out we were both going to be here, I thought it was destiny intervening. I was hoping we could get to know each other a little better."

"Starting with your name?"

He grinned. "You have the right one, but I can't guarantee I'll be using it the next time you see me."

She looked at him seeing the serious expression in his eyes, despite the grin on his face. "I see." Just then they reached the house. "I need to get cleaned up for dinner. Can we discuss the details about tomorrow later?"

She headed for the back stairs and her room thinking about what he had said. So Jack had sent those postcards. When the first one arrived, the innocuous message gave no clue as to who sent it, only saying the person was thinking of her. That one had been mailed from Paris. The second and third had been mailed from other towns, Dover and Amsterdam. Claire hadn't given the first one much thought, as many of her customers sent postcards and some even forgot to sign them. When the second and third arrived with the same unique scroll, she had a strange feeling they might be from Jack. But she had scolded herself for being a romantic; telling herself a relationship wasn't going to happen. And it wasn't. But she was glad to see him again and she would enjoy his company tomorrow.

* * *

Claire thought the parlor was empty when Neil spoke. "Good evening, Ms. Gulliver. How was your day?" He was standing in a shadow near one of the French windows opening onto the terrace.

She smiled. "Please call me Claire. And thank you for asking. I had a very pleasant day. I think it was a good choice to come out here. I'm enjoying the Lickmans and especially their granddaughters."

"Can I get you a drink?"

She nodded. "White wine, please." Then accepting a glass from him she asked, "Where is everyone?"

He shrugged. "David went up to see the girls and get changed, and the others are around. Probably they haven't finished their inspection yet. Would you care to sit?" He indicated a seating group behind her.

"Actually, I'm glad to have a little time with you alone, Claire. I wanted to talk to you a bit. You know? Get to know you better. I see you're wearing the watch. I hope you like it. We decided it was something you could wear as a reminder of our appreciation, without calling undue attention to you."

She nodded, holding her wrist out to admire it once again. "I love it. It's far more than I would ever have anticipated. This trip was more than I anticipated. Vantage is a very special company. I'm sure there aren't many companies in this day which take a personal interest in situations like this."

He agreed. "I believe Vantage is truly a unique organization. That's why I was thrilled to be invited to join them. And, of course, that is one of the reasons I'm dedicated to managing them. I want to ensure they maintain those same qualities even after David retires."

"Oh, will he be retiring soon?"

"Too soon, if you ask me." His smile was tight. "Actually, he had planned to retire at the beginning of last year but then had second thoughts. Can't say as I blame him. He's in great shape; the company is going strong, and he loves his job. So why not work a few more years?"

"Especially when I have Neil doing the hard work for me, hey Neil?" David Lickman headed directly for the bar set out on a cart in the corner.

Neil lifted his glass in a salute. "Glad to be some use to you. It's a privilege to work with a genius like David. Hopefully, we'll be working together for many more years."

"Well, not too many. After all MiMi and I want to do a few things while we're still young enough. And I know Neil well enough to know he won't be willing to wait forever, right?" He winked at Claire. "Neil's ambitious, of course. That's one of the reasons we wanted him. It won't do to keep him in second place too long, or he's liable to get antsy."

Neil nodded his agreement.

"But things will come, when the time is right." David turned to Claire. "And how did your day go?"

She smiled. "I don't know how MiMi keeps up with those girls. They wore me out. It makes me wonder if I should have had some of my own."

"Oh, oh, trust me on this, Claire. It's much easier to be a grandparent or an aunt. A fulltime diet takes all your time and energy for about twenty years and that's 24-7, as they say now. MiMi and I really enjoy the grandchildren in a way we couldn't our daughter. She says we spoil them but we just enjoy them. And we don't have to be responsible for raising them. So we love them, spoil them and then give them back to their parents until the next time. And, as soon as they leave, we collapsc for a while until we get our energy back."

"What's that, dear? Are you telling our secrets?" MiMi arrived and Jack and Wiley were right behind her.

It took a while before everyone had drinks. Then Mrs. Kramer came in and put an attractive tray of hors d'oeuvres down on a coffee table. Claire noticed that no one was talking about the serious issues, instead keeping the conversation on lighter subjects. So she didn't ask any of the dozens of questions she had.

David patted his pocket before reaching in to pull out a piece of paper. "Claire, I almost forgot. Suzanne sent you this." He laughed. "Good thing I remembered or she'd be pinning a note on me like the kindergarten teacher did."

Claire glanced at the paper. It was an itinerary for the next day, starting at the Library of Congress, lunch with Marian Kirkpatrick, and then meeting Jack for the visit to the Vietnam and Korean War Memorials.

She looked up with amazement. "How does she do this? How did she know Jack was taking me to the

Vietnam Memorial tomorrow? And who is Marian Kirkpatrick?"

"Amazing, isn't she?" David nodded. "Actually, not so strange. I understand you told her about wanting to go to the Library and, of course, Jack talked to her about your schedule for tomorrow. Marian Kirkpatrick is our Director of Human Resources. You met her at the Board Meeting the other day. But I don't know what lunch is about. Do you, Neil?" He looked at his protégé and seeing his headshake, he continued. "Well, if Suzanne scheduled it, there is a very good reason."

"Is the schedule all right with you, Claire? If it's too much for one day or if you'd rather do other things, I'm sure Suzanne can adjust it for you." MiMi's concern was touching.

"Are you kidding? I spent all day today trying to keep up with you and the girls; this will seem like a vacation."

When Mrs. Kramer appeared in the doorway to announce dinner, MiMi led them all into the small dining room. Cook had done herself proud. The salmon baked in a light pastry with fresh dill and lemon butter sauce was delightful. The vegetables and salad were more impressive to Claire now that she knew most of the ingredients were grown right outside the kitchen door.

When they finished the English Trifle, loaded with rum and fresh fruit, and sat back to enjoy their coffee, the conversation turned to the more serious purpose of the dinner.

"Well, David, we've done a thorough review of the security measures here, and I think we're both satisfied with the plan. Jack made a couple of good suggestions to Charlie, and we all agree that we need to crank up our level of vigilance for a while. I'm sending a crew out to cover the house for the next week just as an abundance of caution. That way Charlie can stay close to you and Claire without worrying about the security here."

David nodded and MiMi looked relieved.

"What about the party Saturday? The security won't be obvious to the guests, will it?"

"No, these guys will be unobtrusive. Most of them are off-duty police who do this kind of work a lot. We've used them before when we've had special projects. Some will dress so they look like guests while some will work with the valets to make sure all the guests are invited ones. I assume you're using the same catering company?"

At MiMi's nod, Wiley continued. "I'll have a word with them just for safety's sake, but really, MiMi, don't worry. We're doing this so we don't have to worry. If we thought there was imminent danger, we'd suggest you cancel the party. No one wants to risk your family or friends. Just think of us as party insurance."

MiMi nodded again, the worry now gone from her face. "I really appreciate your attention to this, Wiley. The Gala isn't so important it couldn't be cancelled, but it has become somewhat of a tradition. So I don't want to cancel if I don't have to. Really, you've made me feel so much better now.

"And you talked to Percy and Mrs. Kramer?"

Wiley nodded. "Everyone's in the loop that needs to be. It will be a great party. My wife and I are looking forward to it as we do every year." He shook his head with a dole look on his face. "Whoa, wouldn't I just hear about it from her if I told her I made you cancel it. She's been talking about what she's going to wear for a month now."

"Well, Wiley, that sounds like you're not taking your lady out dancing enough," David interjected good-humoredly.

"Can't; my boss keeps my nose to the grindstone."

Neil and David snorted their derision. "You're the one. You love that office of yours." Then they all laughed. They knew how it was when you worked at something you loved; it was hard to go home sometimes.

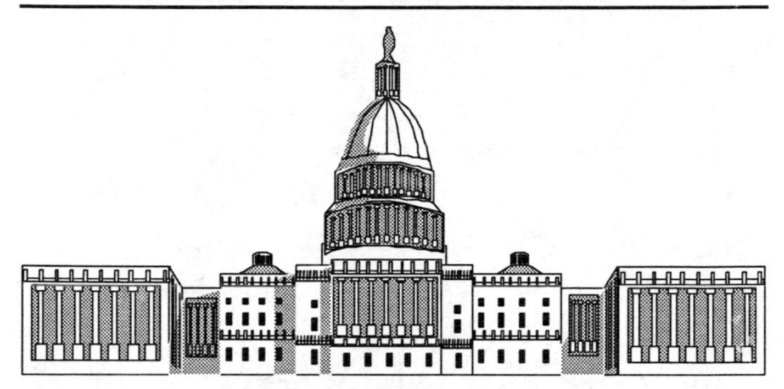

CHAPTER SIX

The Library of Congress was Mecca to librarians. And now Claire had made her pilgrimage. She remembered with embarrassment how before she opened the bookstore, she had spent years learning the routines and systems at the San Francisco Library, where she had worked for so long. Eventually she had almost become smug in her expertise. But that was nothing. This was the ultimate. This was what it was all about. This was the world's largest library.

Charlie had delivered her to the side door this morning just in time for her to join the VIP tour. After the tour she had been met by Amanda Myers, a friend of Suzanne Queensley, who took Claire into the inner-world of the library, introduced her to their process, the staff and the philosophy behind the Library of Congress. Claire couldn't believe her good fortune. She never anticipated she would get such a personal view of the institution she and her colleagues had always regarded with such respect. And if its function wasn't impressive enough the building was awe-inspiring. Each of the reading rooms available to visitors was spectacular, crowned by the Main Reading Room with its soaring domed ceiling, its marble columns and giant female figures dwarfing the reading desks available to researchers.

The Great Hall she was crossing now, served no purpose that she could determine other than to impress the visitors with the importance of the building. The statuary, the columns, the stained glass skylights and the murals were only to please the senses, and she admitted they did. She glanced at her watch estimating she still had about forty-five minutes before she was to meet Marian Kirkpatrick at Neptune's Fountain in front of the building.

Her footsteps echoed loudly on the marble floor as Claire headed down the corridor to the room she had seen on her tour this morning. She had been surprised to learn there was an entire room devoted to Bob Hope's jokes here in the Library. That room held a lifetime supply of funny quips. She needed to see them. She still remembered as a small child, sitting in front of the TV, laughing uncontrollably at his jokes. She didn't know if she understood the humor or if she was joining her parents' hilarity. Her father's love of Bob Hope was one of her treasured memories. And so she had always admired him too.

She had been astounded to learn how he had cross-indexed each joke by subject matter so he could retrieve them easily. If he had a luncheon with the Boy Scouts in Kalamazoo he could retrieve jokes about Boy Scouts, Kalamazoo, Michigan and other topical subjects before he even left home. He kept a warehouse of filing cabinets to hold the material. When he gave the collection to the Library of Congress, they immediately began logging them onto a computer database and kept a separate room in the Library so the public could access them. She didn't want to miss a chance to browse through them.

Claire emerged finally and hurried down the front steps only a few minutes late, but still smiling from the jokes she had been reading. She had managed to write down a few she thought the girls would enjoy, but of course, she read many more in the process of finding those. She shook her head in amazement. Somchow you take someone like Bob Hope for granted. You just think he was funny and he had good writers. You don't think of it like a business. She had learned he used several teams of writers to concurrently write his TV shows, and then he selected the best of each for the final program. But he saved and archived all of the jokes the teams produced. He was smart. He was professional. And he was funny.

She hurried down the steps already scanning the people gathered around the fountain. She immediately recognized Marian from the Board Meeting. The dark red hair was natural, no one would be able to fake the gray hairs sprinkled liberally through it. She was probably in her mid-forties but could have been ten years older or younger. She gave the impression of being a serious person, very simply dressed, no jewelry of any kind. Her hair was expensively cut, her clothes were costly but conservative, and she wore very little makeup. Today she had on a dove gray suit, the jacket off, folded over her arm and a matching silk sleeveless shell. Her feet were shod in Nike's as were most of the women's on the street, choosing comfort and mobility over fashion for their lunch hour jaunts.

"Hi, Marian. I'm so sorry I kept you waiting. I wish I had a good excuse, but I confess I was in there chuckling over Bob Hopes jokes and just lost track of time." She held out her hand for Marian's firm handclasp.

"No problem. Actually that sounds like a better excuse than most. And I came a little early, because I was given strict instructions to make sure you were not left anywhere unattended. But frankly, I was enjoying the fresh air."

Her piercing gaze fastened on Claire's face. "I appreciate you taking the time to lunch with me. I know you have limited time here with lots to see and do."

"Not at all, but I guess I'm not quite clear as to why you wanted to meet with me."

Marian ignored her comment. "Do you mind walking a few blocks? The neighborhood down the street has a few restaurants which are quite good."

They headed down the sidewalk away from the Capital, which faced the Library. After only a couple of blocks the imposing office buildings gave way to a shady, comfortable neighborhood, dotted with restaurants which spilled out over the sidewalks, little shops which displayed a variety of goods and houses, or maybe they were flats, scrunched together, walls connecting, doorways and steps emptying directly into the pedestrians crowding the walkways.

Marian glanced at Claire, a faint smile hovering around her mouth. "You're not the only one wondering why I wanted to meet with you.

"Neil called first thing this morning. He can't stand not knowing everything that's going on. But he's not in charge, yet," she added.

Claire's surprise was obvious.

Marian went on. "I told him the same thing I told Suzanne when I asked to be added to your schedule. I just want to make sure you aren't suffering any ill effects from the trauma you went through last spring. You know we have a large pool of excellent resources to treat our employees in cases of stress? And we would be happy to make these resources available to you. I know symptoms don't surface immediately, and I thought Vantage owes it to you if you need this kind of support."

Marian pointed at an inviting looking restaurant and quickly guided Claire to one of the tables in front, sitting in the deep shade of the trees hanging over them.

"Do you mind sitting outside? It's not too hot yet, although when the breeze dies about three o'clock, everything and everyone will start to wilt. I'm cooped up in the office so much of the time I take every opportunity to breathe real air when possible." She slipped her suit jacket over the back of her chair and picked up the menu for a quick glance.

The next few minutes were spent deciding on lunch choices, ordering and then Marian excused herself to use the restroom while Claire sat back sipping her water and watching the restaurant fill up. As cosmopolitan as Washington was, it seemed it was still only a large village, judging by the number of people who knew each other on the increasingly crowded street. Claire was enjoying the scene, grateful that Marian had chosen to give her a glimpse of what it would be like to work here.

"Oh, good. They brought the drinks."

Claire hadn't noticed when the waitress set down their drinks and now followed with salads.

Marian looked around their table and then, apparently judging they were far enough from neighboring patrons, leaned forward to speak to Claire, who leaned forward in response as if drawn by a magnet.

"I really wanted to have lunch with you so I could talk to you about Carol Daley. I've thought about this for a long time, and finally I decided I would make up my mind when I met you. You seemed like such a normal, common-sense type of person, I decided to go for it."

Claire was really confused, sure that she had somehow missed something important in this conversation. But before she could ask, Marian continued.

"Carol Daley and I were very close friends for many years. As a matter of fact, we were college roommates. When we graduated she went off to a career at Vantage while I went on to graduate school. But we always stayed in touch.

"And it's because of her that I'm here at Vantage. When they were searching for a new director of HR she mentioned me to a member of the search team. And, of course, after hearing her descriptions of Vantage over the years, I was very interested when approached. Anyway, it worked out well and I'll always be grateful for her help."

She paused long enough to push her salad around with her fork, take a sip of her wine and then stare a minute at her plate as if wondering what to do with it.

"I don't think anyone knows we were friends, at least no one in management. Not that either of us tried to hide it. But by the time I started, she was already in the process of transferring to London."

Marian peered at Claire intently, as if willing her to understand. "You see she became involved with a married man and had finally decided to make the break. She thought London was far enough away to make sure her resolve to stop seeing him held. That was four years ago. I know it was very hard for her, but she was determined to break out of a no-win situation.

"That's why I was shocked when I talked to her the day before the incident in London. She called me at the office, which she never did. She was very upset and wanted to talk. He had called her. He said he had divorced his wife and was now free, but she was ambivalent about getting involved with him again. She said the time and distance had given her a different perspective and she wasn't sure she really trusted him. We talked only a short time as I had a meeting. So I said I'd call her back later. There was no later."

When Marian looked up she was blinking rapidly, fighting the tears welling in her eyes. "I'm having real difficulty dealing with her death. But even worse, I just can't believe she was involved in a plot to blow up the airline. She loved Vantage Airlines. And she was always so conscientious. How could she have ignored the rules to allow Rosa access? It doesn't make sense to me."

Claire looked at her helplessly; the sandwich the waitress had delivered suddenly tasteless and dry.

Marian used her napkin to dab her eyes dry, shaking her head. "No, no, I don't expect you to solve this for me, but I wanted you to tell me everything about your encounter with her and what exactly happened as far as you can remember. You know, your impression of her, how she looked, how she acted? I'm hoping something will come up to help explain it to me. Will you do that?"

Claire shook her head as if clearing her confusion.

"Please, I know it's hard for you but I need to know. I just can't believe the Carol Daley you met was the Carol Daley I knew so well." Then she grabbed her purse off the cement by her feet and rummaged around to hand Claire a picture. "This is Carol. Are you absolutely sure this is your Carol?"

A younger version of Carol Daley smiled gaily against the background of a porch somewhere. She handed it back sadly. "This is the Carol Daley I met. I'm so sorry."

This time Marian couldn't stop the tears leaking from her eyes, dabbing again, futilely, with the napkin.

"The problem is..." Claire began thoughtfully, "...the problem is that I'm no longer sure exactly what I remember and what memories have been changed from things I've learned since. I can't trust my memories to be accurate."

Marian nodded. "I understand, but please try. I need some closure or a clue. I don't know why I feel I have to solve this, but it will haunt me all my life if I don't."

Claire understood that feeling. So she went back in her memory to that place in time when she met Carol Daley at London's Heathrow Airport and how grateful she was to have someone else take charge of their group. She pulled up her impressions of the efficient but nice Customer Service Manager, recalling how smoothly she got everyone processed and to the correct boarding area. She talked of the incident at the security gates where the recalcitrant Rosa again caused a problem. And she told how relieved she was when Carol was able to bend the rules to allow Rosa to pass, because leaving her behind in London didn't seem like a viable option.

Marian and Claire sat quietly for a moment, thinking about the incident Claire had just described in detail.

Marian asked a few questions but then shook her head. "There doesn't seem to be anything new for me. I know I shouldn't be disappointed, but..." she shook her head in frustration, "I am disappointed."

"Did you ever meet this man she was involved with? I mean, do you know who he is? Perhaps he has some clues?"

"No, she never told me. In fact, she was so tight-lipped about him I just assumed I would recognize who he was if she used his name. After all, this is Washington, D.C. The city is filled with legislators who are rather well known for their extramarital affairs. So she never gave me a clue," she mused. "Still, maybe she told someone in her family."

Then she said forcefully, "No! No, she'd never admit to them she was involved with a married man. But maybe one of her other friends might know. I know a few of them from years ago. I'll get in touch with them and see what I can find out."

"Marian, did you ever tell any of this to the authorities when they interviewed you?"

Marian was surprised. "I wasn't interviewed. No one asked me any questions about her. I received requests for documents from her personnel file, but that was it."

She looked at Claire thoughtfully. "Do you think I should have? I mean, I can't see how it would impact their investigation."

Claire shrugged. "It wouldn't seem as if it would, but you can never tell what will be important. I think I should at least mention it to Jack. Let him decide if it's something to pursue. After all, you don't know who her lover was, but you do know he arrived back in her life just before the incident. And we know she received at unidentified phone call before she went up to assist us at Heathrow. What if the two were connected somehow?"

Both women lapsed into silence considering the ramifications of Claire's question. The breeze had died down and Claire was suddenly feeling the heaviness of the humid air descending on her. She abandoned the sandwich as hopeless and finished her iced tea. She saw Charlie guide the big dark blue car to the curb and glanced at her watch, surprised at how fast the lunch hour had gone by.

"Marian, Charlie is here to pick me up. Did you tell him where we were?"

She nodded. "I called when I went in to the restroom. Look, Claire, thanks a lot for your help. Go ahead and talk to Jack and see what he thinks. I prefer not to tell Wiley about it unless Jack thinks it's important. I don't mind Wiley knowing, but Neil is liable to make a big deal out of it."

She looked at Claire thoughtfully. "I know I was being indiscreet earlier, which is really not like me. Personnel people are known for being neutral and discreet and I'm usually that way. But today, maybe thinking so much about Carol, I just lost it. I do apologize."

Claire nodded. "Can we give you a ride back to the office?"

Marian shook her head, reaching for what was left of her wine. "No, no thanks. I'll finish up here and wander back. I need some thinking time. But if you remember anything else, please call me directly." She took out onc of hcr cards and quickly wrote two numbers on the back. "The second one is my cell phone, but leave a message at either and I'll get back to you." She tried to smile, not quite pulling it off. "Thanks, Claire. Thanks again for your time."

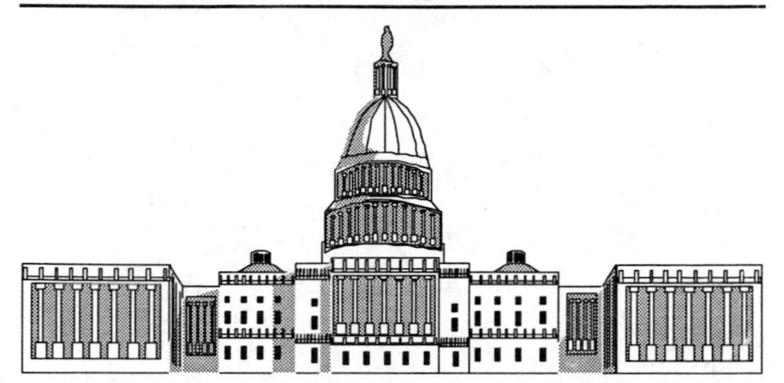

CHAPTER SEVEN

The air-conditioned interior felt wonderful.

"Hope you had a nice morning, Ms. Gulliver?"

"I did. Thank you for asking...and for picking me up. Where do we go next?"

Charlie chuckled. "I feel like a tour director." He closed the door and walked around to the driver's side and when he got settled he continued. "We're meeting Jack at the Lincoln Memorial. I understand he has your afternoon planned. I hope he brought along an umbrella 'cause it's gonna rain."

"That will be a relief. It was pleasantly warm and then it became so muggy."

"Well, our storms don't necessarily mean respite from the humidity. You'll see. But I heard there was a front moving this way, which could give us a break by tomorrow. Just in time for Mrs. Lickman's do."

She had been warned about how awful the weather could be at this time of the year, but actually she thought it had been quite nice. Yesterday afternoon had gotten kind of sticky, but they had been out at the pool most of the time. So she didn't suffer from it. And today she had dressed for the heat, wearing her loose two-piece dress and comfortable sandals, a compromise for tourist activities and still suitable, she hoped, for dinner with Jack. She grinned, congratulating herself for not dressing as the two tourists she saw on the sidewalk—he was in a loud Hawaiian shirt with matching shorts, she in shorts and a halter top, and both were sporting baseball caps with fans built into the bill.

When the car pulled up to the curb in a lot filled with tour buses, taxies and limousines, Jack hurried over to open the door before Charlie could get around the car. He looked cool in a light green, short-sleeved, golf shirt, cream colored linen-like pants, Nike's and a backpack slung over his shoulder.

"Got your umbrella?" Charlie demanded. "Gonna rain."

"No. I didn't bring one."

"I have a spare. Just send it back with Ms. Gulliver." He popped the trunk, rummaged around and returned with a folded up umbrella.

"Thanks." Jack slipped it into his backpack as Charlie left them.

"What else is in there?" Claire questioned, thinking how like him it was to come prepared.

"A couple of hats. Did you bring one?" At her head shake he went on. "I didn't think so, but after a while in the sun you'll be glad to wear this." He pulled out two Day-Glo orange baseball caps.

"Nice color."

"Hey, if we get separated in a crowd you'll appreciate the color."

He rooted around a bit pulling out a book. "A guidebook in case you ask questions I can't answer, and some water because it's going to be hot."

"Pretty impressive. I feel like I'm going on a Scout hike." She put the hat on, ignoring the color.

Jack put on his hat, fastidiously adjusting the brim.

"Okay. Ready?"

She nodded.

Jack moved through the crowd of tourists to the path around the Lincoln Memorial. "I thought we'd start with the Vietnam Memorial since that was top on your list. That way we can stay as long as we want, or at least as long as we can bear the heat. Then, depending on time, we'll check out the Korean War Memorial. It's fairly new and not as well publicized, but I think very impressive. And of course, we'll visit the Lincoln Memorial."

Claire was happy to follow his lead, grateful already for the shade the hat provided for her face. She craned her neck as they passed the Lincoln Memorial. She had seen pictures of it all her life and couldn't believe it was just there with the huge statue of the seated Lincoln for everyone to see. They wandered further down the tree lined path and she didn't even notice the start of the Wall. It was almost a curb of shiny black stone, increasing in size as the path dipped down, and suddenly she saw the pattern on the black granite was really an endless list of names.

The number of people on the path increased, moving in both directions. It seemed a strange mixture. There were families pushing babies in strollers and trying to keep track of little ones darting here and there. Groups of teenagers joked, calling out to each other as they traversed the path, seemingly unaware of the significance of the Memorial. An older couple in front of Claire and Jack stopped abruptly, the woman burst into tears as she traced a name with her fingers. The man with her, most likely her husband, hunched in on himself, his misery showing clearly in the stance his body took.

Claire watched an aging hippy stumble away from the wall and fling himself on the lawn, obviously distraught. Then two more men joined him. These two looked to be successful businessmen, squatting down in their expensive casual clothes, Gucci loafers with no socks and designer hairstyles. They talked earnestly, gestured emphatically, but their faces reflected a horror that made Claire shudder.

Some people examined the Wall closely referring frequently to the notes they held. Some had apparently left tokens, flowers, teddy bears and even photographs which sat by sections of the Wall.

At the end of the Wall Claire was happy to follow Jack from the monument to a row of trees and benches, which looked back on the scene. They shared one of the bottles of water while a slight breeze ruffled the leaves of the trees but only gave the illusion of respite from the heat. They continued to watch the parade of people pass the Wall.

"I've heard so much about it, but I just couldn't imagine it. Does your guidebook say how many names are on it?" Claire finally spoke.

Jack pulled out the book and after a little studying said, "Fifty-eight thousand, one hundred and fifty-six in chronological order beginning at the intersection." He pointed.

"Did you see those men?" She nodded at the men still sitting on the lawn. "After all this time and they're still having a hard time with it. I felt like I wanted to join them, to hear their story." She paused, watching them. "I know it was sad. It's obvious it is still sad."

Jack nodded, his expression unreadable.

"Did you go?"

He shook his head. "I was lucky. But I knew a lot who did. Some didn't come back and some came back different."

"The young man who lived down the street from us went. I was in Junior High School, and I had a huge crush on him. He used to mow our lawn. His family was so proud of him. Then he was killed. The whole neighborhood mourned. It brought the war on television right into our homes. The family moved away the next year and we never heard from them again. I don't think they ever recovered."

"Want to find his name? What year was it, do you remember?"

She looked at him and, realizing she did want to see it, she nodded. "I was in the seventh grade, so it must have been 1970 or thereabouts."

"See all those people up at that end? There are lists of names cross-indexed with where the name is located on the wall. Come on, we'll see what we can find."

Finding his name was satisfying, but locating it on the wall, just one of the thousands, was depressing. It was all that was left of the fun-loving, vibrant young man she knew. They left the Wall the second time in a somber mood and meandered slowly past the Lincoln Memorial again to the other side where the Korean War Veterans Memorial was located. This Memorial had its own black granite wall, albeit smaller and covered with pictures instead of names. This wall led to a pool. The pool, reflecting the black billowing clouds racing overhead, seemed to absorb the light. The afternoon had suddenly become ominously dark.

They turned from the pool back towards the Lincoln Memorial and found themselves facing directly the larger-than-life steel sculptures of the soldiers marching across the field. The last soldier in the line appeared to be nervously checking behind him as he struggled to keep up. In the dimming light these figures looked real. Too real!

Lightning flashed and an almost instantaneous clap of thunder caused the hair on Claire's nape to stand on end and provided an appropriate sound effect for the scene in front of them.

"Guess Charlie knew what he was talking about," Jack muttered as he fumbled in his backpack for the umbrella. "We need to find some shelter. It's going to pour in about..." The umbrella snapped into position and he held it over them just as the skies opened.

People were running for cover in the darkness lit eerily by the flashes of lightning. The thunder spurred them on. Claire, being a California girl, had never seen a storm like this. It felt as if they were in a battlefield with explosions all around them. She didn't need anyone to tell her how dangerous it was. She ran blindly, relying on Jack's arm around her, supporting her, pulling her to guide her in the right direction.

They pounded up the steps with the others seeking refuge, the water bouncing up from the steps as the rain poured down, rolling off the others around them, and drenching them to the skin. They squeezed into the mass of people huddled around the base of Lincoln, under the roof of the Lincoln Memorial. People were wedged in the space tightly almost as if they were all hugging each other, trying to stay as far away from the exposed front as possible.

She buried her face in Jack's shoulder, cringing at each new clap of thunder, feeling the ground vibrate with the fury of the storm.

"I think the worst is over." Jack's voice finally spoke softly in her ear.

She was disoriented. She blinked furiously, realizing her eyes had been scrunched tightly closed as if that would save her. Now it was more like twilight on the large platform and the crowd was not so dense. She could see that many people had already taken the opportunity to leave as the rain let up a bit. She shivered. It wasn't really cold but she was chilled.

"Well, I don't think I'll forget my visit to the Lincoln Memorial." She tried to squeeze some water out of her skirt. Looking around for her hat, she gave up; it could have fallen off anywhere along the way.

They moved to the front, poised on the long flight of stairs and looked over the Mall. It was definitely getting brighter. A few stray beams of sunlight broke through the clouds and hit the reflecting pool stretching out in front of the Memorial. Refracted light danced from the dripping trees, all the brighter against the background of black clouds retreating to the East.

"Well, we're a pretty mess. That umbrella Charlie gave us didn't help much, did it?"

Claire had to laugh. He did look a bit like a drowned cat. Then glancing down she realized she looked as bad, maybe worse.

"I suggest we see if we can find a cab and head over to my place. I think I have enough clean, dry clothes for both of us, and then maybe we can put your things in the dryer." He eyed her dress doubtfully. "I don't know what it's going to do to either of our reputations if I bring you home in an entirely different outfit."

"Oh, I see. This is a ploy to get me up to your place and get my clothes off."

He brightened. "What a good idea!"

She suddenly felt lighthearted, having survived what she was certain was her end. "I don't know about wearing your clothes. I'll feel very bad if they don't fit," she said, dubiously eying his narrow hips. But the thought of dry clothes was really too tempting to even think of refusing.

"Maybe we can even have a cuppa while we wait," he offered tentatively.

That did it, the offer she couldn't refuse. So she headed down the stairs ignoring the light rain as it couldn't do any more damage to either of them.

It wasn't easy getting a cab. Finally, Jack threw himself in front of one slowing for the light and wouldn't move until Claire got the door open and in. They ignored the cabbie's disgust at their wet clothes dripping on his plastic seats. They weren't getting out until he delivered them to Jack's apartment building near DuPont Circle.

Claire used two towels to get dry. She helped herself to a pair of Jack's running shorts and an old sweatshirt with sleeves shortened by a few hacks from the scissors. After donning a pair of white athletic socks and taking a final swipe through her hair with his comb, she felt one hundred percent better.

"Where's the dryer?"

Jack led her to a utility closet containing a washer/dryer stack and she dumped the sodden mess of her clothes in the drum. "I wish I could put my sandals and purse in there, but I guess they'll have to dry by themselves." Then she looked around. It was a small apartment but had been modernized to include the necessary utilities. And it looked comfortable enough.

"Have you lived here long?"

"About two weeks. It belongs to the company. I'm just using it while I'm here."

That explained the lack of personal touches.

"Where do you live, Jack?" she asked, suddenly curious. This didn't look like the glamorous lifestyle the famous agent James Bond led.

"Everywhere; nowhere." He moved into the little kitchen space and spooned tea into a pot before pouring the contents of the steaming kettle over the leaves.

"Where do you keep your things?"

He got out cups, milk, sugar, spoons and a package of something and put them on the table in front of the window.

"What things? I travel very light."

"Everyone has things. You know, pictures, mementos? Stuff? Where do you keep your stuff?"

He brought the teapot to the table, setting it in front of Claire. "Well, I keep some boxes in a cousin's attic. It's just junk, mementos from high school, things from when my daughter was a baby and some stuff from my parent's home that didn't seem right to sell or give away. I guess when I retire I'll get it out. But for now it's easier to do without."

He poured the tea and Claire added milk to hers before taking a sip of the fragrant brew. She picked up the package reading the label, *McVitie's, The Original Digestive.*

"Oh, I love these." She tore back the wrapping with enthusiasm, biting into one of the crunchy graham cookies. "They're so good with tea. This reminds me of being in England. I loved having tea in the afternoons."

"There's a little shop in Georgetown that specializes in English products. I did a run by there last weekend to get tea and a few of my favorite things. Can you find these in California?"

"You know, I haven't looked but I'm going to when I get back. I had forgotten all about them and they're too good for that."

They sat sipping their tea, the swooshing sound of the dryer tumbling Claire's clothes in the background, the light from the window growing brighter as the sun now broke through the clouds in earnest. The rain had completely stopped. Just the eaves and the leaves were still dripping.

"Its not even close to being over, is it?" Her voice was low and calm.

"Pardon?" Jack thought she was talking about the storm.

"I said it's not over. I was just fooling myself. It felt safe out there in California but it was only a myth. It's not over. There are still too many questions with no answers." She looked into Jack's eyes. "And Guiness, or Rosa, or whoever she is has never been found.

"That's why you're here, isn't it? You're still looking for her, still on the case, so to speak."

Jack slowly shook his head. "You've got it wrong. We're still working on it. That's true.... But we have a big group, and then there are the British authorities and Interpol, so it's an even larger group involved with this case. I did my part. Now the rest are doing theirs. I'm here because I'm doing some training for my next assignment. It's just like I told you."

"Sure and how very convenient. You just happened to be following me in the Mall when that weirdo attacked me. Come on, Jack. I'm a big girl. I can take the truth."

"I know it sounds fishy, but that's exactly how it happened. And so far we've not made any connection of that incident to any terrorist activities. I know I said I don't believe in coincidences but sometimes they do happen. And when we find one, then we just have to let it go."

Claire refilled both cups, added milk to hers and crunched into another biscuit. "I talked with Marian Kirkpatrick. She's head of Human Resources for Vantage. Do you know her?"

"Redhead? A little older? "

Claire nodded.

"Well, I talked to her a bit at the meeting the other day, but I can't say I know her. Why?"

"I had lunch with her today."

"That's right; something about stress counseling or something, wasn't it?"

She looked at him strangely. Did everybody know everything about everyone, or did they just think they did?

"Actually, no. Not that at all."

That got his attention.

"Look, Jack. How well did your people check out Carol Daley?"

"Through a microscope. In fact, they're still checking all the details. Why?"

"Well, did they find out, for instance, that Marian Kirkpatrick and Carol Daley were best of friends?"

Jack couldn't hide his surprise.

"Did they find out that they were college roommates and that Carol Daley was instrumental in getting Marian her position at Vantage?"

He shook his head. "I don't know. Maybe I just didn't hear the details."

"Marian was so sure that Carol wouldn't have done anything to jeopardize one of Vantage's flights that she showed me her picture. She wanted to make sure the woman I spoke to was the real Carol Daley.

"I mean, how weird is that?" Claire could almost see the wheels turning in Jack's brain. "It was the same person, no doubt about it. But Marian just can't believe it.

"She says she's known her too long and too well. People don't just change like that. The Carol Daley she knew would never have participated knowingly in any plan to damage Vantage Airlines."

She paused, thinking. "Maybe her part was just a fluke. Maybe she didn't have anything to do with the plot."

"No! No way. There are coincidences and coincidences. But Carol was instrumental in making sure their plan worked. They needed her, or someone, to get that computer through security and on your plane. They wouldn't leave it to chance. They're too professional for that.

"Carol Daley had to be a part of it." Jack was so certain that Claire believed him.

"So, what else did Marian tell you?"

Claire shrugged. "Carol was having an affair with a married man before she transferred to London. That's what kind of person she was. This man was apparently the love of her life. But she felt so bad about the fact that he was married, she broke up with him and moved across the ocean. Marian thought he might have an important position in the government, because Carol was so careful about keeping all hints to his identity private. Marian was sure Carol was protecting him, assuming she would have known who he was if Carol had mentioned his name. The only reason Marian brought that up was Carol called her at the office the day before the incident in London. Carol was upset because he had contacted her after all that time. He was apparently now free and wanted to see her. Marian couldn't talk then and told Carol she'd call her back. But, of course, it never happened," she said sadly. "It probably had no relevance, but it's strange."

"So what did Marian want you to do?"

"Nothing really. She just had to make sure it was really her Carol involved in London, and she asked me to tell her all the details of our meeting in case there was something that would help her to understand what happened."

"Do you want more tea?" Jack asked.

"No, thanks. I'll check on my clothes." She plucked at the sweatshirt. "Not that I don't appreciate the use of yours..."

She found them still a little damp and turned on the dryer for a short cycle. Her shoes and purse were still very wet, but she remembered seeing one of those wall hairdryers the hotels used in the bathroom. She spent a few minutes blasting her purse. The inside had some kind of waterproof lining and was dry but the fabric on the outside had gotten soaked. She considered her sandals, then decided she would just wear them wet and ignore the squishing sound when she walked.

When she returned to the living room, Jack was just hanging up the phone.

"A slight change of plans."

"Well that's a surprise." She laughed. "When have we ever gotten together without a change of plans?"

"You're right. It's becoming a pattern. After dinner I have to go into the office. I want to check on the investigation of Carol Daley. Charlie will come in to pick you up, instead of me driving you home. Okay?"

"Hah, you're afraid to show up at the Lickmans' door with me in my bedraggled state."

He burst into laughter. "That too! It will be better for you to explain it."

"Well, my clothes will take a few more minutes. Are we in a hurry?"

"No. No problem. We're going to a place I heard about in Georgetown. I thought it sounded good and I already have reservations."

Claire looked at him seriously. "By the way, Jack, Marian didn't really want to advertise her relationship with Carol. She's not too keen on Neil knowing her business."

Then she added, “You know, he looks very familiar to me but I don’t know why.”

Jack shrugged. “He’s only been on the cover of every news magazine published during the past year. He probably looks familiar to half the population of this country. I wouldn’t let Marian’s opinion of him color your thoughts. There may be some office politics in the mix there.”

Claire shook her head. “You’re right. I probably have seen his picture and that’s why I think I recognized him.”

“Yeah, and sometimes first impressions aren’t all that accurate. Let’s not forget our first meeting.”

She had to laugh remembering the tangled mess they made with the luggage on the stairs in the hotel in London. With his nasty comments about her ancestors ringing in her ears, she thought he was the rudest man she had ever met. Who would have guessed they would end up friends?

“You’re right. You never, ever, ever know.”

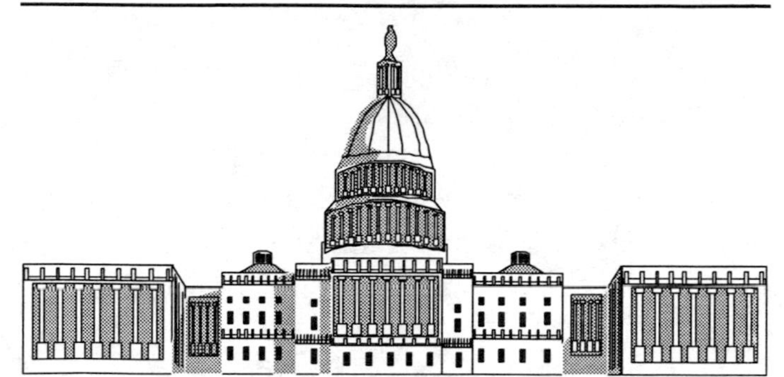

CHAPTER EIGHT

Tuffy's fierce barking turned to excited tail wagging as soon as Claire stepped through the door. She stooped to pet him when she heard MiMi call, "Claire, we're in here if you feel like joining us."

She followed the voice and found MiMi and David in their customary places in the cozy parlor having a nightcap.

"Did you have a good time? Oh, I hope you didn't get caught in that awful storm?"

"Oh, my gosh. I couldn't believe it. I was scared to death. And I understand you have these storms frequently during the summer. How do you cope?" She nodded at David's raised eyebrows and he went to pour her a glass of wine.

"You learn, my dear. And you make sure you don't get caught out in the open, because lightning can be deadly."

Claire believed it. "We took shelter in the Lincoln Memorial along with a few hundred other people. We were drenched. But we did get to the Vietnam and Korean War Memorials before the storm broke."

"Oh good! Aren't they awesome? Every time I go I'm so moved by the experience."

A quiet fell in the room, then David remembered. "Oh, Claire, Suzanne sent another itinerary for you. I left it on the hall table. I think she must have always wanted to be a tour director. She just loves making arrangements for you to see the city."

Claire laughed as she got up, shaking her head at Tuffy, who also sat up in case she was heading outside, and went to get the envelope with the itinerary.

"So, what's on for tomorrow?" Tuffy had resumed his favorite place at MiMi's feet, his chin on her foot.

"Another full day: morning at the Museum of American History, lunch with Doug, afternoon visit to the Capital, and finally, home with David and Charlie.

"This is very nice of you to take such good care of me. I know, I know." She waved her hand. "It's no trouble. But I'm sure it is. And then tonight Charlie had to come back into the city to get me because Jack had a change of plans. I just want to say I really appreciate all that you're doing. But really, I don't have to do all these things. I could just hang out here with MiMi, and the girls, and I'd be happy."

"Claire, we want to do this. Charlie gets paid to do these things. It's his job and he's good at it. And you heard David say how much fun Suzanne is having arranging your schedule. So don't worry about being a burden. We like you. We're grateful to you. We are happy doing things that you appreciate. Let us, okay?"

Claire stared at her a moment and then nodded. MiMi meant every word. The least she could do is be a gracious recipient of their favors.

* * *

Headsville Post Office **American History Museum,** **Washington, D.C.** *Dear Mom,* *Guess where I am? They moved this whole post office into the museum, so I can send this postcard from here. Having a great time. Got caught in a terrible thunder and lightning storm yesterday, but otherwise weather is great. I'm staying with the Lickmans and will tell you all when I get home.* *Love,* *Claire*	*Mrs. Millicent Gulliver* *124 13th Avenue* *San Francisco, CA* *94119*

* * *

"Doug, you're so nice to take me to lunch. Did Suzanne twist your arm?" Claire was happy to see him again. And seeing his conservative business attire, she was especially glad she had run her dress through the washer and dryer before she went to bed last night so she could wear it again today. It was made out of some wonder material that promised to take rough treatment from travel, and so far it had proven to be worth the extra money it cost. She wasn't sure about her shoes. They were a little stiff from the soaking yesterday. But after wearing them for a while they seemed to be loosening up. She realized she had not packed the right clothes. She thought she'd be spending most of her time in tourist places on her own and could wear slacks or casual skirts and walking shoes. But yesterday's dinner with Jack and, now again today, lunch with Doug, meant a dress was more appropriate.

"Not at all. I'm delighted Suzanne could find time for me on your busy schedule. She's tough, you know. She wouldn't put me on the schedule without me ponying up." Claire had fallen into step with him as they moved out the door of the Museum into the Mall.

"So I offered up a visit to the White House. If you're game, of course."

She jerked to attention. "The White House? We're going to the White House?"

He nodded. "If you'd like."

"Like? Of course I'd like to see it, but...I mean, do we have time? Suzanne has me booked solid and I thought the White House Tour takes hours of waiting in line."

He grinned, obviously enjoying her reaction. "It does, unless you know the right people."

"You? You're the right people?"

He nodded smugly.

"You have connections in the White House?"

He nodded. "It sometimes comes in handy."

Claire felt her mouth gaping.

"Have you met with the President? Do you know the Cabinet?" she asked eagerly.

He nodded. "On occasion I have met with them. But, to be honest, I'm a very minor player, so don't think I'm more important than I am. It's just that with my position as Special Assistant to the Secretary of State, I find myself doing many different things and some come to the attention of the movers and shakers."

Claire thought about this as they moved across the large grass circle, called the Ellipse, toward the White House. "But I thought you were attached to the Embassy in London. Actually, I thought you lived there."

He shook his head. "I live here."

She looked at him with speculation in her eyes. "So why did you get involved in my situation? Surely they didn't send you over there just for that?"

He shook his head. "I was there on another matter when MiMi Lickman called my boss. She wanted some special attention for the person who had saved their airliner. And when MiMi wants special attention, she gets it. She's an old time power around here, and no one wants to be the one to let her down. So, I was sent to your rescue. Although it really wasn't a rescue. You seemed to be doing fine."

She looked at him dubiously. "I didn't feel fine. I really did appreciate your support. I thought you were speaking for the entire U.S. Government and I guess I wasn't far off, was I?"

They left the path on the Ellipse and started down Executive Avenue whose half circle enclosed the front of the White House. Claire could now see the endless stream of people lined up along the front of the fence waiting for their chance to tour the White House. She felt a spasm of guilt at bypassing the line, but Doug didn't even falter. He led her to a gate at the side and they went through a thorough security check. After the guards used their wands and the dogs, which were trained to detect explosives, finished their inspection, their names were found on the list so they were admitted.

She felt like a bumpkin, head swiveling, trying to see everything. She needed to remember everything, so she could tell her mother and Mrs. B all about this visit.

Doug's friend in the Secret Services, Pete Marley, met them inside. He explained that one of the duties of the Secret Service was to conduct the tours of the White House and how all the agents rotated through the assignment.

"It's good for us. Keeps us in touch with the people, so to speak. And once in a while someone wants a special favor like my friend, Doug, here. How could I refuse when he said he was trying to make an impression on a special lady?" He winked at Claire. "I hope you're duly impressed."

Claire felt a little embarrassed, sure Pete misunderstood. But not wanting to make an issue of it, she just nodded and followed Pete as he deftly escorted them through the public rooms open that day. He was a font of information, and he managed to have them entering and leaving rooms in between the large tours of sightseers filling the downstairs area.

"When a function is scheduled the State Dining Room isn't open for the tours. Did you see that special on PBS a few years back about the chef and the State dinners he prepares? A State dinner is really a big production. Luckily nothing is planned tonight, so you can see the room; it's the next best thing to be invited to a dinner."

Claire couldn't help feeling awed by what she was seeing. "I keep expecting to see the cast members of

West Wing walking through. I'm a big fan. I thought they should have run for office last election. I bet they would have won hands down." She grinned at Doug and Pete's horrified looks. "Oh come on, don't you think the President could use a team of ace scriptwriters. It would certainly improve his ratings."

They had to laugh at that.

A trio of businessmen passed them, one nodded to Doug.

"So who are all these other people?" Claire whispered.

"Well, remember the White House is a big office building. Lots of business is conducted here each day. If you have business here you're likely to be on this floor either coming or going."

"It's so much bigger than it looks from the outside." Claire couldn't believe how grand it was. She felt a swelling of pride. This belonged to her. She was part owner, and it really was an appropriate symbol of the power of the United States.

"Well, these are the only rooms available today," Pete explained. "If you want to see the family quarters, you'll have to wangle an invitation from the family. And, of course, the West Wing is off limits when the President is in residence, unless you are meeting with him. I can't arrange that." He looked questioning at Doug. "And I don't think Doug has the clout?"

Doug shook his head. "Sorry, as I said, I'm only a very minor player."

"Well, this was wonderful, truly. I didn't expect to see it and I guess I didn't realize how much I wanted to, until Doug mentioned the possibility. Thank you both so much."

Pete shook hands with each of them. Then he watched them exit through the same door they entered.

Doug's hand on Claire's back guided her towards the gate and then around the side of the White House to Pennsylvania Avenue. "There's an old saloon down this way a couple of blocks that has wonderful hamburgers. I thought we'd go there for lunch."

Claire glanced at her watch, still getting a thrill when she glimpsed it. It was already one o'clock. "I'm starved. Do you think I'll be able to make my appointment at 2:30 at the Longworth House Office Building?"

"No problem. It's only a short cab ride away just across from the Capital. Actually, it would be a good walk after lunch, but not in this heat."

"Thank goodness I won't have to walk; I'm feeling a little wilted already."

He laughed. "Well, Washington summers require some getting used to."

He ushered her into the saloon. It wasn't at all the dingy, dark old western saloon Claire had expected. The dark Victorian interior was filled with etched glass panels, mahogany wood and red velvet upholstery in big booths. It was elegant and cool. Claire was happy at Doug's choice of restaurants even before seeing the menu selections.

"I'm going with the burger. And a coke," she told the waiter.

"Me too! But make mine with cheddar and bacon."

They spent the few minutes waiting for their food talking about inconsequential things. Claire told him about the Presidents' Ladies exhibit at the American

History Museum, and the thrill of seeing Fonzie's leather jacket.

Doug talked a bit about his life in the Washington arena. "It sounds a lot more glamorous than it is. And of course the fact that I'm an available male for rounding out tables at dinner parties helps. But frankly it's getting a little old. Or I am. I turned forty a few years back and suddenly things seem different."

"Oh, I know about that. Look at me. I didn't even wait to hit forty before I quit my job and sank every penny I could get my hands on into my bookstore. I shudder now when I think what a risk I took. There was so much I didn't know. My mother tried to warn me but it seemed that after all those years of her cautions, I just wanted to get out there and fly a bit."

"Didn't you ever want to do the traditional things? You know, get married, stay home and have kids."

"That's traditional? How many families do you know where the wife stays home with the kids. I bet there are as many househusbands as housewives these days."

She thought a bit. "I guess I did. When I grew up that's what women did and I just assumed I would too. But then as the years went by I was always going to do it later and now suddenly it's too late—not for marriage, but certainly for kids."

The waiter brought their lunch and the next few minutes they concentrated on staving off starvation.

Claire had slowed down. The burger, big and juicy, was practically gone. She made good use of the large linen napkin and then continued their discussion while she picked at what was left of the sandwich. "You know, the real reason I never got married is I never met that right guy. They say there is a man for every woman, but I've noticed that some women have more than their share while some women have none. And I'm one of the latter."

Doug crunched into his pickle, chewed and then asked, "What about Jack? Do you have something going with him?"

"Jack?" She shook her head. "I hardly know him. I like him. Maybe I liked him better when I thought he was a tour guide. Knowing what he really does is a little daunting. It's pretty hard to get to know someone like him. Who's to know what things about him are true? He has to be secretive. After all, his life may depend on his cover.

"How well do you know him?" She asked Doug.

"I only met him that time in London. But I've checked a bit. He has a good reputation. He's apparently very good at what he does. And I noticed that about him right away. I understand he used to be an inside man, but then one day they needed to fill a hole and he was it. He's been outside since. It must be a hard life."

"I guess. Why did you ask about him?"

"I just wondered if you two were an item. I mean, I've seen how attentive he is both in London and here, and I didn't want to horn in."

She realized her surprise must've shown on her face as she stared at Doug.

"As I get out to the San Francisco Bay Area a couple times a year," he continued, "I thought maybe we could get together for dinner or something."

She was momentarily speechless. Then, recovering her wits, she asked boldly, "Doug, are you hitting on me?"

He smiled. "I guess. I just thought I would enjoy spending some time with you."

"Really?"

She wondered why Doug would have an interest in her and almost as if reading her thoughts he said, "You know, you're a very interesting person. You're independent, intelligent, and adventurous. And," he studied her, "being as attractive as you are doesn't hurt."

"Whoa." She sat back, stunned.

"Come on, why are you so surprised? You must get lots of passes."

She shook her head. "No, none that I've noticed."

"No one ever asks you for dates?"

"Sometimes, but I'm too busy for that." She thought a minute. "But...if you called, I could probably find some time."

He laughed. "Fair enough."

The waiter came to clear their plates and ask if they wanted dessert. Doug asked for a cup of coffee, but Claire only wanted a refill of her Coke. "That was a great burger. Thanks."

While Doug settled the check Claire visited the restroom. When she refreshed her lip-gloss she couldn't resist examining her face in the glass. Doug thought her attractive. Well, Jack had made it plain he was interested in her. Could it be that in middle age she was becoming a siren? As a young woman she had always looked more mature than her friends. Therefore, she was never carded when they went to clubs. And she was a serious type of person, not the kind that young men flocked to. Could it be that she was finally coming into her own? Well, she would just wait and see.

"There's a cab."

"No, not that one. He has his windows down so he's not using air-conditioning. Even riding only a few blocks is a killer without air-conditioning. There's one." Doug put up his hand and the cab cut across the traffic to stop in front of them. He handed Claire in the cab and climbed in behind her. "The Longworth House Office Building, please."

"Doug, you don't have to go with me. Please, I know you're busy. I can go by myself," Claire protested.

"No you don't. I'm delivering you in person. Nothing is happening to you on my watch. D.C. can be a dangerous place, and you seem to attract more than your share. I'm not taking any chances."

He sat back and then said seriously, "I don't know if you know this but we've lost a few young women recently. It's pretty scary. The most recent was going home when she just disappeared. Turns out she was involved with one of the Representatives of your state and there is quite a scandal going on. But the important thing is that she has never been found."

"Yes, I've read about it. My mother called to warn me when she learned I was coming, as if San Francisco hasn't had more than its share of horror crimes."

He nodded. "The night you arrived someone tried to knife you." He shook his head. "Not on my watch. I'm delivering you personally to Jack Doobies' office."

"Who is Jack Doobies?"

Doug grinned. "The Lickmans' Representative to the House. MiMi applied a little pressure. Or maybe Suzanne just implied that MiMi requested the favor.

Anyway, someone in his office will give you a personal tour of the Capital." He shook his head at Claire's alarmed look. "Don't worry. It's in their job description. Most tourists contact their representatives to schedule tours before coming to Washington. They expect it."

Doug went into the building with her, up the elevator and then pointed out the correct office.

"Thanks again for lunch, and for the tour of the White House. It was super."

"My pleasure. I guess I'll see you Saturday night at the Lickmans'?"

"I'm looking forward to it." And she went into Doobies' office.

The intern's name was Marybeth Benigan and she was from Annapolis. She had majored in Political Sciences and Communications, and she was interning before graduate school. She was so young and so enthusiastic.

Claire spent over two hours with her and came away exhausted, informed, and in awe of her energy. They took the underground walkway from the Longworth House basement to the basement of the Capital. It was filled with people moving back and forth. Claire was amused that as important as many of these people were, no one seemed to care the tunnel was filled with pipes and fixtures you would find in any basement. It was just a practical way to quickly move from one building to another without weather concerns. Marybeth, despite her short six months on Doobies' staff, seemed to know a good number of the people they encountered, from security guards posted at strategic points to other interns moving between the buildings to business people who Claire suspected might be Representatives themselves.

And she was very knowledgeable about the workings of both the House and the Senate. They visited both chambers. Unfortunately Congress was recessed for the holiday, but that did give them the freedom to roam about at will. Marybeth was doing such a good job explaining the procedures of the Senate that several other people crowded around listening and then asked questions. She good-naturedly included them in her comments.

By the time Claire met Charlie, waiting patiently for her at the bottom of the Capital steps, she knew more about being an Intern and living in D.C. on the stipend they were paid, than she ever thought possible. She admired Marybeth for her willingness to take on such an adventure. She wondered why she never thought to do something like this when she was young. But she realized she wasn't ready to leave home at that age. She had been overly protected by a mother who had never got over the loss of her husband and guarded her daughter carefully lest she lose her too. And times were different then. Her world was small. It never occurred to her to investigate other opportunities.

She was happy to sit back in the luxurious car and let Charlie take care of everything. Her brain was on overload and when David joined them, she was pleased that he wanted to read the stack of papers he had brought so she didn't even have to keep up half of a conversation.

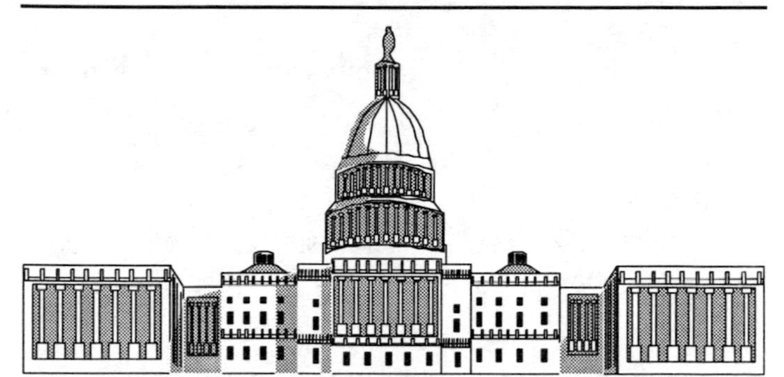

CHAPTER NINE

"Grandpap. Grandpap." Amy threw herself at David, who stooped to sweep her up in his arms.

JoJo didn't want to be left out and moved close to hug him too.

"Welcome home, dear." Then MiMi smiled at Claire. "Did you have a good day?" She waited for Claire's nod before she continued. "David, I made reservations at the Club for dinner so you have an hour to have a drink, change and get there."

"Okay." He set Amy down. "So this reception wasn't really for me, it was to get me moving."

Amy nodded. "I'm hungry."

JoJo disagreed. "We're just glad to see you, Grandpap."

"Claire, this is a very casual dinner. We'll be sitting outside on the dock, so if you want to change, wear anything comfortable and cool. Otherwise what you have on would be fine."

Claire nodded and turned to go into the house, almost tripping over Tuffy who was dancing underfoot. That amused her. She had become so used to the bedlam at the Lickmans' she didn't even register that

Tuffy was barking and jumping for his share of the attention.

'What are you going to wear, Claire?" JoJo asked shyly. "I'm wearing this. What do you think?"

Claire looked at her seriously, and then nodded her head. "Very nice. Yes, I like it. Turn around so I can see the back."

JoJo twirled so the skirt of the sundress she was wearing flared out. It was white cotton with different kinds of fish printed on it.

"I think I have a sundress with me. Maybe I'll wear mine. What do you think?"

JoJo smiled her pleasure.

"I'm wearing my shorts." Amy said proudly. "Gramimi said I could."

"Well, you look very nice too. I could wear shorts. I think I'll just go up and see what I have that will surprise you when I come down."

"What did you do today, Claire?" JoJo was curious.

"I had a great day. I'll tell you all about it at dinner, okay?" And she headed upstairs, hoping for a quick shower before dinner.

The Club was a yachting club the Lickmans had belonged to for years. The dock was crammed with tables and everyone seemed to know everyone. The clubhouse had a large dining room as well, but it appeared to be mostly empty with all the members preferring to sit on the dock. The maitre'd led them through the labyrinth, seating them at a table near the water with a clear view of the marina. At one time, David explained, he had served as the Club's Commodore. That's when they still owned a big motor yacht and spent most of their spare time at the Club or on the Bay.

"I wasn't using it enough. So I finally sold it. We keep the little boats down on the dock for fishing or just taking a ride. And the girls' parents take the motorboat out water-skiing sometimes."

Amy piped up. "I love to water ski."

"You don't water ski," JoJo retorted with scorn.

"I do so!" Then at her grandmother's look, she amended somewhat. "Well, I ride in the boat and watch for when the skier goes down. That's really important, isn't it, Gramimi?

"And I'm going to ski just as soon as I turn ten, Mom said."

JoJo agreed. "I'm ten and I'm just learning. It's lots of fun. But I can only ski when Mom and Dad are with me until I get really good. Probably when I'm eleven, I think. That's why I'm on the swim team. It makes me strong. It will help me be a better skier." JoJo was obviously proud of herself. She turned to her grandmother and politely asked, "Gramimi, can I get some more shrimp?"

"Yes, dear. Amy, do you want to go back to the buffet?"

Amy nodded, getting up to follow her sister to the lavish buffet laid out for the members.

David chuckled. "That Amy, she is really something. She is so positive that she's right. It would be annoying if it wasn't so comical."

"Yes, dear. She takes after someone else in the family, don't you think?"

"What? Are you suggesting me? Moi?" Then he turned to Claire and shrugged. "Well, if it's in the genes, what can we do?"

"Gramimi," the girls were back, excited, "Mrs. Cooley said the kids are going to play games down in the recreation room after dinner. Can Amy and I go?"

"Right now? I thought you were going to get some more to eat?"

They both shook their heads.

"We're full," JoJo claimed.

"Will you keep an eye on Amy? You know some of the games will be too much for her?"

"I can play all the games. I can."

"Amy, you know that some of the games, like Monopoly, are too hard for you. But I'm sure someone will want to play Old Maid or Candyland."

Amy started to pout. "Those are little kids games."

"Amy, you are a little kid," JoJo told her impatiently.

"Am not!" The lower lip hung out even further.

Her grandfather reached over and pulled her into a hug, whispering in her ear. She perked up considerably and followed JoJo willingly.

The waiter cleared their table, and then brought their coffee and drinks.

"Peace at last." David sighed.

"And you only have had them for an hour or so. I had to take a nap this afternoon." Then as if she felt guilty, MiMi explained. "Its not that they're bad. But they just have so much energy, they wear me out just watching them."

Claire joined in the laughter. She knew just how MiMi felt.

They talked a while about Claire's adventures that day and then MiMi explained David was taking the girls to lunch and a movie the next afternoon while the caterers put the final touches on the party preparations.

"You're welcome to go too, Claire, but I'm going into town. I made an appointment at a spa to have the works. And on a hunch I made one for you too. I hoped you might want to join me. It's a nice way to get ready for the party." Her eyes twinkled. "It's a nice way to get ready for anything."

"What a lovely idea. I've never been to a spa but I've certainly heard about them. I'd love to go. Thanks for thinking of me."

"Good. We'll leave with Charlie about 10:30. I expect we'll be home about four or five. The houseguests will start arriving about then. We'll have tea and cocktails in the solarium from five to six-thirty and the Gala will begin about eight. Will your dress need to be pressed? Mrs. Kramer will take care of it if you call her."

"Thanks. Everything is fine. My dress is made out of a silk jersey and it comes out of a suitcase almost wrinkle free."

Claire listened while David and MiMi discussed the people who were and weren't coming to the party. It was a beautiful night. While the day had been hot and very humid, the night was warm and pleasant. The Club's dock hung over the Chesapeake Bay, and on both sides boat slips stretched out holding a variety of cruisers and sailboats. The sun was down and the gray sky was turning to deep blue. She loved sitting there, watching the other diners, absorbing the atmosphere of a life so entirely different from hers.

"I hope you're ready to do your share of dancing, Claire."

"Hmm...what? I'm sorry, I guess I was drifting."

"It sounds like we're having more unattached males than usual. The women will have to be ready to dance, because this band is hot."

Claire had to laugh at David's enthusiasm. "What's hot?"

"You know, doo-wop, YMCA, Harbor Lights, 50's, 60's and 70's. The stuff that's fun to dance to."

"Well, fun for us, anyway," MiMi admitted. "The best thing about giving the party is you can have the food you like and you can choose the music you want played. It's the one night of the year David and I pretend we're young again."

"Yeah, we've got moves." He swayed to the music in his head. "I hope you like to dance because this band gets everyone on the dance floor. You'll see. We had them a couple of years ago and it was the best."

It occurred to Claire that their party was going to be fun. She had expected to enjoy herself, but she was thinking staid, somber and posh. Now it sounded different. She tried to imagine MiMi and David on the dance floor and finally decided she would have to wait to see them.

"Well, I'm afraid I don't get much practice dancing, but I used to love it when I was in school. I'll do my best."

MiMi was counting off unattached males for David's benefit, and Claire interrupted. "Isn't Neil married?"

"Oh, that is very sad." MiMi shook her head.

"Now, dear. It's his life."

"David, I can't help it. I worry about him. He was married to a lovely girl. Then shortly after he joined us they started having trouble and she left him. He got a divorce about a year ago. Of course, it's his business but it's hard enough to carry all the responsibility he does without someone to share it with. He needs someone to care about him." She looked at David.

He nodded as if she had spoken to him. "I don't know what I would do without MiMi. Not only does she support me, but she also lets me know if I get out of line. When you're in charge, it's pretty easy to start thinking you're always right. You've heard of yes-men? Well, every successful person needs a no-man. MiMi is both for me."

MiMi nodded vigorously. "It's a hard job. Sometimes it would be easier to just agree and go on, but I can't. He relies on me to be honest."

David nodded. "And now Neil doesn't have that safety valve. I was all ready to retire last year and turn the company over to his management. Then he separated and started his divorce proceedings. I became concerned about so many changes hitting him at the same time, so I decided to wait awhile and see."

"I'm sure it won't be long until he finds a wife. He must be considered very eligible—nice looking, good job. There are probably dozens of women lusting after him," Claire offered. But she wondered why his wife left him.

* * *

Claire turned in front of the full-length mirror, admiring her image. She spent a wonderful afternoon at the spa. Her fingernails and toenails were a bright, shocking red. She felt her complexion glowing from the facial and her hair looked decidedly different. She always wore it short, so she wasn't expecting the hairdresser could make much difference. But somehow she did. She convinced Claire that some blonde streaking would brighten her hair, which was turning gray, and give her hair a little more body. Then she styled it to give her that tousled look so popular these days. All and all, she thought she looked younger and more modern than she normally did. And there was going to be an over-abundance of single men. She could expect a fun night.

She smoothed the silky fabric over her hips, adjusted the heavy gold and lapis lazuli Egyptian necklace she purchased at the Museum Store in the Stanford Shopping Mall at home. She loved the way the long dangling earrings swayed every time she moved her head. Her dress was very simple, the long skirt was an A-line, and the bodice very plain with open armholes slanting toward the neck leaving her shoulders bare. Modest though it was, the rich blue and the silky fabric made it look sexy.

She stuck her foot out, admiring once again the red toenails in the little gold sandal, amazed yet again at how the shoes stayed on her feet with such flimsy straps. But, as fragile as they looked, they felt good and she was sure that, given the chance, she could dance all night.

Feeling good—no, feeling great—she sailed out of her room ready to party. MiMi and David were near the front door greeting their guests as they arrived, so Claire wandered into the drawing room. The pocket doors between the drawing room and the parlor had been opened extending the size of the room. And all the French doors were opened to the terrace. Most of the furniture had been removed and replaced with little groupings of tables and chairs extending out onto the terrace. A dance floor and bandstand had been erected on the lawn at the edge of the terrace. The band was silhouetted against the bay. And everywhere there were flower arrangements and candles, as well as tubs of flowers and burning torches placed around the dance floor and terrace. It was amazing how the house had been transformed into a fairyland while she and MiMi were at the spa.

The band was already set up, but not yet playing. Several people had arrived, gathered in clumps, drinking and schmoozing. She glanced at her watch and saw it wasn't quite eight. She had debated wearing it, not knowing if it was still considered poor taste for women to want to know what time it was at a social function. But, as it was the best piece of jewelry she owned, she decided she was wearing it to the party.

She headed into the dining room where a long buffet table had been installed. A large bar had been set up in one corner in addition to the waiters circulating with trays of drinks and hors d'oeuvres.

She managed to capture a white wine and a delicious little morsel with a piece of lobster on top.

"Claire, hi. I'd like to introduce my husband. Barry Kirkpatrick, this is Claire Gulliver, the woman I told you I had lunch with the other day." Marian was wearing a frothy black cocktail dress with a full skirt made for dancing. And she was wearing makeup and diamond earrings that looked too big to be real, but might be. This was an entirely different Marian than the woman she lunched with, or the woman she met at the Board Meeting. This Marian looked very glamorous and ready to party.

Barry was an attractive man, older than Marian she guessed by at least ten years. But he was a man who obviously took care of himself and, judging by the expression on his face when he looked at his wife, one who was very much in love.

Claire appreciated his firm yet gentle handclasp and his warm smile. "My wife was singing your praises."

"Barry, do you think you could snag us a drink?" Marian asked gently. As he moved away, she leaned in to whisper to Claire, "Did you talk to Jack?"

Claire also lowered her voice in response, although there was no one within hearing range. "I did. He was going to check on the results of the investigation on Carol Daley, but I haven't heard back from him yet. He'll be here tonight, so whatever I hear I'll let you know."

Marian nodded gratefully. "I talked to a couple of our old friends with no luck. But one of them told me Carol was pretty tight with a woman living in Oregon. She gave me her number, but I haven't been able to reach her. She seemed to think that if Carol shared any information, it would have been with her." Barry returned just then, so she deftly turned the conversation to more general subjects.

Claire talked to several more people and was introduced to Jack Doobies. Claire thanked him sincerely for having Marybeth give her the tour of the Capital. She chatted with Amy and JoJo, admired their dresses and commiserated with them about their curfew at ten that Gramimi had set.

"She forgets we're growing up." Amy's face was so solemn that Claire clamped down on her laugh, which threatened to escape. Instead she nodded seriously.

"I think grandmothers are like that. But anyway, you'll get to have dinner and be here for the start of the dancing. It will probably get pretty boring after that." Amy was not fully convinced.

Claire was talking to Doug, who looked very nice in his white dinner jacket, when Neil and Suzanne joined them. Neil scanned the crowd even while he talked, apparently making sure he saw everyone and spoke to all. Suzanne, in a long kelly green gown, looked completely different than her competent business persona.

"Like it?" she whispered to Claire.

Claire nodded. "Really, it's gorgeous and it looks perfect on you."

It did. The shining green glowed against Suzanne's latte skin, and the long slim lines seemed to give her small form more stature.

"I clean up well, huh?" She grinned. "I don't get to play with the big kids much, so when I get the chance I just have to go all out."

"Well, you certainly did."

"And you didn't do so badly yourself. I suspect all that concern over what to wear was probably a pose. Look at you, girl!"

Their little group swelled and ebbed as others stopped to talk before drifting over to the bar or into one of the other rooms. Several of the Board Members stopped to speak to her. She met some members from the Yacht Club where they had dined, and she learned from Neil's comments he was aggressively campaigning for votes for membership in that same club. She was able to introduce some of MiMi and David's houseguests to the people she knew from Vantage, having met them earlier in the day.

Jack finally joined them, nattily dressed in a black tuxedo. She looked at him with a raised eyebrow. "Traffic problems?"

"No, just checking the grounds with Wiley," he murmured low for her benefit, accepting a non-alcoholic drink from a passing waiter.

A flash of white caught Claire's attention and she turned her head just in time to see Amy racing through the dining room towards the kitchen.

"Oh, oh, I think we have trouble." Claire hurried after Amy not waiting to see if anyone was following. Through the kitchen door she saw Tuffy standing, tail swinging in circles, watching Amy approach. Before she reached him, he playfully turned and dashed across the kitchen, oblivious of the people and the activity taking place.

Claire watched in horror as he ran right between the legs of a tuxedoed waiter, who had just accepted a large chafing dish from one of the chefs. The scene looked as if it had been choreographed for a movie. The waiter, holding the heavy dish, turned toward the dining room, tripped over Tuffy and crashed to the floor, the contents of the dish spattering hot green glop everywhere.

As awful as that scene was, Claire's gaze was riveted elsewhere. Her eyes locked on the man in the chef's hat who had just handed off the chafing dish to the waiter. His face reflected surprise, which then turned to horror. His eyes never left her face as he backed up, turned and abruptly left the kitchen through the side door to the garden.

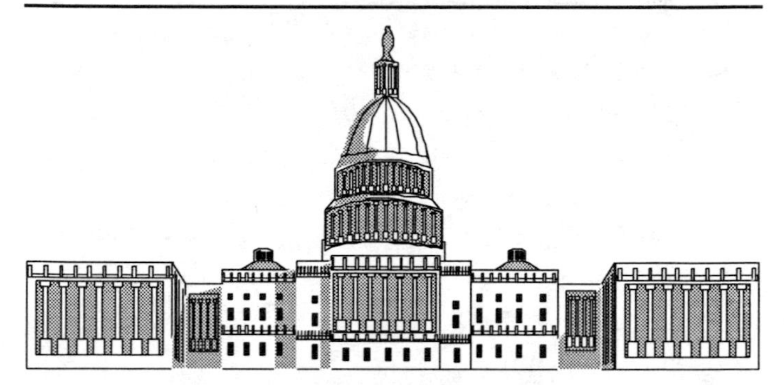

CHAPTER TEN

"Jack, Jack!" Her voice was only a croak. She dashed across the kitchen, jumping over the mess on the floor. When she got to the door she turned around and gestured frantically. "Hurry! Hurry! It was him! It was the guy from the Mall. Did you see him? He just went out the door." Her shaking hand opened the door.

Comprehension chased the confusion from Jack's face. He paused long enough to admonish her to stay where she was before he burst through the door, and then he was gone too.

"Claire, what is it?" Doug hovered over her protectively.

"That man, the one in the chef's outfit, he was the one who attacked me in the Mall. He was here. Right here in the kitchen!" She looked at Doug in horror. "What was he doing here?

"He ran out that way. Jack went after him," she continued. Her body trembled so violently she needed to lean against the door jam for support.

Doug's eyes flashed his anger. "I'm going to find Wiley. You wait here. They were prepared for something, now we'll see how well." And he went back through the kitchen the way they had come in.

That's when Claire realized there was another disturbance in progress.

"Get that dog out of here. What a mess!" Neil was so furious his voice was high pitched, almost a scream. "Who let that...that dog...in here?" His anger caused him to sputter.

Amy quaked in front of him, her lower lip jutting out and quivering. JoJo came into the kitchen and hurried to her sister's side.

"Amy, I told you not to let him out." Her whisper sounded loud in the hushed room. Everyone else froze, not knowing who should do what.

"But I didn't. I just..." she hiccupped, "I just wanted to make sure he wasn't lonely. But..." she started crying, "but he got out when I opened the door and he was being naughty..." a heartbreaking sob erupted, "and he ran from me."

"And see the mess he made?" Neil showed her no mercy. Her tears didn't move him one bit.

Claire moved in to hug Amy. "Don't cry Amy. Tuffy was being bad. But he didn't mean to cause so much trouble, did you, Tuffy?" They both looked at the dog, who paused a moment to return their look, his pointy ears at attention, his head cocked to one side, his open mouth covered with green. He seemed to know they were talking about him. Then he turned back to the green mess, gobbling as much as he could off the floor.

"JoJo, can you grab his collar and drag him out of that mess? Be careful not to get any on your dress."

Claire turned to look at the red-faced Neil. "Neil, really there's no harm done. I'm sure MiMi won't mind; it's only one dish of spinach. And you're scaring Amy."

Maybe it was what she said or the reproach in her tone, but Neil calmed down, probably a little embarrassed by his show of temper. He shrugged, unable to find any more words, turned and stalked out of the kitchen.

Fortunately, the ever efficient Suzanne, who had followed the others into the kitchen, had immediately gone to find Mrs. Kramer when she saw what was happening. They came in as Neil left, and Mrs. Kramer immediately took charge. She started some of the catering staff cleaning up the mess. She talked to the head caterer about how to rearrange the buffet table to fill the empty spot where the soufflé was going to sit. She sent JoJo and Amy to take Tuffy back to the nursery where he was banished until the party and clean-up were over.

"Wait a minute, JoJo." She took a wet towel and cleaned off the dog's face and his paws. "Let's not have him tracking spinach all over the house, okay?" And then at the last minute she took a dog biscuit out of her pocket and handed it to Amy. "And you can give him this before you leave him. With that and a tummy full of spinach soufflé, he'll probably sleep all night."

Amy nodded, her face brightening just a little.

It was amazing how quickly the kitchen was back to operating efficiently. The waiters formed a steady stream, carrying out platters and dishes piled with interesting foods to fill the buffet table. Dinner would soon be served.

Suzanne stood beside Claire. "What did I miss? Where is your friend, Jack? And Doug? And why did Neil look so pissed when he left?"

"You wouldn't believe it." Claire shook her head.

"Well, come on. Let's get out of here before we have another disaster. You can make a believer of me while we have a drink." The diminutive Suzanne took Claire's arm and firmly guided her out of the kitchen.

Claire sipped her wine as she finished the story. "So I don't know where Jack is. I hope he caught that man. And I don't know why Neil lost it.

"And poor Amy, she's so sensitive. She was only worried about Tuffy being lonely." She looked at Suzanne, who shook her head, trying without success to suppress the smile pulling at her mouth and then they both burst into laughter.

"I wish I had been there. But when I saw the dog running right through that waiter's legs, I knew we needed Mrs. Kramer. But see, I missed all the good stuff." She had to sit down at one of the tables near them. She had laughed so hard her knees were weak.

Claire joined her. But her shaking knees were the result of finding her attacker in the kitchen, rather than from her bout of laughter.

"Well, we're not going to get any answers until the 'boys' get back. I suggest we have another drink and join that line at the buffet.

"Oh, there's Wiley's wife. Have you met her?" Suzanne stood up and waved over a very regal looking large dark woman stunningly dressed in a two-piece pale wheat colored silk dress.

"Masie, I don't think you've met Claire Gulliver, have you?"

Masie's smile was warm. "No, I haven't. But I've sure heard about your visit. I hope you're having a good time. I know Suzanne is probably doing her best to make sure you see everything."

"Well, she's doing a fabulous job. If I miss anything it won't be her fault."

"We're just thinking of getting something to eat, Masie. Do you want to join us? I think the 'boys' are out running around the yard. Who knows when they'll get back?"

Masie rolled her eyes. "That Wiley, he loves playing cops and robbers. I just worry that some of the other guys won't know it's a game." She moved with them to the buffet, obviously used to entertaining herself while her husband was working.

Claire followed her plate as it was passed from server to server, each one slipping a selection of delicacies on it attractively. But her mind wasn't on the food accumulating on her plate. She was still reeling from the shock of coming face to face with her attacker in the kitchen. And she was wondering where Jack was and what was happening. She set her plate down on the table they selected and nodded her thanks to the waitress who brought silverware and napkins.

"Suzanne, I saw Amy and JoJo in line. I think I'll just check and make sure they're okay. I'll be right back. Snag me another white wine if the waiter comes around, would you please?"

"Amy, JoJo, is everything all right?" Claire nodded cordially to their Great Auntie Maude, MiMi's aunt, who was standing behind them, apparently intending to supervise their dinner.

Amy nodded sadly. "I told Gramimi and now Tuffy's in real trouble."

"Amy, Gramimi isn't mad at him," JoJo admonished. "She was just disappointed there wouldn't be any soufflé for Grandpap."

Amy nodded. "Tuffy ate it all." She couldn't help the look of revulsion on her face; they all knew she hated the stuff.

"Girls, look lively there. It's your turn. Amy, don't take more than you'll eat. JoJo, make sure you take meats and vegetables, not just sweets," Great Auntie Maude directed them.

"Okay, girls, have a nice dinner. I'm sitting just over there with Suzanne. I'll see you before you go to bed, won't I?"

They nodded, now absorbed in the business of filling their plates.

Claire smiled at Maude before heading back to her table.

She sipped the wine the waiter had delivered, wondering how many glasses she had already. Too many, she thought. But she didn't feel a thing, so she took another sip.

"How's Amy?"

"Fine, just feeling guilty Tuffy got in so much trouble." Claire grinned. "And probably a little disappointed that her Great Auntie Maude is supervising their visit to the buffet table. MiMi is much more tolerant, letting them choose whatever they want and encouraging them to try new things even if they don't eat them. I think Great Auntie Maude's no-nonsense approach is a lot stricter."

"There you are." Doug came from behind her and slipped into a vacant chair at their table. "Dinnertime? Good!" He reached over and helped himself to a piece of succulent looking lobster from her plate. "I hope you don't mind, but I'm starved. It didn't look like you were eating it..." he eyed her plate, "or anything else for that matter." This time he liberated a spear of white asparagus.

"What's going on? Where have you been? Where's Jack?" Suzanne and Claire were anxious, wanting answers.

"And Wiley?" Masie joined in.

Doug looked at her puzzled, so Claire introduced them. She was so agitated she could hardly sit still.

"Relax, relax. I'm going to tell you everything I know. Are you going to eat that?" When she shook her head he pulled her whole plate over in front of him. She automatically handed him her silverware and napkin. He looked over his shoulder and made eye contact with one of the waiters who quickly brought him a glass of wine.

Apparently he was very hungry as he devoured the food on the plate, trying to politely talk around his chewing.

"The man took off in one of the catering vans. Almost ran over one of the men parking the cars. Wiley had the police put out an APB for him and the van. So we're expecting to hear very soon that someone picked him up. It's kind of hard to hide out in a white catering van." He paused to finish the medallion of Veal Oscar.

"Jack talked to the head caterer and got the name of the manager. He's tracking him down now. Your man was hired on recommendation of one of their other employees, because they were short-handed. He was kitchen help—you know, finalizing the food preparation, making it look pretty on the serving trays and then cleaning up the empties coming back to the kitchen. This was his first job with them but, so far, the head caterer here was pleased with his work. They know the man who recommended him and will have some records in their employment files on him. I think we're going to catch up with him pretty soon and then we'll have some answers to our questions."

He looked at the empty plate. "I believe I'll just get a little more. Claire, can I get you something since I ate yours."

She shook her head and drained the glass of wine. It was driving her crazy. Who was this weirdo, and what was he doing in the Lickmans' kitchen? Finding him here was no coincidence!

She accepted another glass of wine without even thinking.

Doug came back with another plate of food, this one heaping. Suzanne and Masie excused themselves to visit the powder room. The band had switched from soft mood music to loud rock tunes and, judging by the noise from outside, everyone was on the dance floor.

Claire realized she was becoming pleasantly sloshed.

Suzanne appeared with a man in tow. "Claire, you remember Cliff Denning, don't you? He wants to dance, but his wife didn't come with him. I'm already promised, but I told him you'd probably oblige."

It was the man she talked to about San Francisco restaurants at the Board Meeting luncheon the other day. Cliff looked embarrassed, but hopeful.

"Of course. I remember Cliff. We have a mutual fondness for San Francisco, don't we?" She got to her feet. "I'd love to dance, but I don't know how good I am."

Suzanne gave her a grateful glance and disappeared.

"Excuse me, Doug, but this music can't be wasted." She excused herself as she followed Cliff to the dance floor. In spite of his stern demeanor and his gray hair, Cliff was a dancer. Claire realized she would have to be a lump of clay to not look good on the floor dancing with him.

"Did you used to teach at Arthur Murray's?" She panted after a particularly complex move.

He just laughed as he swung her into another dance. Then she danced with Neil and then someone she hadn't even met. She had time for a quick swallow of wine before spinning off with David Lickman, who as he had claimed the previous day, did have moves. Doug apparently satisfied his hunger and caught up with her on the dance floor. They danced several dances, one of which Amy and JoJo joined them for a loud rendition of *Y.M.C.A.* with all the required arm movements. Finally she collapsed at a table for a rest while Doug went off to get them some more wine.

Cliff found her again but she begged off, promising to dance with him after she had regained her breath. She sat on the edge of the terrace where the dance floor was clearly visible and watched the Lickmans dance. They were obviously having a great time. Marian and her husband were also surprisingly good dancers, moving as one entity. And Suzanne appeared to be having fun. She hadn't sat down yet as far as Claire could tell. But Suzanne was quite a few years younger than she was, so naturally she had more energy, she consoled herself. Yet, using that line of reasoning she was hard pressed to explain why Great Auntie Maude, who must be years older, was dancing energetically with one of the older male houseguests. Neither the beat of the music nor the lateness of the night seemed to be slowing them down.

The band was very good. Their soft mood music through dinner was deceptive. As soon as dinner was over the four doo-wop girls and one male singer demonstrated their talents, each taking leads in a variety of songs from the past. The sound system had been cranked up to deafening so people had to dance or go inside, as there was no chance for conversation to be heard anywhere near the dance floor. And it appeared that most people elected to dance.

Jack slipped into the chair opposite her, looking a little less dapper than he had earlier. She saw his lips moving but she couldn't hear a word. She shook her head, then motioned for him to follow as she moved inside to a table in the drawing room.

That's when Doug found them with the drinks. He immediately gave his drink to Jack, who needed it more than he did, turned and went back to get a glass for himself.

"Nice party." Jack took a sip and seemed to relax a bit.

"How would you know? You've missed the whole thing. I bet you didn't get anything to eat, did you?"

He shook his head.

Doug having just returned with his drink said, "Well, I don't think you had anything to eat either, did you, Claire?"

She grinned ruefully, "No. I was so disappointed about the spinach soufflé, I lost my appetite.

"So, are you going to tell us about it?" she inquired, "or are you keeping secrets?"

Jack shrugged. "Nothing to keep secret. I didn't catch him." His face clearly reflected his thoughts about that failure. "I didn't even see his face, just the back of his head as he drove out the gate. We have the local police looking for the van, and for him. He won't get far."

"Jack, it was him. I couldn't be mistaken."

Jack looked at her and nodded. "I never doubted you for a minute. Not only am I sure his face was clearly imprinted on your brain, but why else would he have hightailed it out of the kitchen and then steal one of the vans in his effort to get away? No, it was him. But what was he doing here?"

They stared at each other as if the answer was there to see.

"Tomorrow we'll be at the caterer's first thing in the morning to review their personnel files. The police are currently visiting the guy who recommended him, so we may get identification later tonight. We will get some answers," he promised Claire. "Meanwhile, I've missed the fun." He stood up and held out his hand. "How about a dance?"

Claire excused herself from Doug and followed Jack to the dance floor. Just as they stepped onto the dance floor, the band delivered *The Harbor Lights* David had promised her yesterday, and the exhausted dancers smiled gratefully for the respite.

Claire fit perfectly in Jack's arms. They were the same height, although the sandals Claire wore gave her an inch advantage.

"Did I mention how super you look tonight?" Jack murmured in her ear.

"No, I don't think you did."

"Well, you look great. I don't know what you did with your hair but it's nice. And I get goose bumps when those little scarlet painted toes peek out from under your dress."

Claire smiled. "Oh, so you're one of those?"

"Those?"

"Guys with a foot fetish."

"Hmmm. I never thought about it, but maybe I am. Or I'm just developing one."

The band slid into the *Theme from Summer Place* and the dancers glided over the floor. Claire just enjoyed being held. It was romantic, the warm night, the slight breeze from the bay, the stars overhead and the muted light all adding to the mood.

Then the rock music was back, and Cliff was there to claim his dance. Jack headed for the house to find something to eat and Claire gave herself up to the beat. After all, it was a Gala.

***

The black Porsche glided into the deserted parking lot and moved toward the public facilities. This was a popular launching ramp for boaters, so it was well maintained, albeit completely empty at this time of night. He pulled up as far in the shadow as possible and got out of the car.

He looked around but saw no sign of movement. Then out of the darkest shadow he saw something.

"Tony? Christ, are you mad? Calling me at the Lickmans'? Why don't you just take out an ad in the Post?" He couldn't help it. He was mad. Furious!

"It wasn't my fault," Tony whined. "Everything was fine until that dog appeared. And then she was there, just staring at me. She recognized me immediately. I had to get out of there."

Tony's face hardened. "It wasn't my fault. I did everything you wanted. It wasn't in the cards. And now I'm blown. I've got to get out of town. I need my money and I need a ride to the Baltimore train station."

He nodded. "Where's the van?"

"I ditched it a couple miles that way." Tony gestured with his head. "Then I hoofed back here to call you. It was too big, too white and too noticeable to disappear in."

"It wasn't your fault. I saw it." He nodded again, sympathy on his face as he moved forward. "I can't believe the bad luck. Of course I'll pay you." He was very close to Tony now, as he reached into his pocket and brought out the gun. He didn't even pause as he pulled the trigger. Once, twice, and then bending directly over the body, a third time. He wasn't taking any chances that Tony would be caught and able to tell his story.

Then he turned, got in the car, revved up the motor and took off for home feeling much cheerier.

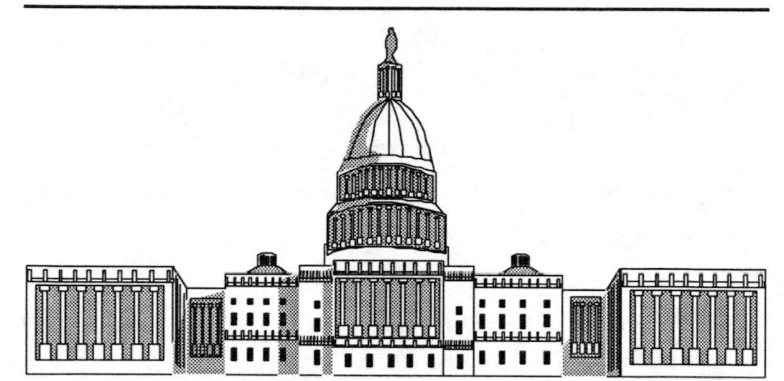

CHAPTER ELEVEN

Claire came awake slowly, aware it was late. She smiled and stretched. It had been a lovely party. It was like something out of a movie, not at all real. The last of the guests left very late and then the houseguests mingled a little before wandering to their rooms.

Doug, Cliff and Jack had all kissed her goodnight. Chaste, friendly kisses on the cheek. Doug murmured he would be in touch. Cliff thanked her for being such a good dance partner and helping him have a good time. Jack, a bit disgruntled, perhaps by the number of people milling about in the foyer, said he would call in the morning.

She grinned. She had felt like the belle of the ball. But now she was starved!

She made fast work of her shower and was downstairs in the solarium in record time, where she noticed that even though she thought it was late, no one but Amy was in the solarium. Claire helped herself to some coffee and juice and made her way to the table where Amy sat hunched over a bowl of oatmeal.

"Why such a long face, Amy? Are you a little grumpy from such a late night?"

She shook her head gloomily. "No, I'm just worried."

"Worried? What's got you worried?" She sat down and took a sip of the fresh orange juice. The sharp citrus tang jolted her taste buds and she drank more, not really paying much attention to Amy.

"What did you say?" She now turned her attention to the child.

"I said Tuffy's sick. And," her voice dropped to a whisper, "he threw up. It was awful. It was green." Her eyes were big and round.

"How sick? Lots of times dogs will throw up, just like babies do."

"He won't get up. When he did stand up he kind of fell over. You know, like he had turned in circles too many times."

"Where is he now, Amy? Did you go get your Gramimi?"

She shook her head solemnly. "No, Mrs. Kramer told us last night to be quiet this morning so Gramimi and Grandpap could sleep in. And I tried to tell JoJo but she just pulled the covers over her head."

Claire sat back looking at the child, thinking as she sipped her coffee. Tuffy was such a bundle of energy she couldn't imagine him sick. She stood up and reached a hand for Amy's. "We'd better go see him, Amy. Then we can decide what we should do."

Amy led her to the far end of the nursery where Tuffy's basket sat. Amy was right. The dog was sick. The dog's normally white crispy hair was limp and matted, and instead of jumping up when they approached, he only opened one eye to look at them and then closed it again. Claire was no expert but it looked serious to her. She held out her hand and touched his nose feeling how warm it was. She thought that meant he had a fever, and she could see the green mess he had made during the night on the other side of his bed.

Amy stooped down close to the dog. Patting him gently on the head she whispered to him, "Don't worry, Tuffy. Claire is here. She's going to take care of you."

Claire felt a tightening in her chest. She wasn't sure what to do. Finally she simply told Amy to stay with Tuffy while she went for Mrs. Kramer.

The kitchen seemed to be back to normal already, even after all the activity of last night. Cook had a couple of helpers ready to prepare breakfasts as people ordered from the solarium.

"Where can I find Mrs. Kramer?"

"Take that door, down at the end. I'm sure she's up by now, but she hasn't been here yet."

Claire tapped at the door, hating to disturb the woman who so competently ran this household.

Mrs. Kramer looked surprised to find Claire at the door but asked graciously, "What can I do for you this morning?"

"It's Tuffy. He's sick. Amy told me, but she hasn't told MiMi or David. I did go up to see him and even knowing nothing about animals I can see he's very sick. I didn't know what to do, so I decided it would be best to get you." The last was said to Mrs. Kramer's back as she had already started moving briskly down the hall toward the back stairwell.

JoJo finally gave up when they traipsed back through the nursery. Rubbing her eyes she grumped, "What's going on? Why is everyone in here?"

"Tuffy's sick," Amy explained. "I told you before."

Mrs. Kramer knelt down beside Amy and looked at the dog carefully. Then standing up she said to Claire, "I'll go down, call the vet and talk to Mrs. Lickman. Can you call Charlie? The number is star 17 on the house phone. Ask him to bring the car around and then come up here to carry Tuffy down." As she went out the door she said over her shoulder, "Don't worry about that mess. I'll send someone up to clean it in a few minutes."

"JoJo, it sounds as if a lot of people will be in here in a very little while, so you may want to take your clothes into the bathroom and get dressed," Claire suggested as she picked up the phone to contact Charlie.

She was right. MiMi was there in a matter of minutes, looking alarmed and rumpled, not having finished her normal grooming cycle when Mrs. Kramer knocked on her door.

"Tuffy, baby. What's the matter with you?" she cooed as if the dog was going to answer.

When Charlie arrived only a few minutes later she instructed him to take the dog, basket and all, down to the car. "I'll get my shoes and be right there."

Mrs. Kramer had returned by then and MiMi stopped. "Oh, my guests..." Then making up her mind she hurried out the door. "They'll just have to entertain themselves for a few hours; I have to go with Tuffy."

"Gramimi, can I go too?" Amy's anxious face looked earnestly at her grandmother.

MiMi paused in the hall. She couldn't seem to make up her mind, so Claire offered, "Do you want me to go with you? I could look out for Amy."

"Would you? Thank you."

Then seeing JoJo come in from the bathroom she said, "JoJo, there you are. You stay with your Grandpap and help him with the guests, will you?" And she was gone.

"Dr. Milhouser, Tuffy's veterinarian, asked if he ate anything unusual, so I told him about the spinach soufflé incident. He asked that I bring a sample, but I don't have any. The caterers took all the trash away with them last night," Mrs. Kramer told them as she headed downstairs with Amy and Claire following.

Then Claire remembered. "What about the towel you used to clean Tuffy last night? Did the caterers take that too?"

Mrs. Kramer thought a minute. "No, I don't think so. I think I threw it in the laundry. That's a good idea, Claire. Wait just a minute." She was back in a very short time with the stained towel in a sealed baggie. "Here, see if this will do."

And they were off. Claire sat in the front with Charlie. MiMi and Amy sat in the back with the dog, crooning softly to comfort him as Charlie drove as fast as the country roads would let him.

They arrived at the animal hospital a few minutes before Dr. Milhouser. But the attendant was expecting them and led them back to an examination room. Claire looked around surprised at how like a doctor's office it was. Not having a pet, she had never had the occasion to visit an animal hospital before. And when Theroux the cat decided to adopt the store, she had called in a veterinarian on wheels to check her out, because Mrs. B had advised her it would result in a lot less trauma on all of them.

When Dr. Milhouser hurried in, Claire could see that he had not intended to spend the Sunday of his Labor Day weekend in the clinic. In spite of his tennis clothes, he didn't seem at all put out with the interruption; his only apparent concern was with the sick dog.

"What's the matter, Tuffy?" He peered closely at the dog, pulling up an eyelid to look into his eye. Then he inserted a tongue depressor in the dog's mouth while he examined his teeth and gums. His assistant deftly inserted a rectal thermometer and Tuffy didn't even flinch.

"Well, Mrs. Lickman, I'm sorry to agree that Tuffy is very ill. I understand there was an incident with some creamed spinach last night?" He picked up the folder his assistant had ready for him on the counter and thumbed through the contents. "Has he ever eaten spinach before?"

MiMi shook her head.

Amy nodded hers. She looked at her grandmother with guilt all over her face. "Well, last Christmas when Mom said I had to eat some," she gulped, not really wanting to confess, "well, Tuffy was under the table and...

"But, he liked it," she said earnestly.

"So he didn't get sick then?"

"Apparently not." MiMi raised her eyebrows at Amy.

"So it's probably not the soufflé. Has he been outside? Could he have eaten any mushrooms? You know, in the woods or out on the lawn."

"I haven't seen him. Do dogs eat raw mushrooms?"

The doctor shrugged. "Not usually. Has he had access to any poisons?" Seeing MiMi shake her head he said, "Look, why don't you wait outside while we do some blood work? Then I'm afraid our only hope is to pump his stomach and hope he responds. It sounds like he threw up a good portion of what he had eaten, so maybe we can get the rest out of him in time. Meanwhile, we'll see if we can get someone at the lab to look at the sample you brought with you."

Then he looked gravely into MiMi's eyes. "We need to know what made him so sick before we can administer an antidote. You need to know that without this information, we may not be able to save him."

MiMi sat down in the waiting room, suddenly old looking. She couldn't stop her tears. "Oh Claire, you must think I'm a dotty old fool. Getting this upset about a dog."

Before Claire could answer, Amy went over and hugged her grandmother. "But Gramimi, Tuffy's your baby, isn't he?"

MiMi cried harder, nodding, hugging the child closer.

Claire turned to Charlie. "You have a cell phone, don't you? I need to contact Jack. And I need his cell number."

Charlie nodded and led the way outside. He punched in the number and handed the phone to Claire.

"Jack? This is Claire." She ignored his surprised greeting. "Jack, we have a sad thing happening here at the Lickmans'. You know the dog, Tuffy? Well, he is very sick this morning. The doctor seems to think it is some kind of poison. He's been questioning the spinach soufflé as Tuffy had eaten more than his share from the floor last night...and he vomited quite a bit of it, but..."

Jack's response was a squawk and then he shouted, "The spinach? Wasn't that what your guy was handing off before he hit the road?"

She nodded. Then realizing he couldn't see, she answered, "Yes, that's what's so suspicious. We don't know what he was doing in the Lickmans' kitchen. But I for one assume he was up to no good."

Jack was silent. Then he responded, "We need to get a sample and have some tests run. Do you have any there?"

"No, it went all over the floor and what Tuffy didn't get went in the garbage. I understand the caterers took all the trash away with them when they cleaned up, so I don't know where it would be."

"Okay, I do. I'll have somebody track it down. Hopefully, it didn't get picked up yet. The guys hate to go through the dump."

Claire shuddered with revulsion just thinking about that search.

"We do have a towel here that Mrs. Kramer used to clean him off last night, and it has some soufflé on it. Would that help?"

"Maybe. Where are you?"

Charlie gave her the address and she repeated it to Jack. "They're going to pump Tuffy's stomach, but that's all they can do until they identify the cause. The doctor is sending the sample we have here to a laboratory for testing. But he thinks it could be toadstools or poisonous mushrooms that Tuffy got into in the woods. I'm more suspicious. I suspect foul play."

"I'll get someone out there to pick up a piece of that towel, and we'll see how fast we can work. Where can I reach you?"

She gave him the hospital's name and number as well as Charlie's cell phone number before going back inside to sit with MiMi and Amy.

The doctor reported that Tuffy's blood work showed no clues as to the source of his ailment, so their only course of action was to pump his stomach. They waited through that, and Tuffy still stubbornly held on.

Then the doctor sent them home as there was nothing more they could do. The towel had been split in two. One half he sent to the local lab for testing. The other half was waiting for the person Jack was sending to pick it up. And the doctor promised he would stay with the dog for the duration of the crisis. "I'll call immediately with any change." His eyes were sympathetic. "Good, or bad."

The ride back was at a much more sedate pace and Claire watched amazed as MiMi pulled herself together, preparing to assume her duties as hostess even though Claire knew her heart was breaking.

* * *

"Jack, we got your guy." Wiley's voice boomed over Jack's cell phone.

"Great! Where is he? I have lots of questions."

"I don't think you'll get many answers, but I'm going there now. Wanna come?"

"Naturally, do you want me to meet you somewhere?"

Wiley gave him detailed directions to the boat launch parking lot and hung up with a telling comment, "No hurry now."

Jack plugged his phone into his car lighter socket; he had already used it so much today the battery was getting low. He headed out of D.C. toward the Lickmans'. They had their sample of the spinach soufflé. It turned out that because one of the vans had been stolen, the caterers had to crowd all their workers, the leftover food and the dishes into the two remaining vans. Consequently, they had left the trash at the Lickmans' and sent someone back early this morning to get it. In doing so, they had missed the scheduled trash pick-up at the caterer's. That was a lucky break. But Jack still sent someone out to the veterinarian hospital for the towel as a back up.

Jack's colleagues made arrangements through the FBI for a laboratory in Maryland to do an immediate analysis. He hoped to hear the results soon. The personnel files at the catering company contained bogus information on the man who fled the Lickmans'. But it turned out the cousin, who recommended him for the job, was a bonafide person. The cousin reluctantly identified the man they were seeking as Anthony Berberson. The police files provided further information on him. He was known as Tony the Pickman, a small-time hoodlum who did anything for hire.

The puzzle was coming together piece by piece. However, they still had no clue as to the purpose of these strange happenings. Tony the Pickman could be the key to this mystery.

Jack pulled off the road behind a pickup with a boat in tow and then waited while the driver maneuvered a u-turn to get back out to the road. A policeman was blocking the entrance to the lot, patiently turning away boaters planning to use this facility to launch their boats into the Chesapeake Bay.

Jack ignored the gesture to turn around, rolling his car forward so he could talk out of the window. "I'm Jack Rallins. I'm to meet Wiley Blackford from Vantage Airlines. Has he gotten here yet?"

The policeman nodded and gestured to the far end of the lot where a group of emergency vehicles, cars and people were clustered. Then he waved Jack into the lot before he stopped another boater who had pulled up close to Jack's bumper. Jack angled his car across the large empty lot pulling up beside a car he thought might be Wiley's.

When he stepped out of the car onto the steaming asphalt, Wiley separated himself from a group of men and motioned him over to the trees bordering the edge of the lot.

"Whew, let's stand in the shade a bit. It's gonna be a scorcher today." The big man had on lightweight chinos and a golf shirt, but was still perspiring.

"Is it him?" Jack wasn't a cop but had been in the business long enough to recognize a crime scene. He had surmised his man wouldn't be alive after Wiley's comments on the phone. The activity in the parking lot confirmed his hunch.

"They think so. You can't identify him. His face is blown away, but his wallet contained identification of one of his known aliases, and they're checking his fingerprints."

"How far is this from the Lickmans'?"

"Not far. It's maybe four miles from the turn off. But it's the other way. You'd expect him to head over the bridges to D.C. or Baltimore. And that's where they found the truck, run off the road about six miles away but on the other side of the Lickmans'. Maybe he had someone waiting." He shrugged. "Who knows? But somehow, I think Tuffy dashing into the kitchen with everyone following was a total surprise. Why else would he have left so early that he had to steal one of the trucks to get away?

"Detective Maynard, over there, is in charge. As soon as he finishes what he's doing I'll introduce you. He's getting some mug shots of this guy for you and Claire to look at."

Jack looked around and saw the half dozen or so cars and boat trailers parked in the lot. "I thought they closed this launching ramp."

Wiley followed his gaze. "Apparently these belong to people who were in the water and gone before the body was discovered. The guy who called it in is over there."

Jack saw the new model SUV with a color-coordinated boat still sitting on the attached trailer. The owner paced around the car while a woman, probably his wife, sat inside the vehicle trying to entertain two young children, who were more interested in watching what the cops were doing.

"He's not having such a good day today."

"No, I guess not."

Detective Maynard approached and offered his hand to Jack. "So, you think you know this guy?"

Jack shrugged. "I may have met him a couple of times, but I can't say I know him."

"Probably just as well. I wouldn't consider him the kind of person who would be a fun friend." He led the way back toward the body, which was now being zipped into a body bag in preparation for removal. "He was definitely killed right here. Three shots, one directly to the head, probably when he was already down. Someone wanted to make sure he was dead. No witnesses that we can find. No vehicles, no tire tracks. And that doesn't get us any answers, does it?" He looked resigned. "Wiley filled me in on some of what has happened over the past few months. Anything you want to add?"

Jack shook his head. "Wiley told you about the arrangement we have working with the FBI? The guy you need to keep informed is Marcus Ng." He slowly gave Marcus' phone number while Detective Maynard scribbled in his pocket-sized notebook.

"When will you have the pictures for us to see?"

"The guy's on his way. He should be here in a half hour."

"Fine, we'll wait. Thanks. Wiley will keep you informed if we come up with anything else. Or Marcus will. Hopefully, you'll do the same."

The weary detective nodded, he knew the drill, and then he turned back to the technicians who were clamoring for his attention.

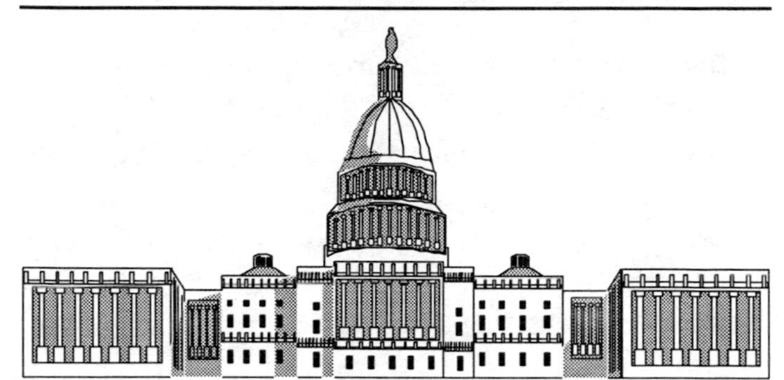

CHAPTER TWELVE

Claire groaned as Great Auntie Maude's ball smacked hers, knocking her out of range for the clear shot she thought she had at the next wicket. This was not the game she thought it was going to be when she agreed to play.

"Why don't you join us for a nice game of croquet, dear?" Great Auntie Maude had asked. It sounded harmless enough even as she explained the house rules in effect. She remembered croquet as a pleasant diversion on a warm summer day. How was she to know they were all sharks just looking for fresh blood?

She looked at the other players. JoJo was playing along with several of the more elderly houseguests. They appeared harmless. She shook her head in disgust at her own ineptitude. She was beaten. She was just glad they hadn't wagered money on the outcome. Then as she watched, Hal, who was related to someone but she wasn't sure to who or how, skillfully sent his ball home.

Amidst the hoopla and hollering she surrendered her mallet and ball. After adding her congratulations to the winner, she headed for the pitcher of iced tea sitting invitingly on the drink trolley. Claire was amused at the sight of Great Auntie Maude, collapsed in a chair under one of the umbrellas, fanning herself as she sipped her tea. She didn't look like she could do harm with a croquet mallet, but now Claire knew better. Hal was holding court, replaying each of his swings, and revealing a strategy worthy of winning a war.

"Well, Hal, you're getting a big head. I think I have to challenge you to another game. Who's up for another round?" Maude, eighty if she was a day, enthusiastically marshaled the players.

Claire had asked her earlier how she kept her energy so high.

Maude had winked and said, "Don't you know that every day above ground is a good day? And at my age I can't afford to waste any good days."

Now remembering that comment she smiled. Maude was an interesting person and in many ways she reminded her of her assistant at the bookstore, Mrs. B. She was sure Mrs. B wasn't as old as Maude but probably not far from her age. But both woman had sharp minds and displayed a curiosity about all aspects of life which seemed to keep them young. Many times Mrs. B's unflagging energy shamed Claire into extending herself.

And, of course, Mrs. B had played a major role in convincing Claire she should sponsor Lucy's tour of Britain last spring; say nothing of her encouraging her to take charge of the tour when Lucy's accident prevented her from going. Yet Claire never blamed Mrs. B for getting her into that mess. The trip had been an enriching experience, which despite the problems and the danger, ultimately increased her confidence in her own abilities.

Now, as she watched Maude carefully select her mallet, Claire hoped that someday she would be another Maude or Mrs. B. Then remembering the events of the last few days she amended her thoughts to include the hope she lived long enough to be like them.

Amy was playing this round. She was too young, of course, but Hal said he'd help her and even JoJo didn't object. Amy had been subdued today and, while most people didn't know why, they all felt the need to cheer her up. JoJo shadowed her sister, solicitously offering advice. Hal encouraged her to knock her ball hard into any others in her reach and the whole group cheered when Maude's ball was sent skidding sideways. Claire was happy to sit on the sidelines and kibitz. It gave her time to think.

Dr. Milhouser had sent them home in time for lunch. Cook had set out a lovely buffet of salads, sandwiches and fruit. Tables were set up in the solarium and on the terrace, which allowed people to sit where they wished. No one seemed to notice MiMi had been absent for the entire morning, so she was spared the subsequent questions and the concerns which would have been heaped on her if anyone had known about Tuffy. And after lunch MiMi excused herself to take a nap. She looked as if she needed one, even though she only said she had a terrible headache. But Great Auntie Maude was more than willing to take charge. Some guests returned to their rooms for a nap. Several headed for the pool preferring their nap on a lounge chair at poolside, and this courageous contingent let Maude talk them into playing lawn croquet.

Claire leaned back in one of the shaded chairs, enjoying the light breeze coming off the bay, which kept the heat from being unbearable. The voices of the croquet players as they coached and heckled their fellow players blended with the calls of birds in the trees, the cries of the gulls over the bay and the hum of bees busily seeking nectar. The heat made her drowsy, or maybe it was the late night. She was just considering going to her room for a nap when she spied Jack heading across the lawn. She sat up suddenly alert. Her heart pounded with anxiety. She realized she had been waiting for him. She was hoping he had some answers for her.

Jack helped himself to a glass of iced tea and then pulled another lawn chair close to hers under the umbrella, so they could share the same pool of shade.

"Looks like a wicket game." He grinned at his play on words.

"You better believe it. Don't they look like nice harmless souls? Well, they're sharks."

"Sharks?" He grinned. "You lost, huh?"

She nodded sheepishly. "How did you know?"

"Oh, I've played a little croquet in my day. The more harmless they look the more ruthless they seem to be."

"Well, they sure suckered me. First a practice round. That wasn't too bad and I was feeling pretty confident, but then we played a *real* game."

He laughed. "I wish I had been here to watch." Then he changed the subject. "How's Tuffy?"

She shook her head, pushing her words past the tightness in her chest. "Not good. Dr. Milhouser wasn't too optimistic about saving him unless he finds what caused it." She leaned toward Jack. "Did you hear from the laboratory about their analysis?"

"I'm still waiting. Hopefully we'll hear soon."

They lapsed into a glum silence. Tuffy would have been having a great time right in the middle of the croquet game if he had been there, perhaps even providing enough distraction to level the playing field.

"Claire, they found our man."

Claire perked up. "They did? Oh my God! What did he say? Did you see him? Did he tell you anything?"

Jack shook his head, now looking even gloomier. "He was shot several times."

The blood drained from her head in a rush; her mouth opened but words didn't come.

"Shot?" she finally stammered. "Shot? As in dead?"

He nodded.

She leaned closer, grasping his arm urgently. "Jack, this is really scary. Why was he killed? What does it mean? What's going on?"

"All good questions. Unfortunately I don't have any of the answers. But I think we all agree now that his attack on you in the Mall was not just a random act of violence in the big city. There is some purpose, some plot, and we haven't even got a clue as to what it is."

"So it is the Guiness affair then?" She managed to sound calm even though she could feel the goose bumps on her scalp.

"We don't know." His face was pensive. Claire could imagine the wheels turning in his brain. "Of course, that was our first thought. But it could be something entirely different."

Claire felt tears well up behind her eyes and she shook her head determinedly, refusing to give in to her frustration.

Then she had a horrible thought. "Jack. Did he follow me? Have I put the Lickmans in danger by coming here?"

Jack looked at her with sympathy. "We just don't know. Perhaps. But remember, Claire, you didn't want to come here. We all insisted. The Lickmans were certain you would be safe here."

He watched her digest his words and persuaded softly, "You are not responsible for this situation, Claire, whatever it is."

But he didn't comfort her. She only thought about Amy and JoJo, Mrs. Kramer, Cook, Charlie, and the Lickmans. They had been so kind to her, and she had apparently led a killer right into their midst.

"What do we do now?" she asked, totally depressed.

He shrugged. "Maybe go in and see what David thinks. Wiley went to update him while I came out to find you."

She got up, putting her empty glass on the table. Amy was engrossed in hitting her ball through a wicket, so Claire waved good-bye to JoJo and headed for the house.

Jack was right behind her, but he was hanging on to his iced tea glass, which he had refilled. His phone gave a discreet little chime. He fished it out of his pocket with one hand, managing to turn it on and get it to his ear without upsetting his iced tea.

"Jack here." His voice was crisp. Then there was a long series of nods, umhs and uh-huhs, then, "Okay. You're sure? All right. Thanks for the quick work." He was walking faster now, Claire almost running to stay with him.

"What? Was it the lab? What did they say?"

He nodded. "It was the spinach. It was botulism. Deadly! Thank God, Tuffy tripped the waiter and knocked it all on the floor, or who knows how many people would be deathly ill right now."

They had come through the solarium and down the hall, bursting into the library without even a polite knock on the closed door. Startled, Wiley, David and MiMi looked at them.

"Jack, Claire? What is it? Is it Tuffy?" MiMi's voice was tight with fear.

Claire went to her and took her hand while Jack repeated the news.

"Botulism? Oh my God!" MiMi collapsed onto a chair near the fireplace. "I've used that caterer many times. They have always been so good. How could they have let this happen?"

Then she seemed to get it. She turned a ghastly white. "Oh, my God. If Tuffy hadn't tripped the man, it would have gone on the table, and who knows how many would have gotten sick." She paused, taking a deep breath; she tried to be calm as she looked to Jack. "Is it fatal?"

He nodded. "Can be, or worse."

"Worse? What could be worse?" David was indignant and clearly frightened. After all, except for

Tuffy's antics, he would have certainly fallen victim to the spinach.

"It attacks the nerve cells. Some victims are paralyzed, their brains only partly functioning. It can cause a person to become a vegetable, if they survive. It's very dangerous."

Still clutching Claire's hand tightly, MiMi put her other hand to her mouth. "Tuffy? Is there an antidote? Can we do anything for him?"

Jack nodded. "The lab technician has already sent some anti-toxin to Dr. Milhouser. It should be arriving there soon. The only problem is that he doesn't know how it will work on dogs. He says it's frequently successful on adults, but they've never used it on animals. So it will be risky."

Almost as if on cue the library phone extension rang and David picked it up. Mrs. Kramer said Dr. Milhouser was on the line.

David nodded. Then asked his wife, "Do you want to talk to him, or should I?"

"You! You talk to him." And then they all sat and listened to David's side of the conversation.

"Well, Dr. Milhouser thinks using the anti-toxin is Tuffy's only chance. I told him to go ahead."

MiMi broke into tears but she nodded, agreeing with him. What else could be done? Claire bent over and hugged her, feeling a big lump in her own throat.

"I don't know what you're thinking, but I think we should get Marcus Ng from the FBI and Charlie and anyone else you can think of in here to try to make sense of this?" Jack looked to David, who seemed dazed but recovered himself enough to nod his agreement.

"MiMi, do you want to cancel your house party? I mean, people will understand." Wiley was concerned.

MiMi shook her head, looking through her tears at her husband for agreement. "We only do this once a year, and I think we should just finish it. We have the cookout scheduled for tomorrow afternoon with all the houseguests and about thirty more people expected. But we're doing all the food preparation here, so that should be safe enough. It's almost easier to go on as planned than to cancel and try to explain why to everyone."

David looked at her intently then nodded. "Whatever you think, my dear." He smiled lovingly at her and she tried her best to return it.

Jack stepped over by the windows and used his cell phone. He looked up and said, "Is four o'clock here okay with everyone?"

They all nodded, and he spoke into his phone again before joining them. "Ng's bringing a couple others and probably Detective Maynard, too. Who else should come?" He looked at Wiley.

"Charlie, and a couple of people who work for me. I'll call them."

"Neil should be here," David said. "Let's meet back here at four."

MiMi went to meet with Mrs. Kramer about details for dinner and the cookout the next day. David said he would call Neil and then go socialize with the guests.

"Claire, we brought some pictures for you to take a look at. You know, to see if you can identify the man who attacked you?" Jack nodded to Wiley who reached into his briefcase for an envelope. He handed it to Claire.

She pulled the little stack of pictures out and looked at them carefully. The photos were of tough desperate men, shot in black and white and none of them looked like people anyone would like to know. She easily separated the two shots of the man in the Mall, the same man in the kitchen last night.

"You're sure?" Wiley looked over the ones she chose, then handed them to Jack. "Those are the same ones Jack picked. I guess there's no doubt we found our man. Too bad we didn't find him sooner."

"Yeah, especially for him," Jack added dryly.

Claire noticed she now had a full-fledged headache and, since there didn't seem to be anything else she needed to do right then, she excused herself, deciding an aspirin and a nap would help her clear her mind before the four o'clock meeting.

Jack and Wiley headed for the kitchen, hoping to scrounge some leftovers to make up for their missed lunch.

Claire's room was blessedly cool. The sheer curtains stirred with the breeze coming off the bay, as well as pleasantly defusing the light in the room. She wondered if the house was air-conditioned, but then noting the opened window decided it was probably the thick stone walls that kept it cool. Her head felt better just coming through the door. She had only been there a few days but the room felt like it was hers.

She had learned on meeting Great Auntie Maude that she usually was given the Rose Room, so Claire had offered to trade with her.

"Oh no, my dear." Maude's smile was genuine, her pat on Claire's arm gentle. "MiMi has told me what a valued guest you are and you should have the Rose

Room. You deserve it. I'm perfectly comfortable in the Garden Room. You enjoy."

So Claire was enjoying it. And after she took an aspirin she removed her shoes and lay on the bed, looking around the lovely room, feeling herself relax, little by little. Her mind drifted as she examined the pieces of the puzzle, looking for clues. She didn't realize she had fallen asleep until she woke exactly forty-five minutes later knowing two things about the situation.

First, in each of the two occasions when she had previously been in grave danger, she had experienced anxiety and nightmares, subconscious warnings that something was very wrong. So far, she had not had that same experience. Did that mean she wasn't in danger?

Secondly, the Guiness group displayed a total disregard for human life in their plan to destroy an airplane containing over three hundred innocent people. And that same kind of disregard seemed present last night, if someone did indeed poison the spinach, which was to be served to the guests at the Lickmans' gala.

But did that similarity mean they were connected? She sat up and put on her shoes, then headed for the bathroom to wash her face and fix her hair suddenly anxious for the meeting to start. Maybe someone could make sense out of this.

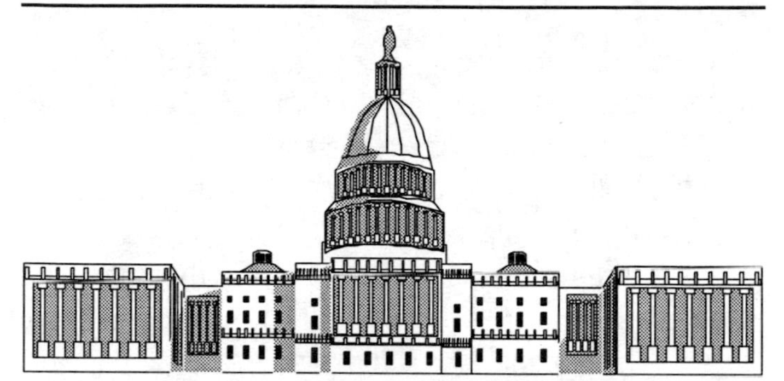

CHAPTER THIRTEEN

The library seemed crowded when Claire arrived. Charlie entered right behind her carrying another chair and set it in the semi-circle that had been arranged in front of the library desk.

"Did you get something to eat?" she asked Wiley. He was easy to spot standing heads above most of the people in the room.

"Sure did." He grinned. "Cook had tucked a few sandwiches away in the fridge." Then he gestured to a smaller man standing next to him. "Claire I don't know if you two have met yet?"

The man shook his head as he moved forward, hand outstretched.

"Claire, this is Marcus Ng, Special Agent with the FBI. He has been assigned to this case and is coordinating the efforts between the agencies involved. And Vantage, of course."

Marcus' hand was firm, his voice somber. "I'm very glad to meet you Ms. Gulliver. I've certainly heard about you."

Claire immediately liked this man. He was impeccability groomed and had an air of competence about him which was very reassuring.

"I look forward to working with you," he continued, releasing her hand. "I know this situation keeps getting more bizarre. But with the talent we have available, I'm sure we'll come up with a solution soon." Then glancing at his watch, he announced firmly, "It's four. Let's get started."

Marcus stood behind David's desk and in a clear strong voice asked everyone to be seated. It took only a few minutes. MiMi slipped into the room in time to take the chair in the front row between Claire and David. Neil sat at the far end of the same row. Jack stood behind Marcus in front of the bookshelves, unobtrusive yet somehow appearing to be the man running things behind the scene. The rest of the chairs were filled with an assortment of people. Some were people who had been in David's office after the Board Meeting, so Claire assumed they were working for Wiley. Wiley was there, of course, in the back where he could watch everything. And Charlie had taken one of the chairs near Wiley.

"Ladies and gentlemen, thanks for getting here on such short notice. I'm sure you'll all agree that we have a unique and puzzling situation confronting us. We need solutions fast to neutralize the situation. So I suggest using the following format to get this meeting going. I'm going to introduce the principals, then, I'd like each of you to stand up and give your name and your affiliation to the group. Bill, over there," he pointed to a man in the row behind Claire, "is going to take notes, so each department will get a copy later.

We will review all the facts we currently have. We'll try to answer any questions you may have, then I'm hoping we can do some brainstorming. Lastly, before we leave we will have decided on how we should proceed and who will do what. Does that sound satisfactory?"

Marcus saw the nods and proceeded. "My name is Marcus Ng. I'm a Special Agent with the FBI, and I have been assigned "Agent in Charge." That means all new information needs to be routed through me to reach all the interested parties. Is that understood?" Again he paused briefly, his eyes scanning the group. "Okay. Before you leave, make sure you each pick up one of my cards here. It will give you all my numbers. We don't want a pertinent piece of information slipping through the cracks because it didn't get reported correctly.

"Now, sitting here in front is David and MiMi Lickman, whose house we are meeting in. David is CEO and President of Vantage Airlines. MiMi is a principal stockholder and a member of their Board. Next to them is Claire Gulliver. Claire is the owner of a bookstore in California and currently a houseguest of the Lickmans. Claire played a key role in thwarting a terrorist attack on a Vantage Airliner out of London earlier this year."

Claire felt all eyes swivel her way and felt her face grow hot.

"Now, starting there," he pointed at Neil and all eyes followed his finger, "introduce yourself and identify who you represent."

"Neil Pinschley, Executive Vice President, Vantage Airlines." Neil was cool and confident, but Claire remembered how he had lost control last night in the kitchen.

Neil sat down and the man next to him stood. "Gary Olson, Sergeant, D.C. Police."

And so it went. Claire didn't even try to remember who was who, and who belonged where. She noted the three women besides herself and MiMi and the rest were men in a variety of colors and sizes. One thing they all had in common, an intense look in their eyes and a grim set to their mouths. They were serious people, here for a serious purpose.

"All right! As you can see, this case touches many different groups and I appreciate you all taking the time to be here to help us.

"Let's begin. We have three separate incidents, which may or may not be connected. But we know something serious is happening and we have one corpse to prove it. The first incident occurred in England earlier this year. Jack, can you give us a recap?"

Jack was brief, packing it all into a couple minutes. The warning picked up by the watchers, the decision to place an agent on the tour, the careful monitoring of all the tour members' movements and the final disappointment when nothing suspicious was detected. Then Claire's dramatic insistence that the plane's takeoff be aborted and the subsequent search, which revealed the bomb cleverly built into the laptop computer. This was the same computer which had accompanied the tour throughout Britain under the control of Rosa Morino. He included how Guiness, alias, Rosa had taken another plane leaving from the same terminal instead of getting on the targeted plane.

And how they had apprehended her in Miami, but before all the congratulations had ended there had been an ambush and an explosion, resulting in dead agents and no trace of their suspect.

He paused a moment. Looking around, he saw Marcus' nod and continued with a description of the attack on Claire on the Mall the previous Tuesday.

Then he surrendered the floor to Wiley, who briefed everyone on their decision to move Claire in to the Lickmans' residence until they found out what was behind the attack on her. He described the steps they had taken to beef up security at the house and for the party. He admitted that by Saturday they had pretty much thought the Mall incident was just the normal crime-in-the-city scenario.

Then he told them about the incident in the kitchen.

Wiley then turned the floor over to Detective Maynard of the Maryland State Police who described the subsequent murder scene and what they knew about the victim. He passed around copies of the pictures of the victim and described the evidence they had obtained from the crime scene.

Jack told them about Tuffy. Claire was gratified to hear the murmurs of shock and outrage over the sick dog from this group who hadn't even flinched at the description of the corpse in the boat launching area. She reached over and patted MiMi's hand. MiMi took a deep ragged breath as she tried to smile at Claire. And they both listened to Jack's description of the search for samples of the spilled spinach dish and the lab report.

"There you have it ladies and gentlemen, a bewildering collection of facts. Does anyone have any ideas?"

"Do we know how the botulism was introduced into the spinach?" One of the women asked tentatively.

Marcus described the search of the caterer's kitchen. A small dish of the soufflé made at the same time for another affair scheduled on Sunday was tested and proved to be botulism free. The team from the Health Department had gone over the recipe, the procedures for cooking and maintaining the heat until serving and found them to be acceptable. Their conclusion at this point, only because of finding Tony the Pickman in the kitchen, was that the botulism had been introduced to the spinach by a foreign means. In other words, it did not accidentally grow in the dish because of mishandling.

"What would be the motive for this Guiness to remove Claire? You say she wasn't the original target and it seems that there are many other people that can now be witnesses, now that they know Guiness is Rosa."

The question came from behind Claire so she couldn't see who posed it.

"Is Claire the target?" A voice asked.

"Who else?" The question came from the back of the room.

"Gotta be!" Several nodded agreement to that.

"Are there other motives to eliminate Claire?" And they all looked at her intently.

So on it went, until Claire was dizzy from swiveling her head to follow the discussion.

"Claire, what about that drug case in San Francisco? Is there any chance it could be the motive for a hit?" The room went silent waiting for her reply.

Slowly she shook her head. "No, no, I'm sure not. As far as I know, I wasn't identified as having any part in it."

"But, I know! There might be others who know. There could have been a leak." Jack looked at Marcus grimly.

He nodded. "Bill, make a note of that; the Bureau will follow that lead."

"What about the Lickmans? Could they have been the target?"

"Motive?"

"Well, their airline was targeted for a terrorist attack that failed." The man shrugged. "Maybe someone decided to take that attack a little closer to home."

"Yeah, didn't you say the spinach soufflé was David's favorite?"

"That doesn't make sense. Then why the attack on Claire? No, Claire is the target, in my opinion."

"Me too. Look at the chain of events. Claire is in the middle of it all."

Everyone nodded. Claire felt as if a lead weight had been placed on her head. She looked around the room. They all agreed and that made her feel guilty. It all seemed to be her fault. When her eyes stopped on Neil she noticed he had a strange expression on his face. Then his eyes met hers and changed. She forced her eyes past him and stopped at Jack. His face, usually immobile, held a look of concern. He, too, obviously agreed she was the target.

Claire was in a daze and her head hurt. She was thinking about what she should do, not even following the conversation, which was bouncing from person to person around the room. She was the cause of Tuffy's poisoning. Because of her, many people could have died or been seriously injured eating the spinach soufflé. She had to get out of the Lickmans' house before another tragedy occurred.

"Okay, that's it. Don't forget to get your findings to me as soon as possible. If anything else comes up I'll pass it on. Let's solve this case. We don't need to wait for something terrible to happen. We need to follow all our leads until we find the answer. Right?"

"Right!" Agreement chorused back. People stood up, shuffling around for their belongings, many coming up to the desk to pick up one of Marcus's cards, some conversing about details. Several nodded encouragingly to Claire as they passed.

Claire sat there even more confused, her musings had left her out of the conversation and she had no idea what the plan was. She turned to MiMi and David. "I'm so sorry. It seems I brought this on you. And poor Tuffy! I feel so bad. I just can't tell you how..."

"Claire, stop!" MiMi was stern. "This isn't your fault. If you are the target it isn't because you deserve it. You didn't do anything bad."

David nodded his agreement, reaching past his wife to pat Claire's arm. "They're going to find whoever is responsible. You'll see. I'm sorry you're going to be confined to the grounds for a few days but I really think its best, don't you?"

She nodded. So that was it. She would stay put while everyone was out there searching. And if no one managed to get by security, she'd be safe; they'd all be safe.

She hoped.

* * *

"You want what?" The tone was incredulous, unbelieving. "What do you think this is? Wal-Mart? You can't just pick one off the shelf."

"Why not? I figure you owe me. Actually, you owe me plenty. If you had done your job last June I wouldn't need help now." His voice was sharp but steady, giving no indication of how close to screaming he really was. Nothing was going the way it was supposed to. It had all been so simple, but then one thing after another had gone wrong. He couldn't wait any longer. It had to be done, and soon.

He tried again, this time he softened his tone somewhat. "Look, I need your help. I know its short notice, but you have resources; you have people who know how to do this. What I need is simple. It doesn't have to be camouflaged. Just make something with a lot of bang. And make sure it's big enough to take a sixty-five footer to the bottom. It doesn't even have to have a timer. Just rig something I can set and still have enough time to get off before it blows.

There was a silence on the line.

"Are you there?"

"I'm thinking. Shut up."

"Now wait a minute." He didn't like being talked to in that way.

"I said, shut up!"

The silence seemed to stretch forever. Then abrupt words, "Okay, I'll talk to her. Call me back in two hours."

"That won't give you much time."

"I said two hours."

"Fine, I'll call you then."

* * *

"Claire, Claire, guess what?" Amy was already equipped with one of her special cocktails.

"What?" Claire looked around hoping for a glass of wine before getting into a long discussion with Amy.

"Tuffy's better. The doctor called Gramimi and said so." She beamed.

JoJo joined them, nodding her agreement. "Gramimi said he was coming home on Tuesday, after all the houseguests leave. He will need a little extra attention for a while, but the Doctor said the anti...the...you know, that stuff they got for him, seemed to be doing the trick."

Claire's smile spread at the news. "I'm so glad. I know how worried you all were. I was worried. It doesn't take long to love Tuffy, does it?"

Hal, from the croquet court, brought her a glass of wine. "MiMi told me you'd want this." He smiled, looking at the drinks the girls were holding. "Looks like you two are doing okay, huh?" And he wandered off to find one of his cohorts.

Claire looked around the large drawing room, which had been made larger by the sliding pocket doors of the parlor opened to make an even larger room across that side of the house.

"So you girls are having dinner with us tonight?"

"No, we already ate. Gramimi said Mom would be mad at her if she let us stay up every night. And we did get to stay up until ten last night, so it's okay."

"Yes, sometimes when all the grownups talk it gets kind of boring." JoJo shrugged. "We had our dinner and after cocktails we're going up to watch a movie before bed."

"There you are, girls. Amy, did you tell Claire how well you did at croquet after she left?" Great Auntie Maude looked proudly at Amy. "Of course, JoJo is a natural. Someday she'll be the champ, won't you, my dear?"

Claire listened with half an ear to Amy's description of her first croquet game, her eyes roaming the room crowded with houseguests and a few others. She noticed a man and a woman over by the French doors leading to the terrace. Even though they had drink glasses in their hands, they seemed to be unusually alert and their eyes were roaming the room carefully. She assumed they were working, either FBI or police.

Great Auntie Maude was telling a story about the girls' mother as a small girl when Claire spied Jack entering the room. He headed immediately for the couple near the doors, so she excused herself and headed that way too.

"There you are, Claire. This is Rodriguez and Mercer, from the FBI. They're keeping an eye on things. We also have three outside. Does that make you feel better?" He slipped his arm around her waist and gave her a little hug.

She nodded cordially at the agents and then said, "Jack, can I talk to you?"

"Sure, excuse us."

She slipped out of his arm and moved to the far end of the room, which, being so far away from the drinks and noshes, was empty.

"Jack, I'm very nervous about all this." He looked surprised.

"Somehow, I think we're looking at this situation all wrong."

"Okay." He paused. "Tell me why."

Claire was really nervous now. It was hard to put her feelings into words. "Oh, you don't have a drink. Did you want one?"

He waved her on. "I'm not drinking, go on. What's your point?"

She flushed, feeling a trifle ridiculous. And then remembering she had been ridiculous more than once in her life, she straightened her shoulders and tried to explain.

"Now let me get this straight," he said when she paused. "You don't feel like you're in danger?" His skepticism felt like a cold dash of water, but she persisted.

"No. I know it sounds silly but, whenever I've been in danger before, something—some sixth sense, an angel on my shoulder, something—warned me."

"And when you were in the Mall and Tony the Pickman was stalking you, did you feel in danger then?" He raised his eyebrows.

She nodded. "Yes. Yes I did. I felt him coming. My hair stood up on my nape. That's why I turned around under that light. I knew something, somebody was there."

She tried to ignore his disbelief. "And on the plane, I almost passed out from fright. I knew! And I had been having all those nightmares before we even got to the airport. It was my subconscious telling me something was wrong."

He nodded.

"And back in San Francisco when I woke up in that warehouse. I knew I had to get out. I know! I know that was a normal reaction to finding yourself in a dark strange place, but that urgency wasn't. I was frantically trying to escape. Something was warning me. Truly."

Now his expression was thoughtful.

"Jack, I read a book a while ago about this. I can't remember who wrote it but he said that in most cases of violent crime the victim has some warning signals of the pending disaster but they ignored them. I believe it. I've always said my Guardian Angel had to work hard. My mother used to tell me my father was up there looking out for me. Whatever! I know I've avoided tragedy more than once, and with no rational explanation.

"And I'm telling you, I don't think I'm the target. I don't think the spinach was meant for me. Somehow we don't have the right answer."

"But you heard the discussion earlier. Logically it is you." Jack's voice was gentle, persuasive.

She shook her head stubbornly. "Think again. Think harder."

"All right! All right, I will. And I'll talk to Marcus later and let him mull this over." Then he shrugged. "Darn. Even if you didn't like the consensus, it made everything a little easier to be focused on a target. Now we have to start over again."

She breathed deeply. He believed her. She was relieved. Now that they could find out the real reason. When they knew the reason they could locate the intended victim, and it wouldn't be long until they knew who was masterminding these events.

"Oops, I guess dinner is being served. We better get in there before they send someone for us." Jack, with his hand on the small of her back, guided her toward the end of the straggling group headed for the dining room.

The room was beautiful. This was the first time Claire had seen it with the table stretched to its limits. The candles were glowing and the dinnerware was gleaming on a snowy white cloth. MiMi directed them to seats down three from David and across the table from her seat at David's right hand. Great Auntie Maude was given the opposite end seat instead of MiMi who preferred to sit close to her husband. Claire didn't know how many guests were present, but assumed it was close to thirty as Mrs. Kramer told her they added another table if they needed to seat over thirty.

Dinner was elegant and delicious. Course followed course as the conversation flowed. On Claire's left was Boyd, David's second cousin with his wife, Edie, sitting between him and David. Boyd was a retired banker who was charming and witty. His wife played straight man for him. On the other side of Jack was Hal and then some of the houseguests, while across the table near MiMi were some neighbors Claire had met at the Gala.

It was in the lull, while the table was being cleared and the desert was being readied, that Edie spoke to MiMi. "My dear, I was so looking forward to your spinach soufflé, but you didn't serve it last night nor tonight. Is David growing tired of it?"

Claire stiffened and alerted Jack. MiMi and David both hesitated, but then David smiled. "You know Edie, I've gone a little off of spinach. I don't think MiMi will be serving it for a long while. Guess you'll have to cook it yourself."

Edie's surprise was visible. "That's hard to believe after all these years, but I know how one's tastes do change. Why, Boyd used to love smoked salmon and..."

Claire turned to Jack. "I guess I don't blame him. It will be a long time before I'll ever try that dish again."

Jack agreed with a crooked smile. "Not that I was so very fond of it anyway." He turned to answer an inquiry on his other side leaving Claire to rejoin Edie's funny story about Boyd and smoked salmon.

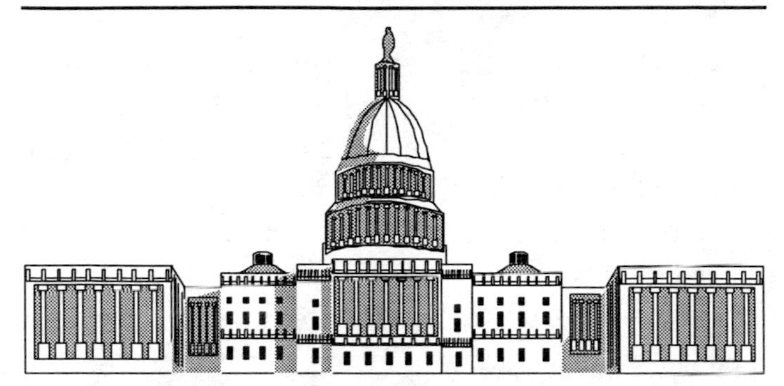

CHAPTER FOURTEEN

Claire came awake slowly, trying to let go of her argument with Liz. She knew it was only a dream, even though it seemed real. But the remembered frustration of dealing with Liz's paranoid conviction that only she knew Rosa was conspiring with strange men in the Camden Market, was haunting. Especially because as it turned out, Liz was right. But Liz was a crazy lady. There was no doubt of that. It had been a relief to the whole group when she left in the middle of the tour because of an injury. Not that they didn't all feel terrible she had been hurt as well as guilty about their relief.

Still, Rosa had been up to no good. And Liz was the only person who suspected her from the very beginning.

Claire turned her head and saw the peachy glow coming through the curtains. It was almost daylight, but too early to get up. So she tried to dispel the effect of her disturbing dream by consciously recalling Liz's strange behavior. She personally had wondered if Liz was having a mental breakdown, or if she was just in that menopausal period. She had been thinking she would have to send her home, she was such a disturbance to the other members of the tour. So, in a way, her accident was fortuitous. But Lucy liked Liz. She had defended her when Claire questioned the wisdom of including her after witnessing her interaction with the other tour members in the orientation meetings. Now Claire wondered, if Lucy had led the trip, if Liz would have been so difficult.

She told herself it didn't really matter now. What happened had happened! And no wonder she dreamed about it. Jack's retelling the story yesterday at the meeting brought it all to the forefront of her mind again. But it would go away, she told herself firmly.

Now she was really awake. She decided to get up. It was going to be a big day around here. The Lickmans were having a cookout. All the remaining houseguests, plus others, would be coming for boiled lobster, clams, corn on the cob and potatoes roasted in the coals. MiMi had told her, Percy Imamura's sons would be doing the cooking in a pit they would dig on the beach. But Percy and his wife would be attending as guests. Also several people from Vantage were coming, including Suzanne, Neil, Marilyn and her husband, and Wiley and his wife. Jack and Doug Levine were also invited. Claire was scheduled to leave on Wednesday and, as she was confined to the Lickmans' estate at present, she wouldn't have had the opportunity to say good-bye to these people if it weren't for the gathering this afternoon.

It was still early when she arrived downstairs. It was too early for breakfast, so she let herself out the door to the terrace. She missed Tuffy. She knew he would have been pleased to accompany her on a walk.

"Morning."

She was startled, then she nodded cordially. "Good morning to you too. Although I suppose you've been out here all night."

"No, just came on an hour ago. Going to be a beautiful day. Hot, but not humid. Good day for a walk."

She nodded, heading down to the dock, noticing the man was quietly speaking into his shirt pocket. She assumed he was notifying other agents she was about. She had forgotten about the FBI agents stationed around the house. It must be a terrible job, mostly boring but always dangerous, especially when things seemed the most boring.

She walked to the end of the dock and sat down on the far end, slipping off her tennis shoes so she could put her toes in the water. She watched the water lap around her feet and the sun's rays bouncing brightly on the water as it rose off the horizon. She was ready to go home. She missed her store and the customers and Mrs. B. She glanced at her watch. For once its beauty didn't distract her. It was too early to call the West Coast, and besides, she realized it was Monday. The store was always closed Mondays. And it was a holiday. Mrs. B was probably over at her niece's house for the day. No, she had two more days here and then she would go home. And she hoped she would quickly settle into her normal routine, which held enough excitement for her. There would be no more muggers, no more questionable chefs in the kitchen and no more worrying about mysterious plots; just the normal business of selling travel books to the locals planning their own adventures.

Suddenly she wished she had stopped for a cup of coffee to bring outside with her. It would have tasted good here by the water. Yearning for home was futile. Retrieving her shoes, she headed back to the house. Now she was hungry. If she was lucky, she would have time to read the paper before anyone else was about.

* * *

Claire laughed with Suzanne at the antics of the children. Today there were several other children for Amy and JoJo to play with, including Suzanne's two nephews who had come with her. Right now, they were playing a slightly altered game of croquet with their own understanding of the rules, and having a great time.

"Suzanne, I can't begin to thank you for all the effort you put into making this such a wonderful trip for me. I can't believe I saw as much or did as much as I did, and in such a short time. Perhaps you should change careers."

Suzanne smiled at that. "I don't think so. I wouldn't want David to know he could exist without my help. But I'm glad you had a good time. I know the Lickmans were worried about that mugging. MiMi especially was distressed you wouldn't get to see the sights because they insisted you come out here." She looked around her. "Not that this was such a punishment, but it's not the Capital. So it was easy enough to set up a few visits. If we missed anything we still have tomorrow to schedule it?" She arched her eyebrow at Claire waiting for her response.

"Oh, no. I mean, I'm looking forward to a quiet day here with the family tomorrow. Anything I didn't see, and I know there was a lot, I'll see the next time I come. Actually, I bet I've seen more than most tourists do in a week." She didn't want to tell Suzanne she was basically confined to the property, as it was obvious Suzanne didn't know.

Suzanne chuckled. "I guess I did have you booked rather tightly. But was there anything you could have missed?"

"Well, maybe the storm at the Lincoln Memorial." She grinned, then changed her mind. "No, actually, I don't think you scheduled that, did you? And frightening as it was, it was still a great experience. No, the whole trip was perfect. And it's thanks to you for arranging it." She reached out and hugged Suzanne, kissing her lightly on the cheek.

Suzanne was embarrassed, but she looked pleased. "Well now, girlfriend, we'll have to stay in touch. Maybe one of these days I'll get out your way and you can schedule some of those wineries for me to see."

"Oh, what a great idea! Would you? Come to California, I mean? That would be fun. I'd love to show you my city and my bookstore and, of course, Napa Valley and Carmel..."

"Whoa, slow down." Then she smiled, her face lighting up. "Well, maybe. It would be fun, wouldn't it? I'll think on it, maybe after the first of the year."

"Hello, ladies. What's going on?" Doug, looking good enough to eat in sandals, white shorts and a green and white striped polo shirt, joined them. "You both look cool and summery." His eyes alight with appreciation lingered on Claire.

She was glad she wore the sundress. Usually it wasn't hot enough where she lived for sundresses. But when she and Lucy were shopping for the dress she wore to the Gala they had seen this. A cookout on Labor Day sounded like just the place to wear a dress such as this. So Claire had let herself be persuaded. Now Doug's admiration made the price tag seem cheap.

Suzanne excused herself to go talk to Wiley's wife while Doug and Claire moved toward the dock, chatting about inconsequential things.

"Hey, how about a boat ride?"

Claire looked doubtfully at the little sailboat.

"No, let's take the other." He led her past the motorboat to the little rowboat and got in, holding it steady against the dock with one hand while he helped her in with the other.

She sat primly in the stern while he untied the rope, took up the oars and pushed them off of the dock. "I haven't done this for a while, so I don't expect we'll go far."

"Well, I can take a turn if you get tired."

"Really? Okay, I'd like to be rowed around. Too bad I didn't grab some grapes from the table."

She laughed, imagining him lolling in the back eating grapes as she rowed the boat.

"Hey, you do swim, don't you?"

"Fine time to ask," she retorted. "I don't see the life jackets."

"I'm sure they're under the seat. But don't worry. This seems like a very stable little craft and, as you can see, no wind and no waves."

"Luckily I do swim and very well, if I do say so myself. When I was a kid we had this gigantic saltwater pool down by the beach in San Francisco. I mean really big. The pool was almost as big as this little cove. No lie," she smiled at him, "the lifeguards used little boats like this to monitor the swimmers. I guess it was getting too expensive and, of course, the property must have been worth a fortune. They pumped the water in from the ocean and heated it, but I remember it was cold, cold, cold. When we learned to swim across the pool, we were good. It was a long distance. Every summer I belonged to a swim club there until they closed it down. I kept up the swimming at the regular pools and was even on the swim team in high school, but finally dropped it in college. There were just too many other things to do."

She noticed they were quite a ways out in the water now, moving along the rocky shore. The sounds of the crowd on shore barely reached them, just the screams of some of the gulls fighting over something on the rocks.

"You know when you learn something like swimming or roller skating or bicycling when you're young, the skills seem to always stay with you. JoJo is a very good swimmer and, while Amy mostly splashes around, she has no fear of the water so she'll probably be good before long.

"How about you? Where did you learn to swim?"

"How do you know I swim?"

"Look at you, so tan. That didn't come from a tanning salon, did it? And you didn't even hesitate about taking out a boat."

He laughed. "I guess I'm more transparent than I thought. " He began telling her about growing up on

Cape Cod and the delights of his summers, which were now his favorite recreational activities. He water-skied, swam and sailed whenever he had the chance and even rowed when he was in college.

"So I suspect my offer of a turn at the oars won't be necessary. Thank goodness!"

They rowed in silence, enjoying the light breeze on the water that tricked them into thinking they weren't cooking in the sun.

"You did use sunscreen, didn't you?"

"I'm slathered with it. Where I live outside San Francisco, we do have sun and heat, but I'm in the store most of the time. So I'm super careful when I do get out. I don't want to go home blistered."

He changed the subject. "I spoke to Wiley earlier and he told me about the meeting here yesterday. I'm very concerned about this situation, but it sounds like they are taking it seriously and doing what they can to keep you safe. How do you feel about it?"

She stared at the shoreline. The children looked very far away.

"I'm ready to go home. I had a wonderful time here in spite of the mugging and the problem with the Gala, but you know...at home I feel safe. And no matter what the Lickmans say, I can't help thinking I somehow led this danger right into their home. I know these things could happen anywhere, but it doesn't seem like it happens at home. I'm feeling pretty anxious."

He nodded, his face serious. "Well, don't take any chances. This Marcus Ng is pretty high powered in the Bureau. I'm sure he's checking everything. And while it might feel confining, I'm sure keeping you on the estate for a few days is the right thing to do.

"Oh, oh, I see the guys digging up food from the pit. We'd better head back. We certainly don't want to be late for lunch." He skillfully used the oars to turn the little boat and reverse their direction, letting the tide assist him in returning to the dock.

Then, as they sauntered up the lawn to the crowd gathering around the tables heaped with food he said, "Look, I'm leaving tomorrow for London for a couple weeks. I have to say I'm a little uneasy about leaving and not knowing you're completely safe. But I guess I have to do my job and rely on Marcus, Wiley and Jack to do theirs. But if you need me, call me. I wrote my numbers down for you. And I will be out your way, most likely before the end of the year. You promised me a dinner date, remember?"

She took the card and slipped it in her pocket, nodded her agreement and then turned in response to Masie, Wiley's wife.

"I saw you out there, sailing around like the Queen of Sheba. I bet it was cooler there." She fanned herself vigorously with one of the fans thoughtfully laid out on the tables. "So Doug, are you providing the rides for the day? If so, I'm next." She laughed at his horrified expression. "Alright. Maybe I can get Wiley out there. I'll just tell him how manly you looked behind the oars. He might fall for it."

Marian, coming up at the end of that comment, shook her head. "No way. He's not going to fall for that. Rowing a boat is work. Give it up.

"I see a nice shaded table over there I'm going to claim. Get your food and come back." Then as they turned toward the tables she added, "And remember to save some for me."

The lines moved very quickly down both sides of the tables and the metal trays provided for the guests filled quickly with clams, potatoes, corn on the cob and what seemed to Claire to be a huge lobster. When they arrived back at their table, two other couples had arrived and at Marian's suggestion they all introduced themselves. Both couples were members of the Yacht Club and one couple was also a neighbor.

Marian reminded them to save her place and one for her husband and left to get her plate. A waitress brought the utensils, big lobster bibs, melted butter and salt and pepper. She took their drink orders and left promising to return right away with the drinks and bread and butter.

"As if we need more to eat," Claire muttered, eyeing the lobster warily.

"Have you done this before, Claire?" Masie asked.

"No, but in San Francisco, we have Dungeness crab which takes a little doing. I'll give this a try. But I hardly know where to start."

"Start with the bib. Trust me on this. It's the right way to start."

They all laughed at Doug's droll statement, and then everyone tied on the big bibs and layered their laps with the matching napkins. Masie ladled the melted butter into the little dishes and passed them around while Marian's husband, who had joined them, dipped the first clam into the butter before popping it in his mouth.

"Yum. Nothing better. Helps get us through the end of summer. Labor Day is always such a paradox. The joy of a holiday hampered by knowing winter is just around the corner. And, of course, for the kids it means time to go back to school."

Then they all began to eat in earnest. This kind of meal required full attention. Wiley and Jack stopped by on their way to the buffet table but when they offered to squeeze closer to make room for them at the table, they declined. They needed to talk to some other folks and promised they'd see them around. Then Percy Imamura stopped by to introduce his wife to Claire. She stood, but was confused when she realized her hands were covered in butter and so she didn't dare shake hands.

Mary, Percy's wife, laughed. "Don't worry, Claire. I'd prefer not to shake hands with you right now, but I'm very glad to meet you. Percy told me how much you admired the gardens. I always like people who appreciate plants and flowers. Sit down, sit down; don't let your dinner get cold. I'll get back to you before the day is over and we can talk then."

Claire got a variety of instructions on how to deal with her lobster. When she finally cracked the large resisting claw and the shell flew three tables over to land in the lap of another guest, everyone applauded. The woman held it up, good-naturedly, for everyone to see. Claire hoped this kind of thing happened with some frequency at a lobster and clambake.

Neil stopped by their table and schmoozed with the Yacht Club members. It didn't surprise Claire to learn that one of the men was on the Club's membership committee.

* * *

"Claire, Great Auntie Maude is going to teach me how to play poker. Wanna play?"

Claire was so full, she didn't know if she could move. After saying her good-byes, she had found a secluded chair for a little rest. But obviously it wasn't as secluded as she thought. "I don't think so, but aren't you a little young for poker?"

"No, Great Auntie Maude and I are going to play together. We're going to win everyone's money. Come on, it'll be fun." She pulled at Claire's limp arm.

"I'm sure it will be, but I think I'm too full of lobster to even hold my cards."

"Jack's gonna play, and Hal. JoJo is playing with Hal. And Grandpap said he'd play later. But we need some more people and almost everyone is leaving. Pl...lease." She tugged at Claire's arm again.

"All right. Okay. Sur' nough. Just help me get out of this chair." She was only gong to be here another day and if Great Auntie Maude had enough energy to play cards then, by gosh, she could too.

"You will?" The smile on Amy's face was worth the struggle to escape the clutches of the chaise lounge. Amy was already headed toward the house tossing over her shoulder, "We're going to play in the solarium so we're out of the way of the people leaving."

When they arrived the card players were already settling in. David's cousin Boyd was there, "Hey, Claire, do you know this game?"

She nodded.

"Then get your money because it'll cost you to play here." He grinned, obviously anticipating easy pickings.

She turned to head for her room and her purse, but Jack waved her back. “I’ll spot you twenty and you can pay me back out of your winnings.” He grinned at Boyd. “You think twenty will be enough?”

Boyd looked at Great Auntie Maude and said seriously, “You never know playing with the big guys.”

Great Auntie Maude just sat there shuffling the deck with professional ease while she instructed Amy on how to arrange the poker chips they had sitting in front of them. JoJo and Hal were whispering, and two spaces at the table were still open.

“Isn’t David playing?” Claire asked while stacking the chips Hal and JoJo had shoved across the table in exchange for Jack’s twenty.

“He’ll be here soon, after he says goodbye to everyone. And MiMi might join us for a while then.” Maude looked around the table, then announced dryly, “Watch out for MiMi. She’s a card shark if there ever was one.” Amy giggled at that.

Claire was a little nervous. She remembered playing croquet with Maude and Hal. She could only imagine how they played poker. But then she reasoned, with Amy and JoJo there, how bad could it get?

And she approved of the girls getting an early education in poker. She had only recently learned to play. When Mrs. B discovered Claire had never played, she immediately rectified that lapse in her education. Mrs. B said all children should learn poker as it taught them risk analysis and math. And a child who learned to maintain a poker face would go far in the world. Claire had come to agree, and it looked like Great Auntie Maude shared that philosophy.

"Hey, have room for one more?" Neil came in the solarium and headed for one of the empty chairs.

"Plenty of room for suckers willing to donate," Hal said with a sly grin. "It'll cost you twenty."

Neil fished his twenty out of his wallet and passed it to Hal while JoJo eagerly counted out another stack of chips.

"All right, ladies and gentlemen, this is a friendly game of Dealer's Choice. Chips are dimes, quarters and dollars." Maude pointed to white, red and blue chips before continuing with her instructions. "Minimum first bid is a dime, and we'll see where we go from there. Remember we have young ears with us and so the language should be appropriate. Now shall we draw for deal?" Maude slapped the deck in the center of the table and everyone drew for high card.

"Hoo, and I'm hot." Boyd flashed his king around the table. "I'm gong for Five Card Stud, jacks or better to open. Ante a dime."

Amy was so excited when she put Maude's dime in the center of the table, Claire thought she was going to fall off her chair.

Boyd took that pot and became even more enthused as he passed the deal to Jack. Jack quietly played the same game but the pot went to Neil. The deal passed to Hal and after he shuffled, he let JoJo deal out five cards to each player. This time it was Five Card Draw, low card in the hand and all like it were wild. Maude and Amy selected a game of No Peeky, and then it got to Neil who introduced Texas Roll'em. Claire won that pot and the deal. Her shuffling was adequate but not flashy as was Maude's. After Neil cut the cards she announced her favorite, Seven Card

Stud, low card in the hole and all like them wild. She had to repeat it twice, but then they started to play.

"Eight of clubs, no help. There's Boyd's ace. Three of diamonds, possible straight flush. Hal, pair of sixes, still bets." She waited until everyone decided if they were in or not and dealt another round."

"Hey, Neil, it was good to see you again today. It's been a while. Let's see, I think it was the end of May, or was it the first of June. Anyway, London, wasn't it?" Boyd asked.

Claire dealt a new card to Neil and saw how the tick in his eye jumped, but his face remained calm as he studied his cards.

"Yep, I'm sure." Boyd nodded certain of his facts. "It was London!" He directed his comments to the entire table. "It's so strange when you run into someone you know clear across the world." Then he peered with interest at Neil. "How did your trip go? Business, was it?"

"Humm, that's right." Neil's face was partially obscured by the cards. "I was on my way to Brussels and stopped over a couple of nights at Claridge's. Actually, I'm on the road so much it's hard to remember which trip is which." He tossed two chips in the pot. "I'll raise a quarter."

"So, you were in London when Claire was there?" Jack asked while he deliberated whether or not to fold his cards.

Neil sat up straighter. "No, as a matter of fact, I had just arrived in Istanbul when I was notified. I was going to head straight back to London, but David said he had it covered. So I finished up my trip as planned." He smiled at Claire as he folded his cards, unwilling to gamble on the final card.

Claire dealt the last card and amidst the groans around the table discovered the low pair of fours she had down had been neutralized by a three. But Great Auntie Maude and Amy gleefully raked in the huge pot and, while Amy was busy sorting and stacking the chips, Boyd started shuffling the cards for the next game.

"Boyd, do you visit London frequently?" Jack asked.

"Well, as a matter of fact, we do. Edie's sister married a Limey and they live there. So, of course, we have to visit often or the girls will break us with the phone bills. Those girls have to talk and talk." He grinned wryly as he announced his game and began dealing.

"Are you and Edie staying tonight?" Claire asked Boyd in an effort to direct the conversation away from London last spring. While Jack and Neil knew about the incident, she was certain Boyd and Hal didn't, and thought Maude probably only knew a little. And besides, she didn't want to talk about it.

"No, we're leaving tonight. But we only live a half hour away and with me retired, we don't have to worry about getting up tomorrow to go to work."

"Hal and I are staying because neither of us is good at night driving. We're leaving early tomorrow. Hal is dropping me off," Maude offered as she smiled at Hal.

Claire wondered suddenly if their relationship was more than distant cousins.

"Well, I'm working. But I'm not going in until the afternoon. I have an appointment in Annapolis in the morning." Neil grinned with obvious anticipation of that meeting.

"Well, well, well. Does that pile of chips in front of Boyd mean that he's winning again?" David came into the solarium and headed straight for the empty chair. He handed over his twenty and stacked his chips.

"Grandpap look how much we have. Great Auntie Maude and I are going to get it all, aren't we, Great Auntie Maude?"

Her great aunt nodded in agreement, her eyes twinkling.

"Well, you're going to have to hurry, because Gramimi said you have a bedtime coming up."

"Oh, no. We were gonna win it all. Can't we stay up later?" Amy's face was woebegone and JoJo couldn't hide her disappointment either.

"Tell you what. We'll play around the table once, which means each person will deal once more. Then you have to go get ready for bed. Agreed?"

They all agreed despite the sad look on the two young faces. "Don't worry, Amy," Auntie Maude whispered. "It's the one who wins the last few pots who wins the most. You'll see."

CHAPTER FIFTEEN

Claire admired the Lickmans' library while she scanned the book titles. MiMi had told her to help herself when she mentioned she thought she would relax on the terrace and read. She felt tired. Too much food, she thought, remembering the feast provided yesterday. And of course her dreams didn't help. All these discussions of the happenings last spring kept her mind in turmoil. This was the second night she had dreamed about Liz. That was disturbing. Liz had been difficult enough in real life. She had been the one member of the tour who didn't fit. And, in fact, her presence and her antics caused Claire no end of problems until she was sent back home after taking a nasty fall and breaking her collarbone. Claire never wished her harm, but couldn't help feeling relieved when she was gone. Maybe her guilt over that was haunting her; because she knew there had to be a reason for the dreams.

That was perhaps what was most disturbing about them. Subconsciously she was processing something that had to do with Liz, or that time. Claire shook her head in frustration, as if she could fling all those disturbing memories into their correct slots and come up with the right answer. She was going to talk to Jack about this when she saw him. Maybe they should review all the pictures from that trip. Maybe something would trigger a memory for her to solve this mystery.

But now she reached for a book on the shelf in front of her. She had heard about this book; it might be an interesting enough read to distract her.

She paused, staring dreamily out the window. Life was just full of surprises, she mused, and probably none more surprising than finding two handsome, exciting men suddenly interested in her. She grinned; the *forties,* it seemed, was going to be a good decade for her.

Jack had stayed late, supposedly to make sure the security was in place after all the guests were gone. Claire smiled to herself remembering his good-bye kiss—well, if she was honest, kisses. No pecks on the cheek last night, and Claire suspected that might have been one of the reasons he had lingered to the last.

She snapped out of her daydream when she noticed the big boat approaching the Lickmans'. It cautiously nosed up to the dock. Someone jumped down to tie the bowline tightly to the dock, then the stern. The man then turned and headed toward the house.

It was Neil.

What a gorgeous boat. Gleaming white in the hot sun it dwarfed the other craft tied to the dock. In fact, it carried its own little boat suspended from arms on the back. And it looked like the kind of boat Neil would own.

She remembered seeing him in his Porsche; he obviously liked the best. Well, more power to him. He had a responsible position, earned top salary and with no family to support, he may as well spend his money and his time on the toys he enjoyed.

She watched him a minute, once more puzzled by that nagging thought she knew him from somewhere. It was very annoying that she couldn't quite place him.

When he disappeared from her view she took the book she had selected and moved out through the solarium to the terrace. She found a chair in the shade of the balcony, got comfortable and was immediately absorbed in the author's world.

"Oh, Claire, there you are." Amy was always seeking Claire out. "Did you sleep well?" Her solicitous manner was a parody of her grandmother's, but she couldn't contain her exuberance long. "Wasn't that a great poker game?"

Amy and Maude had managed to win about ten dollars, which Maude generously donated to Amy's piggy bank. Now Amy was enthralled with the game. Claire had won about a dollar and a half so she was able to easily repay Jack his twenty. She wasn't sure about everyone else but, of course, somebody lost or Amy and Maude couldn't have won.

"I was really good, wasn't I?"

Claire laid the book on her lap realizing Amy wanted to have a conversation. "I think so, maybe because of your skill in playing Yahtzee. It's kind of like poker, don't you think?"

Amy nodded, very serious. "Great Auntie Maude said I'd be able to play by myself when I can count better." Then she added, parroting Maude's rules, "And when I play with my own money and I don't cry when I lose. But you didn't play with your own money, did you? I saw Jack give you some."

"Well, really I did. He was just loaning it to me so I didn't have to go upstairs to get my purse. And I did pay it back, didn't you see?"

"Oh yeah! Well, I can't wait for school to start. We get to learn to add this year, so it won't be long until I can play. I really like poker."

Claire just nodded as Amy rattled on with her perception of the nuances of last night's game.

"Ooh, Claire, look!" She was pointing. "Neil is going to give Grandpap a ride on his new boat and JoJo is going too. Can I go? Can I?" She was jumping up and down with excitement. She wanted to go really bad.

Claire saw Neil and David heading for the dock and JoJo was right behind them. Amy was right; it appeared as if they were going out on the boat. For some reason she felt a stab of alarm and without even thinking why, she stood up and grabbed Amy's arm just in time to prevent her from dashing after her sister.

"No, Amy, wait! You know your mother doesn't allow you to go out on the water without her." She pulled that out of her memory and it sounded good.

"But JoJo's going." Amy wailed. "If she goes, why can't I?"

"JoJo is not going!" Claire was firm. "I'll go down and send her back. You better go check with your Gramimi to see if she needs help getting ready for Tuffy. I'll go talk to JoJo."

Glumly, Amy turned to go back in the house, casting one last disappointed glance at her sister, who had already reached the dock.

Claire hurried across the lawn, waving her hand at the trio. "Hey, guys, where are you going?" She was breathless, partly from alarm and partly from running to the dock.

"Hey Claire, see my new boat." Neil, already halfway up the ladder to the steering platform, gestured expansively at the gleaming cabin cruiser. "David is going out with me for a little test run before I make the final commitment. Want to join us?"

"Oh, but David, Jack called and said he was on the way out. He had something he wanted to show us. He said it was important." She lied but it was the only thing she could think of on such short notice.

"We'll be back before he gets here. We're just going out on the Bay and try a few maneuvers. Come on, it will be fun." Neil urged her, eager to show off his new possession.

She was torn. She didn't want David to go out on this boat with Neil, but she didn't have a good reason why he shouldn't. And it was apparent that he was going to go.

"David," she called out over the sound of the motor Neil had just started, "MiMi doesn't want JoJo to go. She has something she wants her to do."

JoJo's face fell from her disappointment.

"JoJo, you heard Claire. Gramimi wants you." His smile for JoJo was a promise as he projected his voice over the sound of the motor. "Don't worry, Neil will come back and take you out some other time, won't you, Neil?"

"Sure. After I buy it, I'll come and we'll take the whole family. Maybe we'll motor over to the Club for lunch."

JoJo climbed onto the platform on the back and jumped to the dock.

Claire took her arm and bent her head over hers. "Listen, JoJo, I need you to do something important. Can you do it?"

JoJo nodded gravely, understanding from Claire's tone it really was important.

"I want you to hurry up to the house and find Charlie." JoJo nodded. "Tell Charlie to call Jack, right now. He should call Jack and tell him to see if he can get copies of Liz's pictures. You got that?"

"Get Liz's pictures," JoJo repeated. "Okay."

"Right away! Tell him we need them immediately." JoJo nodded her understanding. "And Charlie should tell Jack I went with your grandfather and Neil on his new boat, but we should be back in an hour or so. Can you remember all that?"

JoJo nodded soberly.

"Do it now! You have to find Charlie, right away! Will you do that?"

JoJo nodded again and moved toward the house spurred to action by Claire's intensity.

"Claire, are you coming?"

Neil had already untied the line from the front of boat and he was working on the stern line now while David was at the controls. Claire made up her mind just as the boat started to glide away from the dock, leaping onto the platform, scrambling through the little gate and up the steep stairs to the bridge where

David was deftly steering the boat toward the opening into the Bay.

She moved out of Neil's way as he followed her up the stairs and turned and waved one last time to JoJo before she disappeared into the house, feeling a little foolish now about the urgency of sending that message to Jack. But at the same time she felt relieved for having set in motion a possible solution for the dreams she had been having.

"Well, you're dressed for a sail." Neil nodded with approval at her shorts and tennis shoes.

"What do you think?" He was in an expansive mood. His grin was wide and his eyes sparkled. Even the tick in his eye was barely noticeable.

"It's a wonderful boat," she agreed looking around her at the comfortable table and banquet behind her and the posh chairs in front of the console where David sat.

"Motor-yacht. It's a motor-yacht, not a boat," he explained proudly, eagerly taking over control of the boat while describing the features of the craft to David. "It's got a 15'4" beam and draft of 57 inches..." then noticing Claire behind him, "Go downstairs and check it out. Here, take the forward stairs." He pointed at the door beside his chair.

As she headed carefully down the steep stairs he called out behind her, "When you come back up, bring some beers. We need to christen this vessel."

Claire was astounded by the main cabin. It was like a small townhouse. The kitchen was fully equipped with stove, refrigerator, oven, microwave and even a dishwasher. There was a large TV and a stereo somewhere, because light jazz was playing softly. She moved forward and looked at the console under the windows. It appeared to be equipped with the same electronics she had seen up top, but maybe there were more things here. She admired the buttery soft leather banquet, which wrapped around behind the console so guests could sit and kibitz with the person driving. Then she considered her choice of words. She wasn't sure "driving" a boat was correct. Maybe "piloting" was the right word.

She moved down another level to the master bedroom with a king size bed, its own bathroom and a little office. It looked very comfortable and certainly organized. There appeared to be very little room to acquire clutter on a boat. People who lived on boats must be disciplined not to buy useless knick-knacks at every port they visited. The second bedroom was in the bow and the bed was tucked up into the pointy part. Still it looked comfortable.

She was awed by the grandeur she saw. She had very little knowledge of boats, but after seeing how luxurious this motor-yacht was she couldn't even imagine what the yachts owned by billionaires looked like. They must be mind-boggling.

She remembered the beer and helped herself to three bottles from the generous supply in the refrigerator and then headed upstairs. She had to stop a minute and think, because she needed at least one hand to hold onto the rail to go topside. Finally she stuck one bottle neck down in her back pocket, held two by the neck with her left hand and used her right hand to hold on as she climbed up the ladder-like stairs.

She handed out the beer, toasted with them to the new boat and then settled in comfortably at the table, content to watch the scenery, enjoy the breeze in her hair and wonder why she was still so edgy.

* * *

"Do you have the mugging marked correctly?" Jack asked Wiley.

They were in a conference room at Vantage. Marcus, Jack and Wiley were going over all the pieces, cross checking the data in an effort to find some clue they, and everyone else, missed.

Wiley stood in front of a large white board, using colored markers to draw a timeline of events. Marcus wrote facts on little Post-it notes, which he then attached to the board at the appropriate places on the timeline.

A phone rang and eyes swiveled as Jack grabbed for his jacket, slung over one of the chairs. "That's mine. Sorry for the interruption, guys." He turned away from them and spoke quietly in the phone.

"What? Are you sure? Okay, that's what she said. Okay, yeah. Okay. When was that? Any reason why? Okay. Call me here again if anything changes. Yeah, thanks. And, Charlie, thank JoJo for me. She did a good job."

Marcus and Wiley were waiting expectantly to hear what the call was about.

"That was Charlie. Claire sent JoJo with a message to tell me I needed to get Liz's pictures from the tour in England right away." He was obviously puzzled. "And she wanted me to know she went out on the Bay for a cruise with Neil and David."

"So what do you think? Why did she want those pictures? Do you have them?"

Jack shook his head, too many questions at once. "I don't know why she wants them, but I guess I'd better see about getting them here."

"Do you have them?"

He shook his head. "Did either of you get a set of them?"

No, both had heard about them, but neither Wiley nor Marcus had seen the pictures.

Arnie White was on the Springer Tour and had somehow gotten Liz's exposed film after she left the group. Liz's pictures, as well as the pictures he had taken had ended up documenting Rosa's role in the plot. Claire had retrieved the pictures, along with her own at the photo shop in Conwy before learning of Arnie's fatal accident. She hadn't thought of them again until she found them in her bag in Heathrow Airport.

"Well, I'd better see how to get a set here." He poked a series of numbers in his cell phone, and then said, "Wonder why she wanted me to know she went out with Neil and David?"

"Maybe because we told her she was confined to the house?" Wiley suggested.

Marcus nodded. "Could be. She wouldn't just ignore our instructions."

He and Wiley turned back to their tasks while Jack began his quest of tracking down copies of the pictures.

"Okay, finally. The pictures are on their way to you, Wiley. Can you get into your computer and print them off?"

Wiley nodded. "Sure. I think I have this right." He capped the marker he was using and laid it on the table. “Maybe you can check my times while I’m gone, Jack.” Then just as he was leaving the room, “How many pictures are we looking for?”

“I don’t know. I think two rolls. Maybe you can get someone to print them off for us and you can get back here.”

Wiley nodded, disappearing down the hall.

Jack was checking Wiley’s timeline against the notes he had accumulated when Marcus’ voice broke his concentration. “Excuse me. I didn’t hear all that. I was concentrating. Can you repeat your question?”

“You worked with Claire before, Jack. What do you think? Is she some kind of kook? I mean what’s with this request for pictures from across the ocean. Does she know something, or does she just like attention?”

“Neither. She’s definitely not kooky. I know that. I admit I was a little skeptical first, too. But we were reassured after talking to her friend in the San Francisco Police. I have to tell you, since then, I’ve learned to respect this lady. If she wants those pictures, there is a reason. But sometimes her reasons are based more on intuition than on facts. That’s a bit of a problem for people like us who work from facts.”

Marcus nodded but then said, “Well, maybe not. Some of my toughest cases were solved because of some idea or feeling someone who was working on the case had. So I guess I can understand what you’re saying. But, look at this board. This is crazy. None of this really makes sense. We’re missing something really key to this situation, and it’s driving me crazy.”

“Well, according to my notes, Wiley has the timeline right. Let’s go over your facts on the Post-its. You read them off and I’ll check against my notes.”

* * *

They were moving briskly toward the bridges when Neil finished his beer, turned the wheel over to David and went below. He came back wearing a white yachting cap carrying an ice bucket filled with ice and bottles of beer and some hats for David and Claire.

"This should keep us for a while." He smiled, plucking a bottle out and twisting the top off. "David, you ready for another?"

"Not quite yet. I'm still working on this one. Say, Neil, what did you say the bridge clearance was on this baby?"

Neil tossed one of the hats to Claire with a warning about the sun and took the other one to David as they continued their discussion of the boat, the features and the responses to the buttons they were poking.

Claire set her half bottle of beer back in the ice bucket. The sun was hot in spite of the breeze, and the cool beer was refreshing, but she could never drink a whole bottle before it started to get warm. This was a perfect solution.

She watched the shore as they passed through the narrow part of the bay and under the parallel bridges crossing the Chesapeake Bay near Annapolis. They crossed over these bridges every time they traveled out to the Lickmans' from D.C., but they were different from this angle. From the water they looked much higher and seemed more graceful. She waved to some people on a sailboat they passed as that seemed to be what you did when boating—wave to everyone. She saw a couple of huge ships, one some kind of navy vessel, maybe Coast Guard, and another that looked like a container ship heading down the middle of the bay in front of them. Now in the wider part, the Bay seemed gigantic. Here the far shore had disappeared and the near shore was blurred in the haze, or smog, hugging the horizon.

When she glanced at her watch she saw they had been gone for more than a half hour. Well, so much for Neil's claim they would be back by the time Jack arrived, she thought. But then Jack wasn't arriving, she remembered, trying to let go of her irritation at Neil. She didn't even know why she had been so certain this ride on the Bay was not a good thing to do. It seemed safe enough and she realized, listening to David's and Neil's conversation, they were both enjoying themselves. They obviously weren't looking to turn back any time soon.

Resigned, she sipped on the beer and tried to figure out where that request for their tour pictures came from. Well, of course, it came from Liz. After two nights of fighting with her in her dreams, she was on her mind. Claire was a little embarrassed by her dramatics of sending that urgent message to Jack through JoJo. That was really unnecessary. She was sure he would try to get the pictures as soon as possible no matter how difficult it proved to be and truthfully, she had no idea what she was looking for. She suspected she was wasting his time when they were all trying so hard to make sense out of Tony the Pickman's involvement in this situation.

"Hey, Claire, look lively," Neil called jokingly.

She smiled as she brought him and David a fresh beer, taking their empties and the little twist caps for the trash container near the table. "Don't get sloshed now. I don't want to have to steer this boat back to the dock," she admonished with humor.

"Not likely in this weather. We'll sweat it out before the alcohol can even hit the bloodstream." Then he looked at David. "What say we open her up and see what she can do?"

Claire grabbed for the rail as the craft lunged forward, then carefully managed to get back to her seat at the table, holding onto her hat as she sat back for the ride.

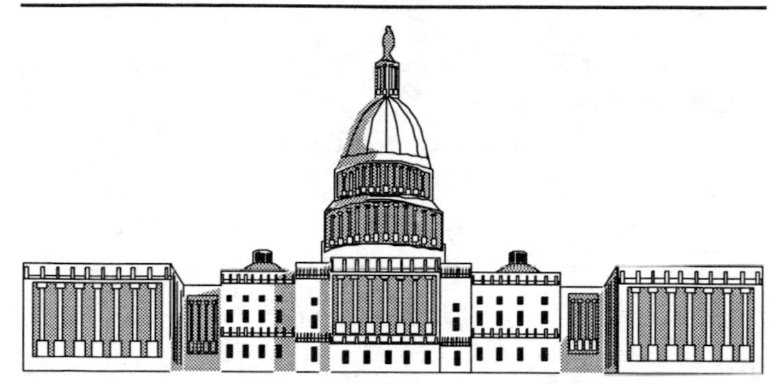

CHAPTER SIXTEEN

The sun was now relentless. Claire moved over near David, who was somewhat protected from the sun by the tinted windshield.

"How you doing, Claire? Want to sit for a while?" David was always the gentleman.

"No thanks. I just thought I'd get a little relief from the sun. I did use sunscreen this morning, but I don't know if it can withstand these rays."

He nodded glancing at his watch. "Whoa, Neil, we've been out a long time. MiMi will be getting worried. We'd better head back." Then he grinned sheepishly at Claire. "Sorry, Claire. I guess we've kept Jack waiting, but Neil and I really get into this boat thing, you know?"

Neil was still steering straight, his manner loose and relaxed. And no wonder as he had consumed most of the beer he had brought up in the bucket of ice. He took a big slug, almost draining his bottle.

"Neil, we have to turn back. Jack is waiting and MiMi will be worried," David repeated.

"I don't think so."

The tone was so nonchalant it took a moment for the words to register.

"Neil, turn around, now." David was becoming angry. He wasn't used to his wishes being ignored.

"We're not going back." Neil turned and looked at them both. "Excuse me. Correction! I'm going back but you, David, and you, Claire, aren't." His laugh, a bit off key, sounded weird.

Claire felt the hairs at her neckline stand up and she looked intently at Neil trying to determine what he meant.

David stood up, angry now. "Neil, what the..."

He sat down just as abruptly. The shock on his face might have been funny, but the muzzle of the gun pointed directly at him was not.

"Neil, what's going on?" This time he remained seated and kept his voice gentle.

"What's going on, he says?" Then Neil snarled, all his good humor gone, "I'll tell you. I'm happy to tell you! You know, David. I was very upset when you changed your retirement date. You shouldn't have done that. You promised me control of the company and then you just decided to postpone it."

"Neil, I thought you understood. It was just a timing issue." David put his hands out to Neil. "The plans haven't changed; they've just been delayed a bit."

"Understood? No, I didn't understand. You promised me the job and then you decide to wait a couple more years. I wanted that job. I deserved the job. Not later. Now!"

"But Neil I made it clear you were to be my successor—" David tried but Neil interrupted.

"I know, I'm the heir-apparent, waiting quietly in the wings." He paused and then said abruptly, "I'll be forty-five next year. Did you know that?"

"Of course, I know it. MiMi and I are already planning a big birthday party for you." Sweat now appeared beaded on David's forehead. He was trying to understand what was happening.

Claire stood frozen at the sidelines of this exchange, not a part of the discussion, but hanging on each word.

"A party? A party." He shook his head with disgust. "I don't want your lousy party. I have my life planned. Did you know that? I've been focused since graduate school on my plan. I've worked endless hours. I did anything you asked of me with no questions. Why?

"Because I was going to be CEO of a Fortune 500 company before I turned forty-five. And I was right on target. I gambled on Vantage and you. I put all my eggs in the Vantage basket. And then you...you decide to delay your retirement for a few years." He screamed the words now. He sat back, visibly trying to compose himself.

"A few years? Christ, your decision destroyed my whole plan. It was too late to move to another company and get on the fast track. I didn't have time for that. And besides, you promised me. So, I decided to do what any top executive would do, take control of the situation. I decided to make sure I would become president of Vantage before my forty-fifth birthday."

His chuckle wasn't funny. He finished the beer he was holding and then, glaring defiantly at Claire, he tossed the bottle over the side, as if she would risk her life to remind him of the litter laws.

When his eyes and the gun muzzle turned her way, Claire tried to shrink into a smaller space at the side of the boat.

"It was a good plan actually," he mused. "No reason it wouldn't have worked. You would've never known what happened. But then little Miss Nosy, here, had to get involved.

"How in the hell did you guess there was a bomb in that laptop? Tell me that!" he snarled at her.

Claire held onto the side of the windshield, drawing in big gulps of air, hoping she wouldn't pass out. She couldn't believe what she was hearing. Neil was involved in the Guiness' bomb plot. It was his plan?

"Do you know how much your interference cost me?"

Then he shrieked, "You bitch, your interference cost me plenty."

His eyes glittered, his head nodded as his voice dropped into a low singsong chant, "Oh yeah, you cost me plenty.

"And it wasn't just the money I paid to that crazy Irish terrorist, although that cost plenty. No. No, what really hurt was the money I lost when the plane didn't go boom, when the stock price didn't plummet. That's what did it. And I had to cover the loss. No matter that it was all hidden behind that dummy corporation; no matter that my whole plan went ka-phooey. I had to use the capital to cover my losses or there would have been an investigation, which might have led to me. I couldn't risk it, so instead of gobbling up enough stock to control the Board as planned, the money went to cover the margin." His malevolent gaze sent shivers up Claire's spine.

David had gone past pale. His skin had a distinct greenish cast. He was breathing heavily, slouched down in his seat. Claire reached out and touched his shoulder wondering if he was having a heart attack.

"Get back. Stand over there where you were."

She moved back, but David straightened as if that slight touch had reminded him of who he was. And that he wasn't alone.

"What are you planning to do, Neil?" he asked, contempt clear in his voice. "What's the great plan this time? And what makes you think it will work any better than your elaborate plan to sabotage our airliner out of London?"

David ignored the red suffusing Neil's face and continued almost as if they were having an intellectual discussion about some obscure point. "I assume Tony the Pickman was yours? And he didn't get it right, did he? He didn't get Claire and he didn't even get the tainted spinach on the table. Your planning and execution skills seem to lack a little something, don't they? Like success? My suggestion would be for you to start re-evaluating your plan."

"Shut up! Shut up, you old fart." Neil's face was almost purple. Then he drew a deep calming breath and the color in his face subsided to a dark red, but the tick in his eyelid was now out of control. "What do you know?

"It was her! She messed up everything. It seemed so convenient when you invited her here. It seemed like destiny was calling to me. So I told Tony to take care of her. I thought it would make us even.

"But she was lucky. Too lucky! But no more!" He looked directly at Claire. "Baby, your luck turned this morning when you came bouncing down to the dock, wanting to go with us. Could you come?

"Hell, yes!

"I wanted you to come. The more the merrier, I say." He laughed that crazy laugh again.

"So how are you going to explain our absence when you show up and we don't, Neil? Tell me that. Bodies float and bodies with bullet holes are very suspicious." The calmer David appeared the faster the tick in Neil's eye beat.

"There aren't going to be any bodies," he said, his mouth stretched into a sardonic grin, "only pieces. And after the fish finish with the pieces, I doubt any bullet holes would show." He watched their reactions. "Actually, I don't intend to shoot you unless you make me. No, I have another surprise. It's poetic really. It will be the perfect end for Claire, here." He nodded with satisfaction at the confusion on their faces. "Yep, it's a shame this gorgeous motor-yacht has to be sacrificed, but life is like that. It's a new boat, not fully tested. There must have been a problem with the fuel line, but no one will ever know for sure because it's going to blow so high over such deep water they'll never be able to recover enough to figure out what happened." He chuckled again.

"Yep, it'll be a miracle that I survive. And everyone will be grateful that I do. Yes, there I'll be, ready and able to assume the role of leadership at Vantage.

"People may mourn you, David, but you'll be gone and I'll be in charge. And right according to plan." His gloating look was too much.

Claire concentrated on her breathing. She felt physically ill. She took deep breaths, willing herself to stay calm. Neil's plan was diabolical. And while she had never taken to Neil, she had never suspected him capable of planning this level of mayhem.

David appeared to have gone into shock. This treachery was so great he was speechless.

Claire's mind was racing. It was unthinkable that Neil could succeed at this plan, yet, he might. Who would suspect him? If Jack or Doug thought the explosion might be part of a plot to kill her, as they had thought the mugging and spinach fiasco were, they would probably never consider Neil as the culprit. After all, he would be the only survivor. His life would appear to have been in as much danger as theirs. She didn't know what disturbed her most; the likelihood of being blown apart, or thinking Neil might get away with it.

She stared at David, willing him to look at her. They had to do something to save their lives. Neil seemed totally unconcerned. Smiling, pleased with himself, he steered down the Bay, only glancing their way from time to time to ensure they hadn't moved.

Not much chance of that, Claire thought. They were both frozen in shock.

And now that Neil had told them his plan, he didn't seem to be in a hurry to put the plan into action. But then Claire remembered he had mentioned deep water. So maybe he had a specific destination in mind for the dastardly deed. If so, she hoped it was still quite some distance away, but she knew better than to count on it.

She wondered, if both she and David attacked him, would they be able to overpower him before he shot them. That seemed too risky. And for all of her concentration she couldn't even get David to make eye contact with her, say nothing about formulating a plan.

Neil was chauvinistic in his attitude toward women. Claire had observed how he radiated his feelings of superiority whenever he interacted with women. She was certain he wouldn't even consider her a threat to him. He especially wouldn't consider her able to physically retaliate against him.

He would be watching David, though. While David was twenty years older than Neil, he kept himself in good shape. In fact, Neil and David frequently competed in various sports so he knew just how fit David was. Yes, he'd be watching him.

Somehow she had to surprise Neil and get that gun. She had to figure out how she could overpower him.

Neil glanced over at her and then at the table behind him. "Claire, make yourself useful and bring me another beer."

Then, impatient with her slow response he barked, "You heard me. I want a beer."

She moved reluctantly towards the table, her mind racing. She picked up one bottle and put it in her back pocket. She then picked up the last bottle with her left hand, keeping her back turned away from Neil as she approached. Her eyes swept over David and she felt a little jolt when she saw his eyes on her. Although his posture hadn't changed a bit, his eyes were alert.

She held the beer out to Neil, who had turned around at her approach.

"Take the cap off, Miss Nosy."

She complied slipping the cap in her pocket at the same time she grabbed the neck of the beer bottle out of her pocket.

"Now look Neil, I can't let..." David stood up suddenly.

Neil jerked around, one hand pointing the gun, the other holding his beer, leaving the wheel free to spin totally unmanned. "Sit down, old man," he roared. The boat lurched just as he fired off a shot at David. The shot shattered the windshield and Neil steadied his gun hand for a second shot when Claire swung the bottle at his head with all her strength.

The bottle shattered. Neil stood there a moment, blood and beer running down his neck. His eyes rolled back and he sank to the deck, the gun and beer bottle falling from his hands. David leapt over him to grab the wheel, steadying the big craft while Claire scooped up the gun. She pointed it at Neil, panting noisily, trying to catch her breath.

"Do you think I killed him?" she whispered.

"God, I hope so." Then commonsense took over and he looked at Neil lying at his feet. "I don't know. There seems to be a lot of blood." Then he looked straight into Claire's eyes, "Thanks. That was great!

"Well, if Neil does wake up, I imagine he's going to have quite a headache."

He turned the boat around. "Think you can find something we can use to tie him up? I don't want to have to be watching him until we get to shore." Then he shook his head sadly. "He's gone over the edge. I don't know when or why, but somewhere, somehow he went crazy."

And then muttering under his breath, "And I didn't even see it."

Then seeing that Claire still stood there looking down at Neil, he said more sharply, "Come on, Claire. Snap out of it. Hand me the gun and see what you can find to tie him up with. Then I'll try out this radio and get us some help."

She looked at him, suddenly feeling faint. She steadied herself by grabbing a chair. "David, we have to get off this boat." Then she repeated tersely, "We need to get off now! Right now!"

He just looked at her.

"David, he was planning to blow it up. Remember he talked about an explosion? We don't know when or how. We have to get off now. Forget Neil. Forget the radio." She looked around. "There, the little boat. We can take that and get away. Just stop the boat now and help me get that little boat in the water." She stuck the gun in her waistband and scrambled down the ladder, calling back, "Come on. Hurry!"

Her fear was contagious. David was right behind her. She was trying to figure out how to operate the wench so it would lower the little silver boat—kind of an inflated raft—to the water, but David managed it with a few flicks of the switch. He held it close to the rear platform while Claire got in. Then he stepped in, moved down to the end of the boat and lowered the motor into the water. It took a couple of tries before the motor caught, and he steered the little craft away from the yacht toward shore.

"Do we have enough gas to reach shore?" she asked, afraid to relax just yet.

"I think so. But if we don't, we have those." He pointed to the oars tucked into the side of the boat.

Claire watched as the distance between them and the motor-yacht lengthened and turned to David. "I guess we made it."

* * *

Jack and Marcus looked up as Wiley held the door for two young men pulling a wheeled cart full of equipment. "Thought we should take advantage of all this hi-tech stuff we have here."

One of the young men, who Wiley introduced as Nick, poked a few buttons on a panel on the wall to lower a screen. The other, named Guy, set a projector on the table and plugged a laptop into it.

"The file came through, but I thought it would be better to project them so we can get bigger images. Any idea what we're looking for?" He looked at Jack.

"Nope, but we'll see it better on the screen. Great idea!" He and Marcus took a seat at the table. Guy already had the first image up on the screen. Slowly they watched the pictures, which could have been anyone's vacation pictures.

"Oh, I bet Claire didn't like that." There was a close-up of Claire. The flash had startled her, because the spoon she was using was in her nose instead of her mouth.

"See anything of interest?" Wiley asked hopefully.

Jack and Marcus shook their heads. Guy clicked the pictures one after another.

"Wait! Go back one."

They all waited and looked at the picture of a crowd of people in a marketplace.

"Can you zero in here?" Jack was on his feet in front of the screen, pointing at a person.

Guy blocked the area and manipulated the computer to enlarge that segment of the picture.

They all stared.

"Isn't that Neil?"

"What would Neil be doing there?"

"Isn't he your executive vice president, Wiley?" Marcus came forward to see better.

"I can't believe it. Jack, do you know where this picture was taken and when?"

Jack stared at the screen, then said slowly, "I think this must be the picture Liz took in Camden Market." He turned and looked at them. "I wasn't there, you understand. I just heard about it."

"That's Rosa." He pointed to the side view of a woman with dark hair. "She didn't want her picture taken. Ever! Everyone knew that and tried to accommodate her. Except Liz. Of course, later we knew why she didn't want her picture taken.

"Anyway, there was this big scene in Camden Market, because Rosa said Liz was stalking her and taking her picture. Liz claimed she was just taking a colorful street scene and didn't even see Rosa. But later she said Rosa was not attending to business. Rosa was supposed to be verifying data in the book for the author, Lucy Springer, but Liz said Rosa was meeting men in all these places instead of doing her job.

"Of course, Liz was a little crazy, or maybe a whole lot crazy. But then, as it turned out, we now know Rosa was meeting with men along the route. Because she was collecting pieces she needed to build her bomb." He turned and looked at Guy. "Can you go back one more picture?"

"Now, there! Zero in on that area."

It was another shot of the crowded market, but this time Rosa's back was to the camera and just over her shoulder they could see a face.

Guy increased the size.

It was Neil, or his twin.

"That son of a bitch!" Jack couldn't believe his eyes.

"Wiley, do you have Neil's schedule for the year?"

"Sure, accounting has records and I'm sure his secretary does."

Jack looked Wiley straight in the eye. "Can you conceive of any reason why Neil should have been in Camden Market, at the precise place and precise time that a terrorist, planning to blow up one of your airliners would also be there?"

Wiley's skin turned gray and suddenly he looked old.

Marcus' eyes glittered coldly. "I think we're going to get to know Neil real well."

"But, why?" Wiley agonized. "Why would he be involved in a plot to blow up one of the airliners? He's going to be the CEO of Vantage. It makes no sense."

"Good question. Perhaps we should ask him." Jack's voice was grim.

"Meanwhile, we'd better go through the rest of these pictures in case we find something else.

They sat quietly as Guy finished flashing the photos on the screen.

Marcus walked to the other end of the room and talked quietly into his cell phone. Wiley gave Guy instructions about printing copies of the two pictures of Neil for their use. He sent Nick back to their offices to gather information on Neil's travel activities, especially during May and June.

Then they sat down to discuss how to proceed.

"Where is Neil now?" Marcus asked Wiley.

"Christ!" Jack looked from one to the other. "Charlie said Claire wanted me to know that she and David were going out on a boat with Neil."

"They're with Neil?" Wiley's voice faltered.

"Maybe not. Wait, let me find out. He pulled his phone out of his pocket.

Charlie answered his cell phone on the first ring, but didn't know if the boat had returned as he was at the vet's with MiMi.

Jack glanced at his watch. It had been hours since Charlie had called him. Certainly they should have been back by this time.

He poked in the numbers for the Lickmans and paced while waiting for someone to answer.

"Hello, hello? Is Mrs. Kramer available? This is Jack Rallins. I have to speak to her immediately." He paused for a moment, then said, "Well, find her!"

"Mrs. Kramer, Jack Rallins here. Mrs. Kramer, did David, Neil and Claire return yet? Can you check?"

"She's going to check but she doesn't think they're back," he said to the anxious faces in front of him.

"Yeah, yeah. Okay. All right. Well, if they come in will you call me immediately? You have my cell phone number? Yes. Yes. Right."

"They're not back?" Wiley asked, his anxiety showing in his stance.

"Mrs. Kramer said JoJo wanted to go, but Claire sent her back to the house. JoJo said that they were only going to be gone for a half hour, because Claire told them I was coming to talk to them about something. That worries me—why did Claire lie? And JoJo is a little put out with Claire. Claire said her grandmother didn't want her to go, but it turns out the grandmother didn't say that at all."

Marcus stood up. "Okay. I'm concerned. Does anyone know the name of the boat or its radio call letters?"

Jack and Wiley shook their heads. Wiley called the Lickmans once more to see if anyone knew what the boat name was.

Marcus called the Coast Guard to find out if there were any problems on the Bay and to alert them they had a situation developing.

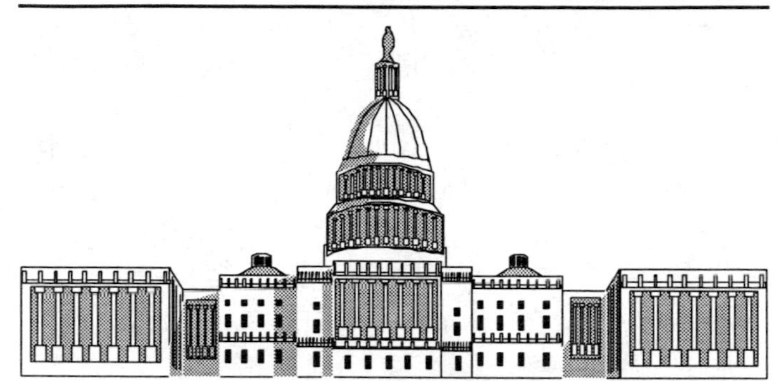

CHAPTER SEVENTEEN

The little boat skimmed over the water, heading steadily toward shore. Claire was calmer now, but every time they went up over a little swell and the boat was high enough to see Neil's motor-yacht she measured the distance between them.

"David, can this boat go any faster?" She struggled to keep her voice calm even though her heart threatened to burst out of her ribcage.

"Not much faster. Why?"

She looked directly at him. "Well, unless I'm crazy, Neil's coming after us."

David twisted around to look. "Unfortunately, you're not crazy."

"I guess the good news is that I didn't kill him. I should have listened to you. You wanted to tie him up. But I panicked."

"Stop it. We were in a hurry! We thought we were heading for safety. For that matter, I should have taken the key out of the ignition and tossed it. That would have slowed him down. Of course, I didn't think of it, then."

They looked at each other glumly.

"What's going to happen? We won't make it to shore in time, will we?"

He shook his head. "Not a chance. But with a little luck we might make it to shallow water." He pointed to some markers in the water a long ways off. "We could get through there and he couldn't." He turned and looked at the approaching boat. "Do you swim well?"

She nodded.

"Well, if you end up in the water and he tries to run you over dive as deep as you can and stay down as long as you can so you can clear the propeller blades. But if he's determined and keeps coming back, I don't think we'll have much of a chance to make it."

His eyes told her it wouldn't be *if*, it would certainly be *when*. "He has to kill us, Claire. You know that, don't you?" His tone was gentle, but certain.

She nodded. No words were needed.

"Well, look in that little locker under your seat and see what kind of survival gear we have. This is a good time to make use of anything we have."

Claire pulled out the box and opened it. The inflatable vests looked like the ones used on the airlines, but if they needed to swim underwater to avoid the propellers they didn't need the buoyancy of the vests. She put them back and, rummaging around, she held up each item for David's inspection.

"There. Give me that."

She handed him the flare gun.

"Let's just see if anyone is close enough to help. If nothing else, it'll give Neil a little more to worry about." He pointed the gun into the air and fired the flare.

They both watched as it burned brightly in an arc, fading far too fast to be any comfort.

"Do you think anyone saw it?" She scanned the horizon hoping to see some other boats appear.

David shrugged looking into the vast stretch of water behind them. "That's the Intracoastal Waterway over there, and it's pretty busy. But I don't know if a big ship, like a liner or a cargo ship would come to look for us, even if they did notice the flare. I guess the best we could hope for would be that someone would radio to the Coast Guard."

"Is there anything else we can do?" Claire asked hopefully.

He shook his head. "Pray. He's going to try to run over us and he's got the speed and power to do it. But, this little baby has maneuverability." He patted the inflatable side as if it was a horse's neck. "I think I can dodge him a few times and hope that gives us time to reach the shallow water. It's like playing Russian roulette.

"Now, when he gets closer, I'm going to run in front of him as fast as we can go. Then when he's almost on top of us, I'll turn sharply either left or right and head around him. You hold on tight to those handles so you don't get thrown out when I turn. It will take him longer to turn and then he'll try again. Hopefully, we can avoid him again. Do you understand?"

Claire understood all too well.

"And if God favors us, maybe another boat will happen along to upset his little game."

They both looked around at the empty sea, but there was still no other boat in sight.

"How will he explain this?"

"Don't worry, he'll find a way. He's good at it. And remember, no one suspects him."

David shook his head. His anger showed. "Damn it, Claire. He may get away with it."

They both looked at the boat which seemed to be approaching even faster.

Their next glimpse of the boat was close enough for them to see Neil at the wheel. He was in control.

Claire felt numb. It just didn't seem right that her life was ending like this. She wasn't ready!

Then at David's signal she grabbed the handles on either side of her and hung on. Her eyes were glued on the big yacht, which now loomed over them and just when she felt a scream emerging spontaneously from her throat, David cut the little boat sharply to the left and scuttled out of the way of the larger craft. But now the little boat bounced and heaved in the wake, almost overturning before righting itself to bob sedately on the swells, the motor idling while David waited to see which way Neil would turn back.

Claire released her grip on the handles, flexing her fingers trying to get the blood circulating again. She trembled. She hadn't believed they would avoid the collision, but they had. Thank God for David's skill.

They sat there silently, watching Neil slow down and go into a big turn.

"He's enjoying this. Did you see his face when he went by?"

David shook his head. "I didn't have time."

"He was grinning. I wished I had a hand free and I would have used his gun."

"Not much chance of doing any harm that way.

"Oh, oh, he's getting ready to do it again. He'll be watching for it this time. I'll do my best, but Claire, remember what I said about diving deep and swimming as far as you can if you go in the water."

The boat was pointing in their direction again and was picking up speed.

The blast was so fierce it actually shoved their boat away. Claire grabbed the handles instinctively and held on as the wave created by the explosion tossed them into the air. She ducked her head as bits of debris rained down on them.

Then it was quiet.

She stirred, brushing some debris off her lap. Then she looked at David. His face appeared frozen in shock. There was blood on his head, dripping down the side of his face and black smudges where burnt pieces had apparently hit him. She imagined she looked as bad as he did.

"David? David, are you all right?"

He nodded, still dazed.

Claire peered around them at the pieces of the boat which floated in the water and at the charred unrecognizable bits which had landed in their boat. Nearer to where the yacht exploded some larger pieces were burning in the fuel on the surface of the water. Otherwise there was no evidence of the motor-yacht, or of Neil.

Neither of them spoke. Claire's ears were ringing and she wasn't sure she could hear, even if David said something.

She had no idea how long they sat there watching the pieces burn and sink. The floating pieces started drifting away and finally she roused herself to check their distance to shore.

"There's nothing we can do here, is there?" Her voice echoed in her ears. Then wondering if David had even heard her, she repeated it louder, almost a shout. That got his attention.

He shook his head and turned the little boat toward the shore once more.

Later he said, “Did you know?”

“Know what?”

“Did you know Neil was involved with the bomb on the plane in London?”

She shook her head.

“So how did you know the boat was going to explode?” He watched her carefully, as if her face could tell him what he wanted to know.

She shook her head. “I didn’t know really. It’s just that when we were on the boat I suddenly remembered what he said about blowing up the boat. Call it intuition. Call it having a good Guardian Angel. I just felt crawly and I knew we had to get off that boat immediately.

“That’s what happened on the plane. And that time in San Francisco when I woke up in the warehouse. I don’t try to analyze it. When my hair stands on end, and my stomach drops down to my feet, I just follow my instinct.”

She stared back at the spot where the boat had been. “I didn’t even guess about Neil. I didn’t like him for some reason. And I thought I had seen him somewhere, but I’m still not sure where that was. He made me uneasy. Yet everyone thought so highly of him, I just thought it was me. Then Amy told me you were going out with him and for some reason I was alarmed. I didn’t stop to figure it out. I tried to get you to wait by lying about Jack coming to talk to us.” She saw David’s surprise but just continued. “When it was clear you were going out anyway, I told JoJo that MiMi wanted her at the house so she wouldn't come. Then I came. As if I could make everything okay..."

"Thank you for that. And for the presence of mind to bean him with that bottle..." He gave a faint smile, "You sure pack a wallop."

"It's the cartons of books I heave around at the store. It builds lots of muscle."

They both fell silent. There didn't seem to be anything else to say.

* * *

Jack hung up his cell phone. His boss was going to notify the English authorities of the new development in this case. The wheels were turning. Solving these cases often seemed to be slow work, but he knew they wouldn't stop until they had the guilty persons apprehended.

Wiley came back in the room after visiting with Neil's secretary, reporting, "Neil is expected in this afternoon. She said she talked to him this morning and he told her he was checking out a new boat and was going out on the Bay with David for a test cruise. She knew the name of the yacht broker, so Guy is contacting him now. Hopefully, we will get the description of the yacht as well as the radio call letters."

"Good work. My office is in contact with the Coast Guard. They are standing by with a couple of search choppers if we need them."

"I feel so useless." Wiley burst out. "We don't really know if anything is wrong, but my gut tells me to do something."

The other two men looked at him sympathetically; they too were sure that the length of time the boat had been gone was an ominous sign.

"Well, one thing I'd better do is call MiMi." His face showed how reluctant he was to make the call.

Jack and Marcus discretely went next door to grab a cup of coffee, giving Wiley privacy to talk to MiMi. When they returned, Wiley was mopping his brow with a big white hanky while listening intently to Guy.

"Okay, Guy's got the information. Neil's been talking to this man about yachts for the past year. Last week he told him he might want to try it out. Sunday, he called him at home and asked if he could take it for a test run on Tuesday. Of course, the salesman was thrilled. He's sure he's got this sale."

Marcus' cell phone rang. He stepped out into the hall to talk and when he returned Jack and Wiley paled at the grim look on his face. "I guess getting the name and call frequency came too late. That was the Coast Guard. A boat responding to an emergency flare found some drifting debris. The Coast Guard is sending their choppers to search the area."

They all stood as if frozen.

"I think we should get out there and see what they bring in. My office is sending a helicopter for us. I assume you both want to go?"

Jack was already on his way to the door.

Wiley ordered tersely, "Guy, stay close to your phone and don't let one word of this out. We don't want panic before we know if there is a reason for it." The big man was out the door on Jack's heels while

Marcus grabbed his briefcase, jammed his papers in it and hurried after them.

They were still in the elevator when Marcus' phone rang again. He turned it on and barked, "Hold on," until the door opened in the lobby and he could hear his caller.

"Okay, they've had a call from another yacht reporting they picked up two survivors," he informed them. "They're on their way to the Coast Guard Station. We'll meet them there." He led them to a dark four-door sedan waiting at the curb, the driver ignoring the heavy traffic which had to swerve around him.

"We're going to the heliport, Bill. I think you'd better join us, so find a parking place."

Jack got into the front seat with Bill, nodding in recognition. Bill had been at the meeting at the Lickmans' and had taken the detailed notes for the meeting. Wiley and Marcus no sooner closed the back doors when Bill pulled out into traffic, reaching out to stick a red light on the top of the car and then hitting his siren.

Wiley said what Jack was thinking. "Did they say who the survivors were?"

Marcus shook his head. "The Coast Guard got the call. The yacht said they were bringing in two survivors in an inflatable raft, who reported their boat exploded."

"The boat exploded and two of them had time to launch the life boat?"

Wiley looked at Jack. "It's got to be them. What are the chances of another boat exploding out there today just when we're looking for them?"

Jack agreed. He tasted bitter acid roiling up from his stomach. No matter how controlled he looked, his nerves played havoc with his body. He just prayed Claire was all right. He cursed himself for not thinking to review all the evidence from London again. Maybe he would have noticed Neil in that picture. Damn, he was getting sloppy! And he hoped Claire wasn't paying the price for his omission.

He braced himself against the dashboard; Bill was using all his skill to maneuver through the heavy traffic, which very reluctantly gave way to their siren and flashing light. He wanted him to go faster but knew he was going faster than was really safe already. He thought about Claire. He really liked her, maybe more than liked her. Even though he knew it was impossible for him to have a relationship and still honor his commitment to the Company, he hadn't completely let go last spring. He thought about the postcards he had sent her. And when he found out she would be in D.C. while he was here, he wasted no time looking her up. Thankfully, as that had probably saved her life.

Still, he thought, she's a survivor. And she's gutsy. He hoped she was using those attributes right now. God, he prayed she was one of the survivors.

Bill pulled into the heliport and they all ran for the chopper, ducking under the rotating blades as they sorted out who would sit where. They fastened their seatbelts, and while they clamped on the headsets that would allow them to have a conversation, the chopper had already lifted off.

Jack felt his stomach lurch and glanced at the others. Bill and Marcus didn't seem to be fazed by their sudden rise in the air, but Wiley looked a little green, making Jack feel better about his own queasiness.

Bill gave the pilot the coordinates where the explosion had been reported, and he skimmed the craft over the bay until he hovered near the area, careful to stay out of the path of the two Coast Guard Choppers searching the surface of the water. They all strained to see something, but there was nothing ominous about the spot at all.

"How far is this from the Lickmans' house?" Jack asked.

The pilot and Bill discussed it and then agreed it might be fifty miles.

"How long would it take them to get here?"

Wiley was more knowledgeable about that. "Well, full out maybe a couple of hours, but just cruising along more likely three or four hours. Why would they be clear down here?"

"I'd hate to even speculate until we get some facts. We know Claire didn't like the idea and that's why she had Charlie call to tell me. And I know from past experience that Claire has good instincts. That makes me think the worse."

Their helicopter had turned and was heading for the Coast Guard Station. They passed a variety of boats on Bay. Any one of them could be the one which picked up the survivors and was transporting them to the Coast Guard Station.

CHAPTER EIGHTEEN

Claire and David stood back and watched Billy John throw the lines to the sailors, who then tied the Emma Louise to the dock.

This yacht had looked big to them when it suddenly loomed over their little boat out on the Bay. But here, tied up next to a Coast Guard Cutter, it was dwarfed. Rhea had called out to them, asking if they needed help. And when they gratefully accepted, she and Billy John had tied their little boat off the stern and helped them onboard. When David explained about their boat sinking and their missing friend, the captain, Rhea's husband Jerry, wasted no time in using his radio to notify the Coast Guard. Then they immediately headed for the Coast Guard Station as instructed.

Rhea had lavishly slopped a rich moisturizer on both of them as soon as they were onboard and had kept plying them with big glasses of cold water until Claire now felt as if she was sloshing every time she moved.

"You all are going to peel, but this will take the sting out of your sunburn and help your skin heal," she explained, overseeing the application of the cream as if they were her children.

Both Claire and David were grateful to be rescued, but neither was inclined to answer the many questions about the fate of their boat. Jerry and Rhea were quick to catch on, concentrating instead on getting them to the Coast Guard as fast as they could.

"Lordy, the poor things. What an awful experience. I told you, Jerry. Didn't I just say that something wasn't right about that kind of boat being out so far on the Bay. Aren't you glad we went over to see if they needed help? They're just about cooked. And they had no water with them." Rhea loved to talk. Fortunately her husband was content to listen and nod. "You know you said you thought you saw a flare a while ago. It must have been them. David said he shot one off."

"Must have been, but I thought it was just leftover fireworks from the holiday."

"Well, anyway, we did see them. I'm sure they would have eventually made it to shore, even if they had to row, which they probably would have, because they didn't have much fuel left. But they would have been in poor shape with all that sun and no water. And even after they made shore there isn't much there. They would have had to look for help." She shook her head vigorously. "No, it was lucky we came by."

David and Claire relaxed in the sumptuous lounge, sitting on towels draped over the chairs to prevent the lotion from staining the upholstery. Billy John laid out some crackers, cheese and cold cuts for them to munch on while he kept them company, entertaining them with tales of his travels with Jerry and Rhea. He had been friends with them for years and frequently joined them onboard where an extra hand was always welcome. The couple spent half of the year traveling by boat between Florida and Newport. And he loved the life on the water almost as much as they did.

"And besides," he said, "they have to have someone around they can beat at Hearts."

Claire had been grateful for his lighthearted chatter, which prevented her from dwelling on the memories of those awful hours on the Bay.

Now, with the boat secured and locked, Jerry and Rhea climbed the ladder to the top of the dock with David following right behind them. Now it was her turn with Billy John bringing up the rear.

When Claire got on the dock she saw that Jerry, Rhea and David had been swallowed up in a crowd waiting for them. She saw Wiley's beaming expression and understood his relief at finding his boss was safe.

Billy John muttered behind her, "Wow, this is some welcoming party."

But Claire had been swept into Jack's embrace and was holding onto him for dear life. For a moment she just rested her head in the crook of his shoulder, breathing deep, trying to clear her mind.

"It was Neil," she whispered as soon as she felt the words could squeeze past the lump in her throat. "He did it. Everything! He was behind the bomb on the plane. He hired the man to attack me in the park. It was his plan to poison the spinach at the Lickmans'."

"We know."

"You know?" She pulled back looking at him with surprise. "How did you know? When did you know?"

"As soon as we started to look closely at the pictures Liz took."

Her eyes opened wide.

"I don't know how you remembered, but Neil was right there. Two of Liz's pictures showed him with Rosa at the Camden Market. They must have had a meeting."

She trembled, leaning on Jack heavily. "That's why I kept dreaming about Liz. That's why I kept thinking Neil looked familiar. I had studied those pictures for hours while I was sequestered in London. Every face must have been burned into my brain. But of course, then, I didn't know Neil. I didn't ever expect to meet him. So when I did, it's no wonder I didn't recognize him."

"Come on. Let's get you inside where you can sit down before you fall down. There will be lots of questions. You know how it is. It will be a while before you can go home."

"Oh, no. You don't mean I won't be able to go home tomorrow, do you?"

He shrugged.

"Jack, I really want to go home. I've been here long enough. Please, please, do what you can to make sure I get on that plane tomorrow."

She knew she was shamelessly working a guilt trip on him, but she didn't care. She wanted to go home to her safe and sane life. The bookstore seemed a little bit of heaven to her right now.

"I'll do what I can, but I can't promise anything."

She nodded, letting him steer her into the building on the far end of the dock.

As they passed the group on the dock she heard David say stubbornly, "I'm not going anywhere or telling you anything until I've talked to MiMi. She must be sick with worry by now."

Wiley handed him his phone and ushered the rest of the group toward the same building Claire and Jack were heading for, leaving David a little privacy to talk to MiMi.

* * *

Charlie drove them up to the portico just as he did the first time Claire came to the Lickmans'. But this time when the door burst open, MiMi led the charge almost bowling David over before he had completely emerged from the backseat. The girls hung on him and MiMi covered his face with kisses. Mrs. Kramer stood slightly back, her face beaming. Charlie held the door open for Claire to get out, followed by Jack. Wiley rode shotgun and he had gotten out behind David. Claire felt tears in her eyes as she watched David's welcome. Then, MiMi swept her into a big hug, murmuring, "Thank you, thank you, thank you," in her ear before turning back to wrap her arms around David once more.

Amy came and hugged Claire tight around her waist. "I'm so glad you and Grandpap are safe, Claire." Her face lit up with joy.

Then JoJo approached, she smiled shyly. "Me too." She hugged her while planting a kiss on her cheek. "I was mad when Gramimi said she hadn't said I couldn't go," she admitted, embarrassed, but she finished her thought. "But Gramimi said you probably saved my life and for sure you saved Grandpap's. So I'm not mad anymore."

This time the tears ran over, sliding down her cheeks as she gave JoJo a big hug. She was unable to speak over the lump blocking her voice, but she was grateful for JoJo's generous forgiveness.

Mrs. Kramer ushered them all into the small dining room where a meal was waiting for them. Cook herself came in to serve the platter of fried chicken as she wanted to tell them how glad she was they were safe.

And they were hungry. Especially Wiley, who worked through the fried chicken, mashed potatoes with gravy, creamed corn, green salad and heaps of golden biscuits like he had been starving for days. Claire found she had an appetite too and concentrated on her food, content to listen as Wiley and Jack told the story.

Like Neil had said, it was a new boat. There must have been a problem in the fuel line. The boat had died and as the electronics weren't working, David and Claire had lowered the life raft to go for help, leaving Neil to guard the boat. After they left he had apparently been able to get it going again and was on his way to pick them up when the boat exploded, right before their eyes.

The girls' eyes were big, their mouths forming an open circle expressing their horror.

"So, how's Tuffy?" David diverted their attention.

"Oh, he's glad to be home, isn't he, Gramimi?" Amy was almost bouncing on her chair. "But he can't run around a lot, so I can't throw the ball for him for a while. That's what the Doctor said, isn't it, Gramimi?"

MiMi nodded fondly at the little girl. "That's right. He's sleeping already in his basket in our room. I'm sure he'll be back to his old self soon."

"But he's never going to eat spinach again. Is he?" Then she looked around the table. "Me either. I'm never going to eat spinach. I knew it wasn't good for you."

Even David had to laugh. And then he nodded soberly, saying, "You're absolutely right, Amy. I don't think any of us will ever eat it again."

"Girls, I'm sorry to say it's long past your bedtime. Say goodnight and go get ready. Grandpap and I will be up in a few minutes to tuck you in."

The girls reluctantly said good night and headed obediently for the stairs. The room felt very quiet after they left.

"Okay, let's hear that story one more time. This time I want to hear all the details." MiMi's eyes were on her husband.

So she heard the unabridged version. She sat back, stunned at the horror of it.

"It was Neil? All along it was Neil. And we never suspected. We didn't have a clue?"

She leaned forward putting her hand over David's. "Are we losing it? Were there clues and we just didn't see them? We thought he was wonderful, so talented and smart. We treated him like part of the family." She shuddered and sank into silence.

Then sitting up straight again she said, "Tell me about these people who picked you up. What were their names?"

"Jerry and Rhea, they own the Emma Louise, and their friend, Billy John. Jerry was going down the east side of the bay to avoid the traffic in the Intracoastal

Waterway and that's how they spotted us. Thank God, I don't think we had much more gas. And, since that part of the Bay is pretty remote, even after we rowed to land, we would have had to get through the sloughs before we found some help. Anyway, Wiley took their addresses as I thought we'd want to do something to thank them for their rescue."

"For sure! Of course, we would." MiMi nodded. "Come on, dear. We'd better go up and get those girls to bed."

David stood to follow his wife. "Wiley, stay a bit longer and meet with me and MiMi in the library. We have work to do."

"Claire and Jack, if you would like, Mrs. Kramer can serve you coffee in the parlor. And then Charlie will take Jack and Wiley back to town when we're through."

Mrs. Kramer appeared as she was conjured up. "Can I get you anything?"

Claire looked at Jack. "I wouldn't mind coffee. Could we have it on the terrace? I feel like some fresh air."

"Of course. And you?" Jack nodded, stood and held Claire's chair for her. They headed through the solarium and out to the terrace.

* * *

Claire relaxed on the little wicker loveseat, facing the inky bay feeling safe with Jack's arm around her. Mrs. Kramer brought a tray with the coffee and a little dish of cookies and then disappeared. It was warm, not muggy, and a gentle breeze came off the water bringing a tangy salt smell.

Jack poured the coffee, put a cookie on her saucer and handed her a cup. "I was afraid I had lost you for a while there."

She nodded. "I was pretty worried myself, as was David." She took a bite of cookie and then sipped the coffee through the cookie she held in her mouth. It was wonderful. Somehow, everything was better tonight, brighter, cleaner, and more hopeful.

"I can't tell you how relieved I am to find I wasn't the cause of this. I was so stressed at the thought I brought this trouble to the Lickmans, that somehow I had put them in danger just because they were being nice to me."

"And it was the other way around."

She nodded.

"Well, I'm sure David and MiMi are thanking God that you were with David and had the presence of mind to attack Neil." He shook his head. "I know a lot of the books tell you to do whatever your captor asks in hopes that he will release you, but if you had done that, you would have been dead." He shuddered.

"Will they find out why the boat exploded?"

"Probably not, but I'd say whoever supplied the bomb wanted to make sure there were no survivors. And you know who I would guess that would be?"

"Guiness? You think Guiness was involved?"

"Who else? Neil was a threat to them. He knew how to contact them. He actually met with them. It seems to me that if Guiness wanted to erase this whole episode this would be a good way to do it. If it didn't work, no problem. But my guess is the bomb was already rigged to detonate at a certain time and if Neil went to set it before that time it would have just detonated when he tried to set it."

She shivered. "I had one of those feelings."

"I know, the Guardian Angel." He squeezed her into a warm hug. "Thank God for Guardian Angels."

Later, the coffee finished, he said, "You know, Claire, I'm thinking of retiring soon."

She looked at him. "Aren't you kind of young to retire?"

He grinned. "In this business you retire young, if you can. Some of us never get the chance to retire. Anyway, I was thinking if I was leading a different, more settled life, maybe we could work something out."

"Something?"

"We're a little old to be pinned. And besides, in my line I don't like to make any promises, but, well, you know?"

She nodded. She did know. They had something going between them, but it didn't seem likely it would go anywhere with his job and her living on the West Coast. But, if he was going to retire...

"What are you planning to do when you retire? Where do you think you'll want to settle?"

"Actually, I was thinking about setting up a little business somewhere, maybe on the West Coast. What do you think?"

She smiled at him. "Sounds good! It would be nice to have you around in case I get in trouble again."

"Hey, no more trouble for you. Do you hear? You definitely need to stay out of trouble. But just in case, I'm going to give you a number to call, day or night."

He took a card and a pen from his pocket and wrote a number on the back. "I'll set it up. Ask for Bernie and someone will help you. Will you remember?"

"Sure, my Uncle Bernie left me his bookstore. I'm not likely to forget that name."

"Memorize the number and test yourself occasionally. You don't want to be searching for that card when you're in trouble and need help in a hurry."

"Oh, there you are." David and MiMi came out on the terrace. "We didn't interrupt, did we?"

"Of course not. We were just enjoying life and the breeze."

"Isn't it heavenly!" MiMi dropped in one of the chairs. "My dear, I just don't know what to say to you. We thought we were saving you and we put you into dreadful danger. I wouldn't be at all surprised if you were quite angry with us."

"MiMi, it wasn't your fault. How could you have known?"

David shook his head. "That's what we say but we feel like we should have known. I just thank God you had the presence of mind to use that bottle of beer. And that you insisted we get off the boat when we did.

"That said, I'm heading for bed. Wiley and Charlie are waiting in front for you, Jack. And, Claire, I'll see you in the morning. Charlie will be taking me in quite early; I have a lot to do. But he'll be back for you around eight, and I'll see you at the office." He bent over her and kissed her gently on the cheek, then helped MiMi out of her chair. And, arms around each other, they walked into the house.

Jack and Claire stood up. Jack put his arms around her and gave her a kiss she felt all the way to the end of her toes. It was a promise of things to come.

"I'll see you tomorrow at the Vantage Offices and we'll go to Marcus' from there. Don't worry. They've promised to make sure you make your plane. Take all your things when you leave here in the morning, as you'll go right to the airport from there."

Claire stood there until the taillights disappeared into the night, then closed the door and saw Mrs. Kramer heading for the terrace.

"Oh, Mrs. Kramer, let me bring in the tray."

"No dear, you go to bed. That's my job. I like to make sure everything is in order and secure, so I can sleep soundly. And besides, you've had a big day. I'm sure you need to sleep. Have a good night. Now that everyone is safe and Tuffy is back, I know I will."

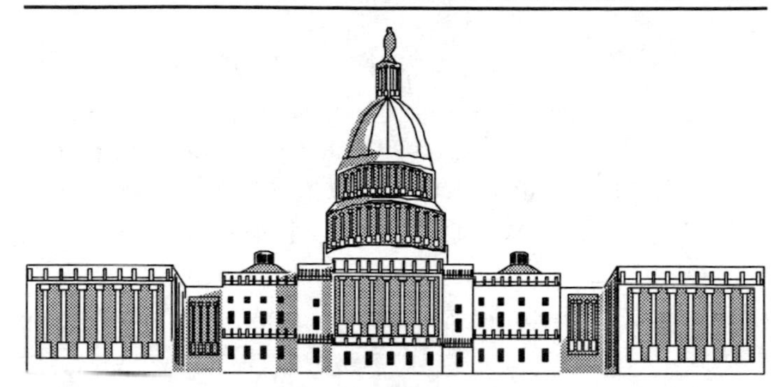

EPILOGUE

Claire was putting books on the shelves when the door chimed indicating a customer had entered. Business was slow; really slow. The collapse of the dot com business caused so many companies to close, down-size and merge, it had affected the entire business community, not just hers. For a while she had fought the decline by promoting armchair travel for those who couldn't afford the real thing, but could dream and plan for when they would be able to travel again.

Then the unthinkable happened. Six days after she returned from Washington, D.C. was Tuesday, September 11.

The shock and horror of her personal experience was almost erased by the universal horror and disbelief at what had happened that day. She, as well as most of the citizens, seemed to move through the following weeks in a daze, fearful of what else would happen; mourning what had happened.

The bookstore business completely dried up for a short time, not that either Claire or Mrs. B seemed to care. But as time went by, the need to survive reasserted itself and once more it was important to put the bookstore in order. Recognizing the public's aversion to travel, they decided to cut the hours they were open, let most of the help go and cancel the lectures scheduled for the rest of the year. She was confidant that interest in travel would resume and, to that end, she and Mrs. B planned an interesting schedule of lectures in the first quarter which they hoped would stimulate business. And just recently the customers were starting to come back, slowly but steadily.

She considered herself lucky for having a cushion of profits, which allowed her to ride out this period without going out of business.

MiMi had called a couple of times, so Claire knew of Vantage's search for a new successor for David, who was now determined to retire as soon as possible. He and MiMi both realized life was too short, and they needed to take the time to do the things they had always planned to do. And, of course, the changes 9/11 had instigated in their industry were adding to their difficulties in managing the airline.

Jack had also called. He told her that Marian had reported Carol Daley told her friend her married lover was an executive at Vantage. And while she didn't remember the name, they suspected it was Neil. Meanwhile they had found when examining Neil's cell phone records that a call to the Vantage Heathrow Advantage Club on that morning in June was recorded. Neil might have been in Istanbul, but he had still been able to reach Carol with his instructions to assist the Springer Tour.

Additionally, they found several numbers he'd called, which they traced to a contact who had a link with Guiness. They didn't have Guiness yet, but they were closing in.

Jack told her about the large contingent of FBI agents working with the Security and Exchange Commission to unravel the complicated setup of dummy companies Neil had developed to assist him in taking over Vantage Airlines. They still hadn't found all the answers but in time they would.

Of course, she hadn't heard from Jack since 9/11, so she assumed he was already on his next assignment. She sighed. She didn't like to think about what he was doing. She just hoped he would stay safe and that he would retire soon. Meanwhile, she had her bookstore to keep her occupied.

"Claire, someone to see you," Mrs. B called interrupting her musings.

Claire struggled to her feet, feeling the time she spent on the floor in the stiffness of her knees. She stretched her legs to get the kinks out and then headed around the shelves to the front of the store.

The man standing at the counter was tall and striking looking in his dark uniform with gold braid.

"Claire?" At her nod, he held out his hand. "Hi, I'm Mike Watson."

She automatically responded with a firm hand clasp. He held onto her hand while he explained further. "I'm JoJo and Amy's father."

"My goodness! Of course, please forgive me. I just wasn't connecting the name."

He smiled, finally releasing her hand. "Well, of course, we've never met but I feel like I know you. The girls have been talking about you nonstop since September. Especially, Amy."

Claire laughed. "I can imagine. I'm so glad you stopped in and I'm finally getting a chance to meet you. I so enjoyed my time with your girls. I'm sorry you were away, but I suppose if you weren't they wouldn't have been there for me to enjoy, would they?"

He shook his head and then glanced around. Seeing Mrs. B had discreetly gone to the back of the store and no one else was about he said, "Maggie, my wife, and I can't tell you how grateful we are to you for keeping those girls from going out on the boat with their Grandpap and Neil. I don't know what would have happened if you hadn't been there. And David told us how you saved him as well by knocking out Neil and insisting you both get off the boat immediately." He blinked rapidly, tears suddenly welling up in his eyes. Then clearing his throat he said, "Maggie told the girls she thinks their Guardian Angels sent you to help us."

Claire felt herself blushing. "Oh, dear, here I was thinking I was a harbinger of bad luck to your family and now you tell me I was a tool of the Guardian Angels. Really though, I just thank God I was able to help."

She smiled a little nervously. "Do the girls know all the details? About Neil?" That worried her. They were so innocent, it didn't seem right that they should be exposed to the wickedness that almost took their Grandpap.

"No. No the standard story was bad enough. We don't want them to have nightmares for the rest of their lives." Then he shrugged. "Little good it does to try to protect them with the whole world going crazy and right on the television in front of them. There was no protecting them from that. But they know that you're the heroine and that you saved their Grandpap's life.

"Which is why David and MiMi asked me to visit you." He reached into his inner pocket and pulled out a creamy business size envelope with her name on it. "This is for you from David and MiMi." He handed it to her and smiled as she struggled to open it.

It was only three months ago she was at the Lickmans' and she thought that week would haunt her forever. But that was before 9/11 overshadowed it all.

Claire scanned the letter and then picked up the little plastic card, looking at the front and back and then back at Mike.

"They wanted to reward you for what you've done for them, for our family and for Vantage Airlines. It isn't often that one person makes a contribution of such magnitude as yours. They felt an exceptional reward was warranted. MiMi wanted me to tell you they were sorry it took so long to do this, but she said she was sure you understood."

Claire nodded. Of course, Vantage had been fortunate none of their planes had been involved in those terrorist attacks, but all the airlines were impacted. The decline of travelers was minor compared to the safety issues involved.

She looked at the little card, turning it over in her hand once more. It looked like a credit card but it was embossed with the Vantage Airline logo and stated it was a VIP Diamond card. According to the letter it would get her first class complimentary travel on all Vantage Airlines and on many of their affiliates. It would give her standby priority, over all Vantage employees and she would have all the privileges of their Club rooms for her lifetime. It was hard to digest what that meant. It seemed to be an incredible reward.

"There have only ever been three of those cards issued, and this is the fourth. The last time one was made it was for MiMi's father when he retired. So we all hope you will appreciate it, and use it often. We want you on our airplanes as often as you'll come."

Claire didn't know what to say. It was a grand gesture. Too grand! Actually, she had been thinking that she might never travel again. But of course she wouldn't tell the Lickmans that, or Mike Watson.

Mike bent over. "And Maggie and I wanted to do something for you, ourselves. Amy and JoJo thought this would be the perfect gift for you."

He set his black satchel on the counter. He opened it and scooped up a little white ball and set it on the counter.

"Tuffy-Two, for you!" he exclaimed proudly.

"Oh, how darling." Claire reached for the tiny stuffed animal. It was perfect, just what the girls would think to give her.

Then it moved. Two bright black eyes peered up at Claire. She actually jumped back, startled to find it was alive. She couldn't help herself. She tentatively extended a finger and a tiny pink tongue licked it. She was in love.

"Oh, he's so cute. He doesn't look real."

Then she looked up at Mike. "Tuffy-Two? Is he related to Tuffy? Is he a West Highland Terrier?"

He nodded proudly. "This is Tuffy's nephew, or something like that. By the way, Tuffy is back to his normal self and I understand you had a role in saving his life too. So you see, Claire, we're all very grateful to you and we hope you'll remember that every time you see little Tuffy-Two here wag his tail at you.

"Mrs. B, Mrs. B, you have to see this," she called out loudly enough to reach the back of the store.

She was cradling the tiny dog under her chin while he wiggled and struggled to get closer in order to lick her all the better, when Mrs. B arrived.

"This is Mike Watson, JoJo and Amy's father."

Mrs. B's face lit up and she put out her hand to shake his. "I'm so glad to meet you. I've certainly heard all about your wonderful girls. I feel like I know them." Then turning to Claire, "And who is this?"

"This is Tuffy-Two. The girls sent him to me as a gift. Isn't he just adorable?" Then her face clouded. "But what will Thoreau think?"

Mrs. B shook her head. "Don't you worry about Thoreau. I'd be willing to bet that she will think this puppy is for her. And before you know it, she'll be raising him as if he was hers. I can't wait to see if she can train him to use the litter box."

They all laughed. Tuffy-Two had just become an integral part of the bookstore.

The End

If you enjoyed this book, or any other book from Koenisha Publications, let us know. Visit our website or drop a line at:

Koenisha Publications
3196 – 53rd Street
Hamilton, MI 49419
Phone or Fax: 269-751-4100
Email: koenisha@macatawa.org
Web site: www.koenisha.com

Coming Soon

Intrigue in Italics

the third novel in the Claire Gulliver Mystery series
by Gayle Wigglesworth

Koenisha Publications authors are available for speaking engagements and book signings. Send for arrangements and schedule or visit our website.

Purchase additional copies of this book from your local bookstore or visit our web site.

Send for a free catalog of titles from

KOENISHA PUBLICATIONS

Founder of the Jacketed SoftCover™

Books You Can Sink Your Mind Into